FEDORA II

More Private Eyes and Tough Guys

Other books by Michael Bracken

Fiction

All White Girls
Bad Girls
Canvas Bleeding
Deadly Campaign
Even Roses Bleed
In the Town of Dreams Unborn and Memories Dying
Just in Time for Love
Psi Cops
Tequila Sunrise

Other anthologies edited by Michael Bracken

Fedora: Private Eyes and Tough Guys
Hardbroiled

FEDORA II

More Private Eyes and Tough Guys

edited by

Michael Bracken

BETANCOURT
& COMPANY

Doylestown, Pennsylvania

Fedora II
A publication of
BETANCOURT & COMPANY, PUBLISHERS
P.O. Box 301
Holicong, PA 18928–0301
www.wildsidepress.com

FIRST EDITION

For
The 2001–2002
Waco High Football Lions:
Tough Guys who should have gone all the way.

Table of Contents

Introduction

Michael Bracken

There's nothing cozy between these covers. The private eyes and tough guys in the following stories are like dark shadows in even darker alleys.

Fedora returns.

Stories in the first *Fedora* were short listed for both the Edgar Award and the Derringer Award. Michael Collins' "The Horrible, Senseless Murders of Two Elderly Women" was nominated for an Edgar by the Mystery Writers of America and my story, "Cuts Like a Knife," was nominated for a Derringer by the Short Mystery Fiction Society. Additionally, the anthology received a Bronze ADDY Award for its cover copy. That's a tough standard to establish, but the five authors returning from the first *Fedora,* and the nine authors appearing for the first time, may have moved the bar even higher.

In the following pages you'll meet nine private eyes, four criminals, and one security guard — tough guys who walk the mean streets without glancing over their shoulders.

But when you finish reading these dark, dark tales, you just might.

Michael Bracken
Waco, Texas
September, 2002

The Watcher on Sin Street

Dan Sontup

I'm not one to fight too hard against temptation, especially where beer and broads are concerned. So, since my office was right next to the bar in the hotel lobby, I gave in to the impulse and stopped in for a quick one — beer, that is — before starting my night's work.

Banana Nose Amanda was in great form as I entered the bar. She was regaling her fellow hookers with the tale of her discovery of the secret spanker on our street. The moment definitely had possibilities.

I managed to squeeze into the corner and stand near my usual stool at the end of the bar, which someone else was occupying at the moment. I caught the eye of Eddie behind the bar, and he nodded and started to draw a glass of tap beer. While I waited, I turned my attention to Amanda.

We called her Banana Nose, usually with affection and never with malice. It was just that she had the same type of prominent beak and was about the same size as Eddie Arcaro, the jockey the railbirds loved to call by that name as he booted home winners at Belmont and Aqueduct, the New York tracks where we nighttime denizens of West 47th

Street sometimes spent our afternoons when we weren't heading for Brooklyn and Ebbets field to root for the Dodgers, or to the Polo Grounds if we were Giants fans, or to Yankee Stadium, or to a movie over on Broadway or the show at Radio City.

We didn't always go out in the afternoon for ball games or other entertainments, but we who worked through the night on 47th Street — musicians, hookers, barflies, night workers of all kinds, plus some assorted lowlifes and, in my case, a scrabbling, usually disheveled part-time private eye and part-time unpaid hotel detective — we were the ones who slept past noon and had the rest of the day free until night came. Getting away from the street during the day helped change the pace of the lives we lived at night.

In our street crowd, even though I had the good plebian name of Mike, I was often referred to as Scoop, a nickname right out of a Hollywood movie, mainly because I had briefly been a journalism major at New York University on the GI Bill, that great project of a grateful government that paid tuition for returning vets of World War II. After a year at NYU, I decided the journalistic life wasn't for me and, after knocking about at various unhappy jobs, I started the decade of the fifties by working for and finally obtaining my PI license from the State of New York. It wasn't exactly my childhood fantasy come true, but it did seem to promise a lifestyle that might make me less unhappy than I'd been at my other endeavors.

I wasn't a real hotshot as a PI and didn't get too many cases coming my way, so when I lucked out and met Max, the hotel owner, through bartender Eddie, I jumped at the offer Max tossed at me. It was a chance to get an office and a room rent-free in return for being the night shift house dick for Max's group of three sleazy hotels on West 47th Street, between Sixth and Seventh Avenues, better known as Sin Street in feature stories in papers like the *Journal-*

American.

My office — if you could call it that — was a small windowless cubbyhole off the lobby that accommodated me, a desk, a file cabinet, two chairs, and a waste basket. There was barely enough room for me to sit behind my desk, and if anyone over two hundred pounds with a big gut came to my office, it was a tight squeeze to sit in the chair opposite my desk without part of the visitor's body overlapping my desk. There was even more of an overlap if a big-breasted woman was in the chair, but I seldom had that pleasure.

As for the free "room" that went with this rent-free office, it was another cubbyhole, also without a window, that was entered through what looked like a closet door in the corner of the office. It wasn't much bigger than a real closet, and in there I had an old war surplus army cot, a small cabinet, a chair, and in one corner, behind a plastic curtain, a bathroom area just big enough for a stall shower with tin sides that I kept hitting my elbows against as I turned in the shower, the tin reverberating with a hollow sound that made me feel I was showering inside a bass drum. And, oh yes, there was even a small sink and a toilet better suited to one of the Seven Dwarfs than a six-footer like me. Well, it wasn't much, but it was home.

I was more at home in the bar, and had a lot more room there, even on crowded nights like this one. The crowd here, as always, was made up mostly of barfly regulars and hookers using it as a pit stop between turning tricks on the outside or in one of the rooms upstairs. Since each trick who went upstairs in any of Max's three hotels brought in money, Max didn't object, as long as I kept things quiet. I went along with this and did a good enough job, mainly allowing only free-lance hookers in, no pimps, so that our three hotels had the reputation of being the elite establishments of all the other sleazy joints on good old Sin Street.

And now, according to Amanda, we had still another

sinner on our street.

"I'm telling ya, he wasn't much taller than me," she said to those around her. "He was a little runt, standing in front of that fancy art store over on 46th, and — get this — he was playing with himself while he pushed his nose up against the store window."

"And naturally you offered to help him out," one of the hookers said, followed by whoops of laughter from a couple of the other girls, followed by the loud guffaw of one man at the bar.

"What else did you expect a friendly girl like me to do?" Amanda said. "I tell ya, it's cold out there, even for January. He had a red wool cap down around his ears and a big black overcoat, and his hand was inside his coat between the buttons, but I knew damn well what he was doing. And when I said, 'Like me to do that for you, Mister?' he jumped a foot in the air and pushed himself back against the store window. Good thing the store was closed for the night, otherwise they might've called the cops on us, him backed up against the store window and me getting ready to move up closer to him to sorta give him the idea, get him in the mood, ya know."

"And you know just how to do that, right?" one of the hookers snapped out.

This time the man's laugh rang out before the other hookers joined in, and there was something about that laugh, a hardness to it, that made me look for him in the crowd. I spotted him sitting in my old spot at the end of the bar. He was big, lots of plastered-down black hair, a chin dark with stubble, and his lips were pressed tight together like he had cut off the laugh right in the middle.

Amanda shook her head, a rueful smile on her lips. "The old charm wasn't working this time. The closer I got to him, the more scared he looked. I stopped and looked up over his shoulder and there was enough light from the street lamp to let me see what he had been pressing his nose up against the glass to look at." She paused and looked around dramatically. "It was three little framed pictures in a row in the window. The first one was of a man, guess you'd say he was dressed like one of those peasants in Europe, and he was dragging his woman into a barn. In the second, he was sitting down on a bale of hay and had pulled her across his lap and her skirt was all the way up and her panties down, and he was raising his hand high with one of her shoes in his fist. In the third, his hand was kinda blurred, guess it was to show that it was moving up and down, and the woman's butt was a nice rosy red."

"He was spanking her?" Eddie asked from behind the bar. "With her own shoe?"

Amanda gave him a small smile and a lifted eyebrow, and said, "No. He was fanning her because it was a hot night." She laughed sharply. "Whaddya think he was doing. Of course, he was spanking her. That's what the whole bunch of pictures was all about, dummy."

There were some whoops of laughter from the others, and Eddie actually blushed.

"Anyhow," Amanda went on, "when I saw this and put two and two together, I figured I knew how to get this little runt worked up just right. I moved a bit closer to him and said, 'Nice pictures up there on the wall, mister, huh?' He just looked at me, still scared-like. I say to him, 'You like to spank me?' His eyes went sorta glassy, and he croaked out, 'Can I watch?'"

"A watcher," one of the girls said.

"Right," Amanda said. "I tell him, 'Watching will cost you thirty bucks, that's three times the going rate. You and your buddy are ten each, and the spanking is another ten.'

"His eyes get even glassier, and he says, 'I don't have a buddy.'

"'Find one,' I say to him. 'Bring him along with you, and we'll do it.' I tell him he can find me here at the bar if he don't see me on the street, and he nods his head, not scared anymore. 'I'll see you later,' he says, and then he scoots past me and moves fast down the street. That was two hours ago, and I ain't seen him since."

"Don't hold your breath waitin' for him," one of the girls said.

"You do the spanking scene before?" another one asked.

"Couple of times," Amanda said, "but not with strangers. Ya never know how rough they might get. I was just teasing the little runt." She laughed, "Maybe I'd let him do it by himself instead of just watching. He's too small to do any damage."

She started to move down the bar. "Time to get back to work for me, ladies."

The big man sitting on my stool reached out as she went by and quickly patted her on the rear. She turned to him and snapped, "Don't handle the merchandise, Mister!"

He laughed that hard laugh of his again and clipped it off right in the middle. He said, "Just letting you know I don't get rough, honey." He grabbed her again and twisted her around and slapped her lightly on the rear. "Now, that didn't hurt, did it?"

Amanda swung backhanded and caught him a stinging blow on the cheek. You could hear the slap loud and clear. The man got up from his bar stool and moved toward her. I shouldered my way between them as the crowd cleared away from us, leaving the bar stools spinning and empty. Out of the corner of my eye, I saw Eddie reach under the bar where I knew he kept a baseball bat and a samurai sword. He vaulted over the bar like a giant bear, baseball bat in hand, and I felt a surge of relief. I was in no mood to see a beheading.

The man and I faced each other in the small cleared area at the end of the bar. Eddie began to edge closer to us. The man looked down at the floor, then up at me and said,

"Aw, shit . . ." and swung his right fist at me.

It was almost too easy. Not only had he telegraphed the punch, but he was also off balance. I blocked his punch with my left arm, grabbed hold of his hand with my right, turned and twisted, and before he could realize what was happening to him, I had his arm twisted behind him in classic hammerlock hold. He bent over double and grunted with pain as I forced his arm up into his shoulder blade. Eddie came around in front of him and let him see the baseball bat hanging low in Eddie's grip.

"Gonna go quietly?" I asked the man and pushed his arm even further up his back. He stood the pain for a moment longer, then nodded his head.

I released my hold slowly, then let go of him completely. He straightened up and rubbed his arm and glared at me. Eddie hefted the bat.

"Later . . . ," the man said to me and turned and walked away and out the door.

Eddie grinned at me. "Nice going, Scoop."

"My hero," Amanda cooed and touched me on the chest.

"Shucks, 'tweren't nothin'," I said in my best cornball imitation.

Amanda winked at me. "Well, thanks anyway." She patted her hair in place. "Time to go back to work." She headed for the door.

"I'll walk you out," I said.

She looked up at me and took my arm, and we walked out into the hotel lobby like a couple of swells.

Carl, the night clerk, glanced up at us and smiled. Everybody liked Banana Amanda.

"Watch yourself out there," I said to her at the door to the street. "That guy may still be hanging around."

"Not to worry," she said. "I can take care of myself. You know that."

I nodded and watched her leave, then waved to Carl and went to my cubby-hole office, where I had originally been heading when I sidetracked myself for a quick one at the bar. I settled down behind my desk and tackled the paperwork that had been piling up for the last three days. I finished it in about an hour, then looked in at the bar, waved to Eddie, and started on my nightly rounds of our three hotels.

I checked out the first one and was heading for the second one, huddling into my coat against the cold, not even thinking about the man whose arm I had twisted and sent out into the night.

That was my mistake. He'd been thinking of me.

I turned down an alley, taking a shortcut to the next hotel, when I heard a step behind me. I spun around, and there he was. He was close enough for me to smell the booze on his breath.

He didn't telegraph his punch this time. It was a left uppercut into my gut. It knocked the breath out of me. His right hand came across and hit me on the side of the jaw before I could even begin to recover from the gut blow, and I went down hard, real hard. My head bounced on the concrete of the alley, and it was like I was paralyzed.

I couldn't move. I lay there, my eyes shut, trying to keep from passing out, unable to even blink my eyes open. I heard his shoes scrape next to my face, and then his booze breath hit me as he bent over me.

There were swirling lights inside my head. I heard him gasp out loud and then his frightened voice jarred in my ears. "Oh, sweet Jesus, I've killed him!"

I heard his shoes scrape again, and then the sound of running feet. The lights in my head swirled even faster, going round and round like pinwheels. Then the lights blinked into darkness, and I passed out.

I didn't know how long I'd been there when I finally and slowly came to. It was still dark in the alley, but that didn't tell me anything except that it wasn't morning yet. I got to my feet by inches, then stood up, half-erect and leaned against the alley wall. It took a while, but I was finally able to move my legs. I staggered out of the alley and made my way back to my hotel, not paying any attention to the voices of people passing me on the street, knowing that they were looking at me and wondering what had happened, but all I cared about was getting back to my room before any cops saw me and started to ask questions.

I stumbled through the hotel lobby, saw Carl give me a surprised look and start to move out from behind the desk. I waved him back with what little strength I had left and made it to my office and then into my tiny room and flopped down on the coarse canvas of my Army cot and passed out again.

I was awakened by someone shaking my shoulder and calling my name. The shaking was making my head pound with pain, and I pushed the hand away.

"Mike, wake up." It was Carl's voice.

I managed to open one eye and could see him through a hazy blur, bending over me. I tried to sit up. He helped me.

"It's Amanda," he said. "She . . . I think she's dead."

That got me awake, not fully, but enough so that my mind started to function. I almost fell getting off the cot, but managed to make my way to the sink in my corner bathroom and stuck my head under the cold water faucet. That brought me up out of it. The pain was sharp, almost blinding, but I was most aware of what Carl had just said.

"Amanda? Dead?"

"Room 314," Carl said. He was already heading out of my room. I followed behind him, unsteady on my feet, but staying erect and moving as fast as I could.

We went by his lobby desk, heading for the elevator. I took a quick glance. The floor-to-ceiling iron gate at the inside stairs next to his desk had been pulled shut and was locked. It was against fire regulations, but it was the only way we could make sure no one who didn't have legitimate business in the hotel could either sneak in or out without the man at the desk knowing it.

Room 314 was part of the business of the hotel, but not exactly legitimate. It was one of the rooms reserved for use by our freelance hookers from the bar who brought their tricks up there if they didn't have another place to go. The fact that Carl had told me Amanda was in 314 was all I needed to hear to know the probable reason for her being there.

The elevator was small and creaky, with room for maybe four skinny people. As it made its way slowly up to the third floor, Carl said, "Amanda came in a little after three this morning, and —"

"Three?" I said. "What time is it now?"

"Almost half-past four. You were out for a long time, Mike. Are you sure you're okay now?"

"I'll make it. What about Amanda?"

"Like I said, she came in a little after three. She had a short, little guy with her."

"She came in from the street?"

"Yes. The bar was already closed."

"This little guy, you know him?"

"No, but since he was with Amanda, I guessed it was okay. He did look funny, though."

"Funny?"

"He had on a long, shabby overcoat and a red wool hat pulled down over his ears, and he kept his head down and sort of scurried along behind her and —"

"The watcher," I said, remembering.

"Huh?"

"Tell you later. You say she's dead?"

"The little guy, too, Mike."

"What?"

"Both of them, yes."

We were off the elevator now, and a moment later Carl stopped at 314. He pushed the door open, and I stepped inside. The smell itself told me it was a death room.

Amanda was half-on and half-off the bed, bent face down over the edge, her legs dangling, one shoe on, the other on the floor. Her neck was twisted at an unnatural angle, her head turned almost completely backward. Her skirt had been pulled up, her pants were down around her thighs, her almost childlike bottom covered with angry red marks.

The little man was hanging by his belt from the inside of the closet door. His belt had been buckled around his neck, the other end looped and tied over a clothing hook on the inside top of the door. His tongue was black and sticking out of his mouth. His beltless pants were hanging loose on his narrow hips. An upturned chair rested on its side below his feet.

"I found them like that," Carl said. "I haven't touched a thing."

"You came up here and found them?"

"Yes. After Amanda and the little guy had been up here for almost an hour, I rang the room phone to see how long they were going to stay — in case one of the other girls wanted the room, you know. There was no answer. I tried again a few minutes later. When they still didn't answer, I locked the stair gate and came up here. I knocked at the door. No one answered so I let myself in with my pass key.

I saw this and got out fast and came down and got you. I didn't touch anything, Mike. Not a thing."

I took a quick walk around the room. "Call the police now," I said. "Not from this room phone. Do it from your desk downstairs. I'll wait for them here." He started to leave. "And Carl . . ."

He turned to me. "Unlock the stair gate and open it before the cops get here," I said, then added, "No one came down the stairs or the elevator while they were up here?"

"No one, Mike."

I waved him out, and was alone in the room with the two bodies.

I walked around the room, but didn't see anything that told me any more than what I had already seen and thought about. There was a small beaded purse on the dresser that I recognized as Amanda's. I opened it. The only thing inside was some folded bills. I took them out. Three tens. Thirty dollars. What Amanda had said she'd charge the little man for watching. I put the bills in my pocket. Better with me than in the precinct property room, or in some cop's pocket.

I went out into the hall, leaving the door open, and reached into my shirt pocket and took out my pack of Lucky Strikes. I needed a cigarette. I had smoked two of them by the time the two homicide detectives arrived.

They were both older, bulky men in rumpled suits. One of them had gray hair, the other was bald.

I identified myself and went inside with them. They did a quick scan of the room and the bodies, then turned to me. I told them everything, starting with what Amanda had told us about the little runt with his nose up against the store window looking at the spanking pictures, and the scene with Amanda and the man who swatted her in the bar, and what I had done to him and what he had done to me in the alley. I told them everything, left out nothing.

They didn't take notes. They just listened to me, the

three of us standing there in that death room with Amanda bent over the bed and her reddened naked rump up in the air, and all I wanted to do was to take one of the blankets and cover her, but they hardly even glanced at her.

"Here's my take on this," the bald one said when I had finished. "She picked up the little guy and decided to let him make his spanking fantasy come true. He had her across his knees, sitting on that chair" — he pointed to the overturned chair at the feet of the hanging little man — "and then while he was spanking her, he either pulled her head back by her hair or by putting his hand under her chin. Add to the sensation of dominating her. It got rough, and he yanked too hard on her head and broke her neck. He panicked at the fact that he had just committed murder. Couldn't face the consequences. Hung himself by his belt."

I couldn't hold myself back. "What are you saying? It doesn't make any sense. You think he had the strength to snap her neck like that, a little guy with small hands and skinny and . . . hell, I already told you he was a watcher."

"Maybe not this time," the gray-haired one said.

"Yep. That's the way I see it," the bald one said.

"Sounds about right," gray hair said.

"You can go now," the bald one said to me. "We'll wrap things up here. We know where to reach you if we need to talk more with you."

I was being dismissed, and so was Amanda, her murder being written off as accidental death during rough sex, the perpetrator then committing suicide. All neatly tied up and ready for the closed-cases file at the precinct. No way, I told myself. No way at all.

The gray-haired detective must've sensed my feelings. He took me aside while his partner checked the room out one more time. "Look," gray hair said to me, "you gotta understand what we're facing here. We're overloaded with cases, a lot of them frankly more important than the deaths of a hooker and her trick."

"You're writing her off," I said.

"Not really. The case isn't closed, just put on the back burner, but you can be damn sure my partner and I are not going to forget it. Any moments we have, any spare time between other cases, we'll be going over the file on this one. And, of course, if anything turns up, if you, for example, turn up anything new" — he handed me his card — "you give us a call."

"That's the best you can do?" I said, not bothering to keep the bitterness out of my voice.

He gave a slight shrug. "Under the circumstances, considering our case load and other factors, like who's involved, unfortunately not someone of importance or standing in the community, under those circumstances, yes, this is the best we can do at this time. I'm being as honest with you as I can. Please understand that."

I let a long moment go by, staring him in the eye. He didn't flinch or drop his gaze. I turned and left the room.

I went back to my office, my rent-free office with my rent-free tiny room and bathroom, and flopped down on my Army cot and stared up at the ceiling. I let my thoughts drift for a while, then narrowed them down and starting thinking things through, focusing hard on every aspect of the night, this night in which Amanda had been beaten, mauled, humiliated, and murdered.

I fell asleep thinking and woke up still thinking and looked at my watch and saw that it was eight-ten in the morning. I got off my cot, stripped, showered and shaved and put on fresh clothes, and went out and had breakfast of coffee and a buttered roll at the corner Nedick's, trying to ignore the smell of hot dogs that they already had on the grill for the day's trade.

I went back to the hotel. Dave, the day clerk, was behind the desk.

"I heard what happened, Mike," he said. "A damn shame. They got any idea who did it?"

I shook my head and looked at the closed door of the bar. "Eddie here yet?"

"In back, at the loading dock."

I went behind the desk, past the open stair gate, and through a door in the rear. I could hear Eddie manhandling beer kegs in what we called the loading dock, but which was just a small concrete area with a freight elevator and a steel roll-up door that opened onto an alley where trucks made deliveries. Eddie saw me and sat down on a keg and looked at me.

"Amanda . . ." His voice trailed off.

I sat down on another keg.

"What happened to your face, Mike?"

"That big guy we threw out of the bar last night, he came at me in an alley."

Eddie gave a low whistle.

"He got away," I said. "Knocked me down with a sucker punch. I hit my head on the ground and passed out. He took off."

"He was out looking for trouble," Eddie said.

I shrugged. "Got more important things on my mind right now, Eddie. I want you to help me sort things out, if we can."

"I'm listening."

"I was out for a long while after he knocked me down. Then I went back to my room and passed out again. Carl woke me to tell me about Amanda and the little guy she brought to 314 with her."

"He was in the bar last night."

"The little guy?"

"Yeah. He came in just before closing, said he was looking for Amanda. I threw him out."

"I didn't know that."

"You haven't been around till now. No big deal. He came in, I tossed him out, he probably saw Amanda on the street, she took him upstairs with her." He paused and looked down at the ground. "It ended bad."

"It did. I've been thinking hard about what happened, Eddie, thinking real hard. Some of the pieces are starting to fall together."

"Wanna talk it out, Scoop? Bounce some ideas off me, maybe that'll help."

"It might. You know, at first I thought that big guy we threw out of the bar came back, and he was the one who broke Amanda's neck like that, getting real rough while he's spanking her. That little runt didn't have the hands or the strength for something like that. Besides, he's a watcher, we know that."

"Makes sense so far."

"Not if you examine it closely. For one thing, the big guy got all terrified when he thought he had killed me back there in the alley and then ran away. Not as tough as he tried to look. But that's not the real reason I ruled him out."

"It isn't?"

"Only Amanda and the little guy went up to 314. Carl saw them come in from the street. The big guy wasn't with them. And nobody came down the elevator or the stairs after Amanda and the little guy went up."

"So then it was just the two of them up there," Eddie said.

"You'd think so, but I just can't see the little guy having the strength to break Amanda's neck, and second, hanging himself with his belt out of remorse. It just doesn't fit in with the little we know about him."

"I don't think I follow here, Mike. If it was just the two of them and the big guy wasn't with them and the little guy couldn't do it — hell, that don't make any sense."

I waited a moment, then said. "It makes sense if there

was a third person with them."

"A third person?"

"Yes. Someone the little guy got to do the spanking so he could watch."

"And how did this other person get past Carl at the desk. How did he get upstairs?"

I swung around on my keg and stared at the freight elevator, then turned back to Eddie and waited.

"I don't like where this is leading, Mike."

"Let me put together a scenario here, Eddie. Let me show you where all the hard thinking I've been doing has taken me." I paused. Eddie was silent, staring at me. I went on. "Here's how it could have happened, Eddie. You tell me if I'm way off the mark." He was still silent. I said, "The little guy comes to you in the bar. He asks you to be the spanker while he watches. He's managed to scrounge together the thirty dollars Amanda said would be the price. You agree. The little guy goes out and gets Amanda, and the two of them come into the lobby from the street, where Carl sees them, and they go up to 314 in the elevator. Meanwhile, you've closed the bar and go back here to the freight elevator and go up to the third floor and join them, and Carl, of course, doesn't see you since you're back here and he's out front at the desk."

Eddie found his voice. "You're way off, Mike, way off on that."

I went on. "It's okay with Amanda if you do the spanking because you're not a stranger to her, and she trusts you not to get rough. She's helping the little guy with his spanking fantasy, and she's making some money at it, and she's with a friend — you. But then you get carried away and hit her real hard on the butt, and she tries to fight back, and that's when you grab her under the chin and yank back, only you do it too hard and snap her neck."

He looked at me and said nothing.

"You've killed her," I said, "and now you realize it was in front of a witness. So you break the little guy's neck and hang him up by his own belt on the closet door and turn over the chair to make it look like he committed suicide. Then you go back down in the freight elevator and out the building through the back alley."

He looked at me for a long moment, then said. "You're overlooking one thing, Mike."

"And what's that?"

"Why should I go through with that whole weird spanking scene in the first place? To make the little guy happy? That's nuts. Why should I want to do that?"

"Well," I said, "he had his fantasy — and you had yours."

"My fantasy?"

"You got real interested in the bar when Amanda was talking about the picture where the man was spanking his woman with her own shoe. She even twitted you about it, remember?"

"You're wrong, Mike, dead wrong."

"Her shoe was on the floor next to her body, Eddie. If I'm dead wrong like you say, then the police won't find your fingerprints on the shoe, or anywhere else in the room for that matter. Right?"

It happened fast. His face crumpled, and he put both hands to his head and rocked back and forth on the keg.

I got up from my keg and said, "I'm going inside and call the detectives from the desk, Eddie. You thinking of running off before they get here?"

He shook his head.

I left him there. I thought of Amanda as I made my way to the front desk. I didn't want to remember her bent over the bed in that room, half-naked and with her head twisted. I knew how I wanted to remember her — the way she was earlier that night, alive and laughing and joking with all of us there in the bar. That was how I was going to remember her from now on.

Amanda would have liked that.

Expect Consequences

O'Neil De Noux

"Once a man breaks a law, he can expect consequences. Not just some of them. All of them."
Web of Murder
Harry Whittington, 1958

As I carry Camille's casket through Lafayette Cemetery, on this bright, spring morning, it occurs to me, this is the first time I've helped bury a client. It's also the first time I bury a lover.

I'm pallbearer number six. Lucien Caye, thirty-one years old, private investigator. I'm in my black suit, dark sunglasses hiding my standard-issue, Mediterranean brown eyes, my face freshly shaved, my brown hair freshly cut.

We lay the casket on a roller next to the walled tomb where Camille will be sealed inside. I step back, through the strong scent of roses and stand next to a large, concrete sepulcher with small, concrete angels kneeling on top.

Lafayette Cemetery, like all New Orleans cemeteries, is a little city of the dead, with crypts and sepulchers, its walls filled with oven vaults where we seal up our dead above ground. There are trees here too, magnolias with their dark green leaves and towering oaks with gnarled branches.

The priest begins praying, as alter boys swing silver bowls back and forth, spreading the pungent odor of incense among the gathered and I think back to the first time I saw Camille Javal, nearly a year ago, May 22, 1949, a Monday.

I was reading the morning paper at my desk, feet propped up, coffee cup next to the small revolving fan on the corner of the desk. There was an article on the front page about former Secretary of Defense James Forrestal killing himself. He jumped from the sixteenth floor of Bethesda Hospital the day before. He was suffering something like battle fatigue. I'd been there, on that damn beach at Anzio, with long-range German artillery raining hell on us.

An article near the bottom of the page caught my attention, about a body found at one of my favorite hotels, the Jung.

"The body of Texas sales executive Milton Hines was found . . ."

The outside door of my building opened and I looked over at the smoky-glass door to my office as a shadow moved behind it. I pulled my feet down as the door opened and she stepped in.

She wore a gray skirt-suit and black high heels, her wavy hair hanging to her shoulders, hair so dark it looked black until she stepped into the sunlight streaming through the Venetian blinds and I could see the brown highlights. A slim figure at five feet-five inches, Camille leveled those wide, blue-gray eyes at me and asked, "Are you the detective?"

Definitely a New Orleans accent with its flat *A* sound, as if Brooklyn had a southern variation. Her pouty lips were painted a deep crimson.

I stood, introduced myself and waved to one of the

chairs in front of my desk. She sat and crossed her legs, propping her black purse in her lap.

"What can I do for you?"

She looked at the Venetian blinds. "I'm a little embarrassed to say this, but I think I've been taken advantage of."

Figured there was some lucky bastard out there.

"How?" I asked when she didn't continue. The fan blew a whiff of her perfume my way. Nice. Very nice.

"I need you to find someone for me." She turned back to me, her lower lip quivering. "His name is Byron Barr and he's been staying at the LaSalle Hotel. On Baronne Street."

I knew the place. Not much of a hotel.

"I think he took my broach." She pulled a photo from her purse and passed it to me. "I had it appraised last year. It's very valuable."

It looked it, a golden scarab with a large emerald in its center and a dozen diamonds dotting its legs. A piece like this would be hard to sell, unless he was smart enough to break it up, sell off the jewels.

"When did you last see it?"

"Day before yesterday. I had Byron over for lunch and I was wearing the broach." Her voice faltered for a moment. "When he left, I saw it wasn't on my jacket, so I searched the sofa." She looked at the blinds again, "Where we had been sitting. But it was gone. I searched my entire house."

She took in a deep breath.

"We were supposed to have dinner yesterday, but he didn't show and doesn't answer his phone at the hotel."

The creamy complexion of her face became red. "I want you to find him and see if he took my broach."

"Have you called the police?"

She shook her head and looked at the newspaper on my desk. Understandable. She gave me her address on Prytania Street and her phone number and a two hundred dollar retainer, which was too much, but I figured she could afford it with that ruby ring on her right hand and the diamond bracelet dangling from her left wrist.

"Do you have a picture of Barr?"

She shook her head and I asked for his description, which she gave me in detail — Thirty-one years old, six-feet tall, thin, with sandy-brown hair, blue eyes and "brilliant" white teeth to go with an ever-present smile. He wore expensive clothes and smiled a lot.

Barr and I were the same height, that's the only similarity.

"When can you start on this?" The quiver was back on her lips.

"I'll walk out with you." Standing, I led the way out, grabbing the coat of my tan suit, opening the doors for her.

"Where's your hat?" she asked as we stepped out on the banquette.

"Never wear one. It messes up my hair."

She almost smiled, thanked me and stepped over to her car, a shiny blue, 1949 Tucker sedan. I watched her climb in and took a minute admiring the lines of her car, nearly as nice as her lines, as she drove away.

Climbing into my gray, pre-war 1940 DeSoto coach, I eased my way up to North Rampart and hung a left. The LaSalle was on South Rampart Street, just on the other side of Canal Street. I parked at a meter, dropped in a nickel, and went into the foyer of the three story, red brick hotel that had seen better days.

The day manager, a heavy-set ex-fireman told me Mr. Barr checked out the day before. A five-dollar tip got me inside Barr's room on the second floor. It was a small room, with a double bed, wash basin, a two drawer dresser, one hardback chair and a narrow closet. The maid hadn't gotten to the room yet. She came every third day. So I rooted around and found two things in the wastebasket — a white linen shirt with a torn sleeve with the initials *A.J.* on the pocket and a wadded up piece of paper with a name and a number: Hines 337.

Hines?

It took a few seconds to click in. That was the name of the body at the Jung. I searched the room again, but couldn't come up with anything else. On my way out I asked the manager what he knew of Barr.

"Never seen him."

I parked at another meter alongside the Jung Hotel, back on Canal Street. Ten stories tall, this brown brick building had one of the biggest ballrooms in the city, as well as a very fine café inside. I found the hotel detective, George Crane, drinking coffee in the corner table of the café. Crane had been my sergeant briefly, when I was at the Third Precinct, before the war. Retired from NOPD, he had a nice cush job now.

"Until something like this happens," he told me. In his late forties, with a lot less of his light brown hair, he was a couple inches taller than me, but much beefier now that he was retired.

"At least we have a suspect," he added.

"You do?"

"We got witnesses." He grinned at me.

"That's good. Was Hines staying in Room 337?"

"How'd you know that?"

"Your suspect, is he a white male, thirty, six feet tall, thin, sandy hair? Smiled a lot."

"Bingo!" Crane was impressed.

I showed him the piece of paper I found in Barr's room.

"Let's call Homicide."

We went to the desk phone and he called Lieutenant Frenchy Capdeville.

"What's the name?" Frenchy asked when Crane put me

on the line.

"Byron Barr." I described him and told Frenchy he might have stolen a broach. I described the broach.

"What's your client's name?"

"I'll give you that if we get the broach."

Frenchy hung up without thanking me.

Crane patted me on the back. "Now they have a name."

He invited me to join him for lunch so we went back into the café. He ordered two oyster loafs. As I sipped my coffee-and-chicory, Crane told me Hines was bludgeoned to death. The suspect was seen talking with Hines in the lobby the afternoon of the murder. Hines was killed during the night. Later that night, our suspect was seen taking the elevator down from the third floor. Flirted with the elevator operator, a new girl, pretty. He convinced the garage attendant that he was Hines' son and drove off with Hines' Cadillac.

Hines was well known, staying at the Jung every three months as he came through town. Even the garage attendant knew he had a son. And the suspect did have the car keys.

"Thank God criminals are stupid," Crane added as our oyster loafs arrived and we feasted on the deep fried oysters stuffed into a half-loaf of French bread.

No wonder he was getting fat.

My office, on the first floor of a two-story, gray building at the corner of Barracks and Dauphine Streets, was in the low-rent section of the French Quarter, away from Canal Street and even the tourist attractions, Jackson Square and St. Louis Cathedral. My apartment, directly upstairs, gave me access to the lacework balcony that wrapped around the corner of the building.

Camille's Tucker was parked on Barracks, in front of the building. As I parked behind her, she climbed out and hurried to me, didn't even let me get out.

"Byron called," she said, leaning in my window. "From Mississippi. He wants to meet me."

It took several questions to get the entire story out. Barr said he was calling from a pay phone in Pass Christian, on the Gulf Coast. Asked her to meet him at the Jourdan Café on Highway 90 at a place called Henderson Point at six P.M.

"I don't know where that point is." She said wringing her hands as she backed away to let me out of the car.

"I do. It's just the other side of Bay St. Louis."

"I need you to come with me." She bounced on her toes.

"Sure, but there's no hurry. It's less than three hours away."

I started for the building, figuring I'd call Frenchy Capdeville before leaving, but Camille was already climbing in her car. I went over and told her we didn't have to leave right away, but she started up the engine, so I took off my coat and climbed in. Even in the confines of the car, her perfume wasn't overpowering, but it was effective.

Readjusting the holster of my Smith and Wesson .38 snub nose, on my right hip, I sat back and let her take me away. Her skirt was up past her knees, giving me a good view of her sleek calves. A woman's legs in nylons always got my attention, especially legs as shapely as Camille's. I tried not to stare.

The Tucker's ride was smooth, like a much larger car. Camille pointed out its features as we made our way to Gentilly Boulevard to Chef Menteur, which became Highway 90 as we left town. She told me about the disc brakes, pop-out windshield, padded dash, all-round independent suspension, and a smooth-as-silk automatic transmission.

We caught the bridge at The Rigolets and watched a tug push a dozen barges from the gray-brown water of Lake Pontchartrain through the pass toward Lake Borgne and the

Gulf of Mexico beyond.

I told her I had gone to Holy Cross and she said she'd gone to Sacred Heart High School. Figured, her being an uptown girl. She told me her parents were both dead now. So were mine, which turned those blue-gray eyes to me for a lingering moment.

"Any brothers or sisters?" she asked.

"Nope."

"Me either." Again a lingering look, followed by, "How old are you, Mr. Caye?"

"Lucien. Unless you want me to call you Miss Javal for the rest of our lives. I'm thirty."

A smile crossed her lips for the first time. "I'm twenty-six."

I wouldn't have asked, being a southern boy, but she volunteered.

"Are you a vet?" Her eyes were wide and searching.

"Regular Army. I was a Ranger in North Africa and Italy."

"My father was killed in Normandy. D-Day, plus three. He was a captain. Engineers."

Past The Rigolets, we moved from swampland on either side of the road through thick forest. Eventually, crossing into Mississippi, we drove though piney woods laced with scrub oak.

"How long have you known this Byron Barr?"

"Three weeks," she said with a hitch in her voice. "Met him at the Blue Room. Lena Horne was performing. We sort of bumped into one another and . . . one thing led to another."

The Blue Room at the Roosevelt Hotel brought in top-notch entertainers. I saw Martin and Lewis there last year.

She told me Barr was an actor and a singer.

"He's been on Broadway," she added with some excitement. "Lately, he's been doing nightclubs throughout the south."

After a while she said, "What he needs is a break. A real break. Hollywood maybe."

Or more gullible females.

We made it to Henderson Point just before four. The Jourdan Café sat on the gulf side of Highway 90, in a long curve coming off the bridge across Bay St. Louis. A yellow, one-story brick building with a row of windows facing the highway, the café had an oyster shell parking lot with a lone black pick-up truck parked there.

I spotted Barr through the windows, as he sat at the counter in an expensive navy blue suit. Camille didn't see him until we walked in. She let out a high-pitched noise and stopped in her tracks.

Barr was in the middle of signing *Little Brown Jug* for the blonde waitress, who leaned across the counter, staring at him all googly-eyed. I hate that song, so I didn't mind tapping him on the shoulder, so he'd turn to see Camille behind he.

"Baby!" He jumped off the stool and scooped her in his arms, doing a little twirl with her. He was smooth, all right, even introduced Camille to the waitress, Miss Ruby Stevens, formerly of Miami Beach. Ruby looked about thirty-five, buxomy with tired blue eyes, but still a pretty woman.

Grinning widely, Barr stuck his hand out to me and introduced himself.

"Lucien Caye," I said, shaking his hand firmly. He returned the firm grip, then let go and pointed us to a booth next to the windows. He slid in, patting the seat next to him for Camille, who slid in the other side. I sat next to Camille, pulling out my Smith and Wesson as I sat, holding it next to my right leg.

Camille noticed it and tensed a moment, her eyes bulging. I gave her a reassuring look as Barr ordered coffees for everyone, including the two men in coveralls in the back booth, obviously from the pick-up.

Barr reached across the table and took Camille's left hand in both of his.

She was right, his teeth were brilliant white, his eyes as blue as the sky.

"I'm so glad you came," he told Camille.

She pulled her hand away. "What happened to you last night?"

He leaned back and raised his hands to show fresh bruises on both. "I got into a little scrape." Again with the big smile as Ruby put cups and saucers in front of us and filled our cups with coffee, leaving cream and sugar bowls. Barr scooped three heaping spoons of sugar in his and stirred.

Camille touched the side of my leg with her left hand as she told him, "Remember my broach. The scarab?"

Barr gave her an innocent-eyed look.

"It's missing."

"Did it fall off? You know. The sofa?" The big smile disappeared in a look of real concern. He was an actor, all right.

"That scrape you were in," I asked. "Was it at the Jung Hotel?"

"As a matter of fact, it was." He picked up his cup and took a sip, hand straight and steady. "What are you, some kind of cop?" The smile again, all joking.

I told him I was a private investigator and he put his cup down and leaned forward.

"Like Sam Spade or Philip Marlowe!" He sat up excitedly. "I'm intrigued."

"That scrape involve a Mr. Hines?" I asked. I could feel Camille staring at me.

Barr nodded slowly. "Ol' Milton." The smile was back, directed to Camille. "That's why I couldn't meet you for dinner. There was a problem."

Camille leaned back, out of my line of sight, and

grabbed my pants leg and twisted. Ruby came back from helping the men in the back and sat on the nearest counter stool.

"What kind of problem?" I asked.

"It all got out of hand and I think I might have killed him." Barr smiled, shrugged his shoulders and took another drink of coffee, his eyes moving from mine to Camille's and back to mine. Ruby let out a gasp.

I slid out of the booth and let him see the .38 in my right hand. Ruby tumbled from the stool. Barr just leaned back and shrugged again, smiling and looking from me to Camille.

"Keep your hands on the table," I told him, then asked Ruby to call the Sheriff's Department.

"Lucien," Camille's voice was deep and firm. "What's going on?"

I nodded to Barr. "You tell her."

He reached for her hands, but she pulled them away and slid out of the booth next to me.

"Can't we just talk this out? Like in *The Maltese Falcon.* The gunsel. They talked it out."

I heard Ruby in the background getting the Sheriff's Department to hurry.

Getting nowhere with me, Barr turned the charm on Camille, telling her it was all a bad mistake. He didn't mean to hurt Milton Hines, it just happened.

"And you can't bring him back, so I panicked and ran. But I called you, didn't I, Baby?"

A black Ford with a gold five-point star on the side and a red bubble-top police light, skidded into the parking lot. I slid my revolver back into its holster and stepped between Barr and the front door.

Two khaki-clad deputies stepped in, both bigger than me, both wearing straw cowboy hats and gold badges with Harrison County Sheriff on them.

"Ruby?" The nearest deputy said and Ruby pointed to me.

I pointed to Barr and told them he just admitted killing a man in New Orleans. The deputies looked confused, so I turned back to Barr and asked him what he'd done with Milton's Cadillac.

"It's around the corner at Summer's Motel."

I explained to the deputies how Milton Hines had been murdered and if they'd call Lieutenant Capdeville, NOPD Homicide, he'd confirm the story.

"Ain't nobody callin' nobody," the nearest deputy declared. "The high sheriff'll be any minute."

Ten minutes later, the high sheriff showed up, parking a gold Cadillac in the oyster shell lot and climbed out in his own khaki uniform and cowboy hat.

"Dis here," the nearest deputy announced as the sheriff entered, "is Joe Yule, High Sheriff 'a Harrison County."

Yule smelled of cheap aftershave and smiled as much as Barr, only his smile was more reptilian.

"Go on," the nearest deputy prodded me, "tell da' high sheriff 'bout dat murda."

I laid out the facts again, feeling Camille grabbing the back of my arm as I spoke. Sheriff Yule rubbed his abundant chin and leered at Barr, who rolled his eyes as if was I telling quite a yarn, and finished off his coffee. He lifted his cup to Ruby who promptly refilled it. I couldn't be sure, but it seemed Yule recognized Barr, or recognized his type.

Yule stuck a hand out toward Barr and asked, "You got da' keys to da' dead man's Cadillac?"

Barr reached into his coat pocket. I guided Camille behind me and moved to my left, leaving the high sheriff in the line of fire, if Barr came out with a gun. He came out with a set of keys he deposited in the high sheriff's palm.

Yule passed them to his deputies and told them to go search the Cadillac. Turning to me, he asked if I was carrying a weapon.

"Yes, sir," I opened my coat and turned my holster his way. He took out my .38 and stuck it in his pants pocket.

"And just who are you, anyway?"

I explained, making sure I put in how I was the ex-police.

"Y'all came here lookin' for trouble?"

"No, sir. I came with her. And I called you right away."

Ruby backed up my story, to which Sheriff Yule asked her for a piece of pecan pie to go with his coffee. He rested his butt against a stool by the counter and nodded for Camille and me to make ourselves comfortable. We took stools away from Barr, Camille keeping her hand on my shoulder.

Ruby slid a huge slice of pecan pie toward the sheriff, along with a cup of coffee. She put fresh cups out for Camille and me. I took a sip. Wasn't bad for pure coffee.

After downing two mouthfuls of pie, Sheriff Yule wiped his mouth with his shirt sleeve and told Barr, "You in a heap 'a trouble, boy."

"I know I am." Barr shrugged and smiled, like he just couldn't help what he did.

"You ever been 'round Biloxi?"

"Sure. How can anyone forget Biloxi?" Barr grinned at Camille and me.

"You ever been to da' Starlight Hotel?"

"Sure." Barr leaned back and nodded. "Starlight. Starbright. What star do I see tonight?" He sang it.

Yule took a hit of his coffee, then said, "A man who looked an awful lot like you left da' Starlight a month ago with the hotel owner, Art Jefferson. You have any idea what happen' to Mr. Jefferson?"

Barr nodded. "Yeah. I killed him." He fanned his coat. "This is his suit I'm wearing."

I had to catch Camille and move her to a booth, where

she recovered slowly, batting her eyes at me, squeezing both my hands. I looked at Barr as he told the Sheriff and Ruby how Art Jefferson had let him audition for the Starlight, sing and dance.

"We were drinking Bourbon and I saw Art spiking my drinks, giving me twice as much Bourbon as he gave himself. He asked if I had a place to stay and offered to put me up for a night or two, so I went home with him.

"That's when he grabbed me and we fought and I had to kill him. He was a pervert, you know. But he had good taste in clothes." Barr fanned the coat again.

He looked at Camille and must have seen the expression on her face because Barr became suddenly serious. "I was desperate, Baby. For money. *For money,* Baby. That's all. That's the only trouble I've ever gotten into."

What about murder?

Camille covered her face with her hands and Barr shrugged. He looked up at the sheriff and said, "You see, I have a weakness for beautiful women." He nodded toward Camille and then at Ruby who snorted at the fool.

"I have da' same weakness," Yule said. "Only I ain't a moron."

Another deputy arrived and Yule told him to keep an eye on Barr. Yule called out to me, "What's the name of dat lieutenant back in N'Awlins?"

I gave him Frenchy's name and the direct number to the Detective Bureau and Yule went in the back to use the phone. He came out ten minutes later, while Camille was in the ladies room.

"I have something else for you sheriff," I said and Yule stepped over. I told him about the shirt I found in Barr's room at the LaSalle with the initials *A.J.* on the pocket.

"Sounds like more 'a Jefferson's good taste in clothes."

"I'll make sure you get it."

"Good. Now we're all goin' down to the office for some

statements. Ruby, you gon' hav' ta' close up a while."

It was almost midnight before Camille and I were finished. Yule gave me back my gun and asked if Camille was gon' be all right.

She nodded.

Yule told us the shoes Barr was wearing belonged to the Jung Hotel victim. "This boy's bad news."

I had a question. "What exactly is a high sheriff? Is there a low sheriff?"

Yule chuckled. "Naw, da' boys just like to kid me, like I'm da' sheriff of Nottintum. You know, like in Robin Hood."

Sheriff of Nottingham? Jesus!

As Camille and I stepped into the dark Mississippi night, I asked why she hadn't mentioned the broach to the Sheriff.

She turned those big blue-gray eyes to me and said, "Can we spend the night here?" She moved her face up toward mine and turned her head and I met her lips half-way. It was a soft kiss, a very soft, gentle kiss that nearly rocked me on my heels. She pulled away and took my hand.

I drove the Tucker back into Bay St. Louis and found a stately-looking hotel, once a Victorian mansion, in the center of the small town. No, we didn't do it. We took separate rooms. Her idea. And I had a hard time falling asleep, thinking of her lying in the next room.

She looked just as beautiful the next morning, waiting for me out on the front veranda. She had another surprise for me. She wanted to see Barr, so we went back to the Sheriff's Department only the judge wouldn't allow any visitors. No bail. No visitors.

On our way out of town, we passed Frenchy Capdeville in his black prowl car, barreling along Highway 90 as if there was no speed limit in Mississippi. Camille said nothing the entire way home. It was a fast ride home in a car with a "rear-mounted flat-six helicopter engine."

She kissed me again, before letting me out on Barracks Street. The same, soft kiss, no tongues, but it still rocked me.

She called me once a week after that until Byron Barr's trial.

Sometimes we talked about Barr. I told her I thought he was such a show-off, he couldn't help bragging about what he'd done. The papers were full of his exploits and his picture. Camille agreed but I could tell it was reluctant.

Sometimes we talked about world affairs.

In June, we talked about how Truman called the nation "hysterical" over Reds, how the nation "isn't going to hell, despite the wave of anti-communism hysteria." She agreed with Truman speaking out against screening books taught in schools.

I had just finished reading the paper that day. Jake La Motta knocked-out Marcel Cerdan to capture the middleweight title. I mentioned it in passing and she jumped right on it, glad an American had retaken the title.

In July, when RCA announced the invention of a system to broadcast color television, she called all excited about it. I had to admit I didn't even have a black and white set yet. I told her I went to movies a lot, invited her to come along, but she declined. I asked her out a dozen times, but she always said no, but thanked me for asking.

In early August, we talked about the Ingrid Bergman scandal, how Hollywood's latest Joan of Arc left her husband for another man, Italian film director Roberto Rossellini.

Later in August, she called to ask if I could take her to Byron Barr's trial. No problem. She stayed on the line, upset over the death of Margaret Mitchell who was hit by a speeding car in Atlanta. She hoped they'd find a sequel to *Gone With The Wind* among her papers. I had to admit, it was a pretty good book and a great movie.

I had driven by her place enough times to recognize she'd had the camellia bushes removed from the side of her immaculately white, three-story, Greek Revival house with a front gallery along its second floor, supported by six Greek columns. I found out she lived with an aunt and uncle. But I'd hadn't seen her since our foray into Mississippi.

I parked my new 1950 Ford four-door sedan in the crushed-rock driveway and watched her come down the wide staircase from the gallery. She'd cut her hair, but not too short, and wore another gray outfit. I recognized it as part of the new "Dior" look (I've always liked looking at models in the advertising sections of the paper). She wore a light gray silk jacket with rounded corners and a neatly nipped waistline over a pleated skirt that was only about ten inches from the ground, too long. Not figure-hugging, but elegant on Camille, who'd look good in a burlap sack, especially a short burlap sack.

"Is this a new car?"

"Yep." I explained how I picked out a Ford because it's like every other car on the road. I needed to blend in. Can't imagine a PI riding around in a red sports car. Actually my black Ford served another purpose. It was identical to NOPD's unmarked prowl cars. Civilians wouldn't notice, but criminals might and leave me alone on stakeouts.

At first she didn't seem nervous, sitting next to me with her legs crossed, that same perfume stirring my pulse. When I parked on Tulane Avenue, just down from the courthouse, I noticed her hand shaking as she checked herself out in the mirror of her compact.

The Criminal Courts Building was a foreboding place, a gray concrete hulk at the corner of Tulane and Broad with the barbed wire Parish Prison attached to its rear. Built as a WPA project, the building had all the charm of the German Reichstag.

Moving down the long, marble hall, the sound of Camille's high heels echoing off the high ceiling, I recognized George Crane in the crowd outside the courtroom. The hotel dick wore an ill-fitting, blue seersucker suit, his eyes lighting up at seeing Camille. Crane introduced me to David Meyer, a short man in a white suit and a reporter's notepad in hand. I introduced Camille, who grabbed my hand and held on, to fend off the leering men.

"I hear you're the man who put it all together," Meyer tells me.

"Who told you that?"

He points to Crane who winks at me because he sicced the press on me. Helluva joke. I told Meyer he's got it wrong, but I can see he's not convinced.

"The trial sure came around fast," Crane says.

"That's because Barr waived all pre-trial motions," Meyer explained, which I could see perked Camille's curiosity. "He could have stood trial in Mississippi first, but the high sheriff told me the D.A. wasn't keen on it," Meyer continued. "Afraid Barr would get a sympathetic jury, killing an alleged homosexual."

Meyer's high-pitched voice grated on me and I tried to walk away, only Camille hung in place.

"Killing a prominent businessman in a swanky New Orleans hotel is another story." Meyer nodded to punctuate his statement.

I'd noticed the case had generated a lot of publicity, just hadn't read the bylines to know Meyer was the one milking the case.

"The wonderful Mr. Byron Barr has been holding press

conferences in parish prison." Meyer checked out Camille again, from head to toe, causing her to move behind me.

"Sings and dances for us and the other prisoners. The man's quite an exhibitionist. Claims this is all because he loves women." Meyer questioned Camille. "Did he know you?"

Camille pulled me closer.

"Guess not." Meyer nodded to me. "Sorry, pal. It's just Barr gave me the names of two women here in town and both thought they were engaged to him. He's quite a character."

Camille squeezed my hand so hard it hurt.

As the trial started, we remained in the hall. In Louisiana, witnesses are sequestered. We can't watch the proceedings. We're also not supposed to talk about the case in the hall.

Camille and I sat in a bench across the wide hall, away from everyone. I spotted the Hines family, clumped together just outside the courtroom, the widow still in black and two grown sons, one with a pretty good looking red-headed wife.

Ruby Stevens came late and I almost didn't recognize her in a lavender skirt-suit that was a little too short. She really had nice legs. All made up, with her long blonde hair hanging free to her shoulders, she looked very nice. Smiling shyly, she came up and asked if she could sit with us.

She sat on the other side of me from Camille and immediately announced she felt Byron Barr was insane. Camille leaned over me and agreed, saying she'd hired a doctor who would substantiate it.

When she turned those gray-blues to me, I asked, "You're working for the defense?"

"I don't want him to hang."

When I was called to testify that afternoon, I noticed Barr was wearing Jefferson's suit, or more-likely a pretty good copy. I wondered if he was wearing Hines' shoes as I took the witness stand.

He smiled and waved at me as I was sworn in. He smiled through my entire testimony, leaning forward, listening intently as I explained how I'd put two and two together to come up with four. It didn't seem like much to me, although the D.A. played it up as if I'd solved the Jack the Ripper Murders.

Yes, I went to the LaSalle and then the Jung and called Homicide. Yes, I went to Mississippi and Barr confessed to me. I had to add that he actually confessed to Sheriff Yule and there were others present. Even Barr's defense attorney, the famed mob lawyer Robert Modini, acted as if he was in awe of what I'd done. I figured he was going to paint the police as being incompetent.

Camille wore a charcoal gray skirt-suit the following day. Ruby wore yellow and kept making eyes at me, you know, staring into my eyes for long seconds as we sat in the hall.

I had a hard time reading the newspaper. David Meyer laid it on thick with a story he entitled: *Private Cop Solves Murder.* At least he spelled my name correctly, while making me look like a mix of Sherlock Holmes and Mike Hammer. He described me as having "piercing brown eyes."

Jesus!

Ruby testified the second day and like me, was asked to stay around until testimony was completed.

Camille wore a pale gray dress the third day, another "Dior" type with a matching jacket. Ruby wore a different yellow dress that was almost transparent when she stood next to the large windows with the sun beaming through.

Camille was upset, not because of what Ruby wore, but because she was never called to testify.

"I guess the D.A. doesn't want to muddy the water with too much redundant testimony." I told her. "Defense lawyers love to search for inconsistencies in witnesses' stories."

Camille couldn't understand why the *defense* didn't call her, although it did call the psychiatrist she hired. Meyer came out and told us her doctor testified that Byron Barr suffered from a neurological disorder, only the judge cut the testimony short because the state had produced two doctors who testified Barr was legal sane.

"He keeps humming," Meyer said. "He greets each juror, waving and winking. He even broke into a little tap dance after the jury filed out."

"Crazy," Ruby said.

"So this neurological disorder," Camille cut in. "That won't help him?"

Meyer shrugged. "He's been screwing up for too long. He got a dishonorable discharge from the army last year for sleeping with a colonel's wife."

I could feel Camille stiffen as she sat next to me.

She was just as stiff the following evening when the jury returned with its verdict. We were allowed in and sat at the rear of the courtroom, Camille holding my left hand in both of hers.

The judge had Barr rise and he bounced up and waved at the jury.

The jury found Barr guilty of murder.

The words echoed through the room, accompanied by gasps and mumbling. Byron Barr just nodded, then shrugged, turned and smiled at the crowd — the place was packed with mostly women.

The judge asked if Barr had anything to say.

"Yes." Barr opened his arms and addressed the jury. "Gentlemen, you have my best wishes."

Camille was so pale, I thought she was going to faint.

It rained that evening and I watched the black clouds over the rooftops of the lower Quarter, watched the rain pelt the roofs, bounce in the street below my apartment balcony, wash across my building in sheets.

My doorbell rang, so I buzzed the downstairs door and stepped out on the landing. She came up the stairs wearing a black raincoat and hat and I didn't realize it was Ruby until she took off the hat and shook out her long, blonde hair.

I held my door open and she stepped in without a word.

I don't think we said ten words that evening.

She started taking off her clothes on the way to my bedroom and I followed. Ruby wasn't the woman I wanted but I've never turned down a good woman and she was good. Very good. She wore me out actually, a fucking maniac, literally.

We started slowly after both getting naked quickly. The first part of her body I touched were those full breasts and round nipples, softly squeezing them as I leaned forward and kissed those lips.

Her pubic hair was dark brown and so soft to my touch as she lay back on my bed. Ruby reached for the lust, pulled it from both of us, crying out as I slipped inside her, gasping as we fucked, grunting when we came.

I barely caught my breath before she said, "Fuck me doggie style."

And I did. More than once.

There was nothing between us beyond the sex and the next morning Ruby returned to the piney woods of Mississippi. I returned to work and never saw her again.

Thanks to the publicity from David Meyer's articles, I had a lot of business all of a sudden. Camille called me every evening between the verdict and the day the judge sentenced Byron Barr, but she stayed away from the sentencing.

I sat next to Meyer in the same courtroom, even more crowded than before, still women mostly. Byron Barr came in wearing the now-famous navy blue suit and a huge smile. He actually tap danced to the defense table.

The judge asked if Barr had anything to say before sentence was pronounced.

"Not really, your Honor."

The judged sentenced him to death by hanging.

Gasps echoed through the courtroom. Two women cried at either ends of the room.

Barr opened his arms once again and said, "Thank you, your Honor. I'll try not to make a fuss." He turned to his audience and said, "It was money. Wasn't for lack of it, I'd have never gotten into trouble."

He pulled his arms down and stuffed his hand in his coat pockets. "I never intended to harm anyone." He looked up at the ceiling and in a deep voice, announced, "My only weakness is beautiful women."

Meyer wrote it all down verbatim.

Outside the courtroom, he grabbed my arm and asked why Camille wasn't with me. "She's visited him in jail more than any of the others," he said, which sent a sickening feeling through my stomach.

"She brings him a rose every time, a blood red rose."

I thanked him for keeping her name out of the paper. He said I owed him for that. "Don't forget," he reminded me as I walked away.

That evening, when Camille called I asked her about the broach.

"Oh, that's gone I guess," she said in her sad voice. "I heard about the sentence on the radio this afternoon. Are they really going to hang him?"

"They usually do."

She changed the subject, telling me how she was upset the Russians got the atom bomb. "It's the worst news I've heard, since the war."

I told her it was inevitable. Military advancements never

remained secrets long.

"I guess you're right. Like gunpowder. The Chinese had it for centuries, just making fireworks with it until the Europeans found out about it and realized they could blow up things with it."

Boy was she ever right.

Camille didn't call the next evening, nor the next. I called and left a message with the maid, but our regular night talks had ended.

Byron Barr stayed in the news. David Meyer kept my name in the news too, even reporting the results of my subsequent investigation of the internal thefts at D. H. Holmes Department Store. I expected the store to publicize how they caught two middle managers stealing from the registers, but didn't think they'd disclose they'd used a private investigator, much less mention my name.

Of course, I gave Meyer some inside scoop, which dressed up his story.

I owed him, after all.

I was beginning to think I'd need a secretary or maybe a partner with all the business I got from the publicity. The busier I got, the more I thought about those sad, blue-gray eyes, and the elegant line of Camille's face, and those crimson lips and sleek calves.

Camille called later in the year, telling me she'd just read a book by a British writer about a grim future. The book was *1984*. She called in February when the same writer, George Orwell, suddenly died. I told her she was right about the book and how I thought it was the best book I'd read in a long time.

In March, she called, furious about Klaus Fuchs, who was sentenced to only fourteen years for giving the Russians the atom bomb.

"And look at Barr's sentence," she complained.

I let her go on, never telling her I thought Byron Barr was getting what he should have expected. The bastard sure garnered enough publicity, holding press conferences in jail, entertaining the newspapermen.

Byron Barr composed a song for his execution and, according to David Meyer's newspaper account of the hanging, sang it on the way to the gallows. It was called, *I'm Fit as a Fiddle and Ready to Hang.*

Barr's last words to the assembled was, "Don't forget me."

Camille called at eight o'clock that evening.

"Can you come over?"

I was there in fifteen minutes.

She opened the large carved wooden door, stepping from behind in a white slip, a brandy snifter in her left hand, her hair loose around her face, those pouty lips painted cherry red.

I closed the door and followed her swaying hips through the foyer into a study, where she sat on a dark green sofa and crossed her legs. She pulled her slip up over her knees.

"I'm sorry," she began. "Do you want a drink?"

I shook my head. "Are you drunk, little lady?"

"This is my first drink." She raised it and took a sip, making a face as the liquor went down.

I sat in the love seat across an ornate wood and glass coffee table from her and told her I didn't think she drank.

"I don't. This is a special occasion."

"It is?"

"Yes. And you know why." She took another sip and put the snifter on the coffee table. "He's gone."

Uncrossing her legs, she leaned over to an end table and picked up a white envelope. She tried to toss it to me, but it fell next to the coffee table. I picked it up.

The envelope had Camille's name on it but no stamp.

As I pulled the letter out, I figured he gave it to her in person. Yep, it was from Barr, all right.

> Dearest Camille,
> I hope you will miss me as I have missed you. I am sorry for putting you through all of this. Don't forget me,
> Byron

Camille blinked back tears, her lips trembling as she said, "He probably sent the same note to a dozen women." She tried to laugh, but it came out as a cry. I moved to the sofa and put my arm around her, pulling her to my chest as she cried.

Just as I was thinking I'll never figure women, she stopped crying and asked, "Am I pretty?"

I let out a long breath. She pulled away and looked into my eyes, wiping hers with her fingers.

"Am I pretty?"

I nodded slowly. "My God, you are beautiful. Absolutely gorgeous." I cupped my hands around her face and drew her to me. She closed her eyes and pursed her lips and I kissed them ever so softly. I felt that kiss through my entire body. Our lips began to move against each other's as the kiss intensified. Her mouth parted and our tongues touched and I moved her across my lap. I felt her arms around my shoulder as she hugged me closer.

She pulled back and kissed my lips again and again, in a frenzy, then sank her tongue into my mouth for another long, passionate French kiss. I felt my fingers creep up and pushed down her slip strap and bra strap.

Camille pulled her mouth from mine, and pressed her forehead to mine and whispered, "I want you to come up to my room with me."

I nodded.

"I want you to make love to me on my bed."

She stood and pulled my hands up to her and led me through the house, turning off lights as she went, to a spiral staircase and up to the second floor.

Camille's bedroom was pink lace and white furniture, her bed, old fashioned with a lace canopy atop, one of those beds you had to climb up into. She climbed on and I followed as she lay on her back. I hovered over her face and kissed her again and slowly undressed her.

Camille Java's body was like alabaster — creamy pink and soft-warm that sent rivets of fire-passion through my fingers as I caressed her, felt her up, kneading her full breasts, fingers sinking into the her soft, silken pubic hair.

She was the most loving woman I'd ever touched. As our passion rose and I looked down into her eyes, I saw such emotion there, it surprised me.

"Yes," she gasped as I sucked those sweet nipples. "Oh, Lucien."

I went down on her, kissing her pubic hair, licking her clit, sticking my tongue inside and moving it around, causing her to pull my hair, driving her hips up and down.

When I crawled up and sank into her wet pussy, her eyes widened and she gasped again, calling out my name. We French kissed through most of it. I held back, slowing my hips, lifting up to look down at her face as it filled with pleasure and she was go goddamn gorgeous.

After, as our bodies struggled to return to normal she told me she had wanted to give me what Byron Barr never had.

Then she gave it to me again.

Jesus!

It rained the next day and the next, nearly flooding the streets.

I called Camille three times, but the maid said she

wasn't in, even at eight o'clock in the evening. I left messages.

The third morning, Frenchy Capdeville woke me with a phone call that left me sitting up in bed, my heart aching, my eyes burning. She left me a note on her end table next to the empty bottle of barbiturates she used to leave this world.

He gave me the note at the morgue.

My Dear Lucien,
Thanks for all your kindness. Please don't forget me,
Camille

And it occurred to me, as I stood there with shaking hands, I should have expected this.

I look up at angry, gray rain clouds moving overhead as the graveyard workers hurry to seal up Camille's oven tomb with quick-drying mortar. They'll have to put her headstone on later.

The rain comes and I stay, letting it slap my face, pepper me with heavy drops. I keep staring at the quick-drying mortar. I know she's lying in there in another gray dress, her arms crossed.

Don't know what I feel exactly as I stand here, except a terrible loss.

Don't know what I've learned from all this, except I'll never forget her.

How could I?

Your Weekly Beating

Anthony Neil Smith

Craig was paying me a lot of money to keep him out of jail because I figured out what happened to his college freshman girlfriend I'd been hired to find. He stole her heart, literally, with a post digger before burying her in his backyard by the pool. But this guy kept several million socked away in dirty schemes: fake stocks, embezzlement, gambling set-ups, real estate scams, not to mention the inheritance. So I told him to pay me four grand a week, cash, and I'd forget what I knew. My only condition was that he endure a weekly beating at the hands of my friend Dole Gray. It made me feel more justified in taking the money, I guess.

I told the parents it was a lost cause. "No evidence." (Not counting the foil wrapped lump in Craig's freezer.)

The father, Mr. Eastman, sat in my office then, fuming. "I don't understand, Mr. Davidson," he said.

"Please, just call me David." My friends called me David Junior, but it's not my real name. I didn't want my past to catch up with me.

Mr. Eastman stood, placed both palms on my desk and leaned closer. He was a banker, a compact man with dark hair and a clean face, thick eyebrows. He looked strong in a typical way. Playing dirty, I could take him, no problem. He said, "You told us you were close."

I rolled my head. "I never said close to *what,* did I? I went where the evidence led. How about you pay half, then? I'm fair."

Eastman cursed under his breath the whole time he made out a seven hundred dollar check to *Davidson Investigations.* I didn't let it bug me. After all, Biloxi was new to me, bigger than my hometown, and one unhappy client wouldn't sink my rep. I had landed here six months earlier on another case and liked the area so much that I stayed. Let this one unsatisfied gentleman say what he will, but it didn't stop me from putting the down payment for my Audi TT convertible with leather seats and baseball stitching. *Thank you, Craig Ryan, you murdering bastard.*

Craig disappeared one weekend, missed a payment, and I got pissed. His money was keeping me in beer, gasoline, and my new car. But I figured I'd catch a double next weekend. When he didn't show then, I bit a thumb and cursed myself. Should have jumped sooner when I had a better chance to hunt him down. Call me a softie, I guess, giving him that much space.

I called Dole and told him we had some real detective work to do. Most of our skip trace jobs recently had been easy. Bribe the right people at the phone company, casinos, and credit card providers, and it seems like everyone's got neon targets on their chests. I figured Craig would try harder to stay lost.

Dole and I parked a few blocks away and walked to Craig's place, on the beach in Gulfport. The guy was only thirty-two, and his dead parents left him this whopping two-story fake antebellum. Whatever potential he had was snuffed right then. No need for ambition. But the house was impressive, with a well-kept yard and nice garden full of purples ands yellows surrounded by green. Craig's Jaguar was in the driveway. I touched the hood as I walked past. Ice cold.

"He missed his beating." Dole said.

"What about the week before?"

"No, I got him then. He didn't say anything out of the ordinary. I figured he'd paid."

"When's the last time you saw him?"

Dole smiled. "That was it, beating day. If I were to see him more often, I might gain a little sympathy for him. I don't need that messing with my head, David."

We wandered up the path to the front porch, climbed the steps. Both of us tried to blend in with the neighborhood, in dress slacks and sports coats. Dole had to bend down to keep from getting whacked by the ceiling fans on the porch. He's a big son-of-a-bitch, hovering just over seven feet tall. And built, too, all steroids. He used to play basketball in a minor league, got drafted by a Gulf Coast team that was here only a few months, but Dole liked the place and stayed. Besides, his probation on an assault charge wouldn't let him cross state lines for a couple years.

I rang the bell. A long wait. I rang again and pressed my ear to the amber glass in the door's center. No footsteps, no voices. I tried the doorknob — locked. I pulled out my picks, worked the mechanism and had us inside in less than a minute.

"Slow poke," Dole said as he walked past.

Inside, things smelled bad, but not dead. Newspapers scattered on the hardwood floor, dirty spotted carpet on the stairs, and a set of golf clubs blocking the doorway. I kicked them out of the way.

"Do you think he left in a hurry on his own, or did he have help?" Dole said.

I tried to get a sense of the place — scuff marks on the floor, the golf clubs left in haste, things not fitting together.

Did he run because of me, or did he have bigger troubles?

I said, "Damn, should have pegged him on midnight, right after due day. And charged interest."

"We can find out pretty quick if anyone else wanted him out of the way."

"Good place to start. First, how about we try the bedroom?"

We started up the stairs, past watercolors of ocean scenes, trying to figure out the green and white spots on the carpet. Then we got dive-bombed.

A fucking *dragon,* I thought. Came out of nowhere whirling and shrieking and nearly clawed my face. I ducked. Dole made some *Euowww* noises and swiped at the thing. When it started away, turning for another run, I pulled my pistol and took dead aim, shot the monster out of the sky. It bounced off the floor, settled and rolled around, a big red blotch on its side. An African Gray Parrot.

"Just great. Why'd you shoot it?" Dole said. "Those things talk. It could've told us something."

I shook my head and kept climbing.

Craig's bed was unmade, the room lights still on. We checked the closet, under the bed, the adjoining bathroom. Looked like everything was in place, nothing missing. If he ran, he wanted to start from scratch. No notebooks or paper scraps with flight info or hotel reservations scribbled. A few clothes on the floor, bags still in the closet, and the clock radio at bedside softly crackled a rock station.

Dole sat on the bed, smoothed the sheets. "Why was that bird out, anyway? Think he'd have a cage, so someone dropped the ball there."

"Then where would the cage be?"

He shrugged. "The kitchen? The den?"

We dragged ourselves back downstairs and found the den. Dark and cluttered, four recliners, three couches arranged in rows, all facing a big screen TV. The bird cage was near the window, and it was knocked over, the door open, bird seed spilled onto the floor. A computer desk against the far wall was clean except for a closed lap top. I picked it up, feeling Craig owed something valuable. Dole stepped over to the recliner that had several remote controls on the armrest. It was navy blue, almost black in the dim light, but looked splotchy. Dole's nose was almost touching the seat, hands on his knees as he balanced himself in a crouch. Finally, he took a *TV Guide*, opened it to the middle, and pressed that face down into the seat. Then he lifted, turned it my way, being careful. The pages were soaked red.

"Blood or soda?" I said.

"Blood, David."

I let out a breath, long and hard. "There goes my car."

In the Audi, Dole made a few calls to bookies he knew from his playing days, then to a few "all weather" informants. I drove along the beach, air blasting high while the temperature outside edged ninety, wondering if Craig was dead or just really hurt somewhere. Not that he didn't deserve it, but greed made me worry about him as if he were a brother. I saw girls in short-shorts on the Boardwalk outside my window, but imagined Craig's cold dead body in the woods at night. And imagined myself in a used Dodge Neon.

Dole pressed the off button on his phone and grinned at me like, *You're not gonna like this.*

"What?"

"Apparently, Craig pulled Doctor Hopkins into an investment scam, but Hopkins has friends who understand those types of things. The story is, Hopkins called Craig. Craig started out nice, then went tough-guy ballistic, saying 'You knew the risks! This wasn't get rich quick!' Hopkins hangs up, waits a few minutes, then picks up and makes another call, says, 'Teach him.' There we are."

I yawned. I get sleepy when depressed. "Think we should just drop in?"

Dole froze. "That's a joke right?"

"Of course. We'll go to the office, use the normal channels."

Because you have to be nice if you want to talk with Doctor Hopkins. You don't have a choice.

Mac Hopkins used to be a doctor until he got into trouble for prescription fraud, dealing pills on the side. So he went into cocaine back in the late seventies. He bailed out a decade later and invested in the local casinos, played the stock market, and built himself a nice fortune. We don't know what the fuck he really does nowadays, but it seems that if it's dirty and sure to make people rich in some illegal way, Hopkins's shadow is right there out of the corner of your eye.

I'm not surprised that he and Craig have problems, then. The kid's dopey, not half-aware of what the *real* underground map of the Coast looks like: New Orleans crime families, plus those wannabe Dixie Mafia hicks and the Asian drug gangs, and self-made men like Hopkins sitting pretty with their slices of the pie, smart enough to not get greedy.

I've dealt with him a few times, usually to my benefit, since Hopkins is a generous bastard who likes rubbing in how much power he has over little folks like me by *giving* us shit, making life easier, providing leads, handing over hundreds like they were bookmarks. Pure evil.

This visit, I'd have a complaint.

We waited in Hopkins's dining room, drinking rich coffee brought to us in fine China cups. Then we were left alone, and we didn't say a word. Some guys were dumb enough to talk before going in to see Hopkins, only to have their traitorous words repeated back to them minutes later. Usually the last thing they ever heard.

Dole took a noisy sip and clattered his cup against the spoon on the table, said, "Man, good coffee. This is the type of stuff I keep saying I should treat myself to, but I always end up buying cheap shit, whatever's on sale."

"Yeah, it's good," I said. Too nervous to play the game.

"I'll bet it's fresh ground. That's another thing. I'd need a grinder. I should make myself buy one, you know?"

That's when the short guy with frameless specs and a nearly shaved head stepped in, asked us to follow him.

The house was all dark wood and yellowish lighting, lots of candles, and old thick oil paintings in ornate frames hung on the walls. Real Oriental rugs on the floor, and old tables with early twentieth century cut-glass lamps on them glowing a circle only wide enough to show off each lamp. We followed the skinhead guard to the library, a small room with floor to ceiling bookcases, full of works by British authors from the last half-century (last time I was here, I checked). A case against the wall closest to us held thin volumes of poetry next to modernist pottery. I always felt uncomfortable and envious at the same time when I was in here. If the chairs had been old recliners instead of high-class leather, and the shelves full of techno-thrillers, maybe I'd have felt more at home.

Hopkins sat in a low leather chair, the most comfortable in the room. His feet were covered with Reeboks, propped on a stool, and he held a glass of white wine. Jeans and a lightweight sweater. He didn't have much of his blond hair left, and thankfully he seemed to be letting it go gracefully. The skinhead waved his hands towards two straight backs and asked us to sit. We did. Skinhead left.

"I trust you've been taken care of all right," Hopkins

said in a weak Southern drawl.

Dole said, "Yes sir. Good coffee."

"Glad you like it. Just good ol' Colombian. I've got plenty if you want a sack of beans."

"You don't mind? I can't impose."

"Fine, fine. No trouble. You've got a grinder? Never mind. I'm sure there's an old one around here you can use."

Dole nodded, so gracious and humble. "You don't have to do that, but thanks, if it's no trouble."

"You didn't come for the coffee, right?" He took a mouthful of wine, swallowed. "What can I do for you gentlemen?"

Dole looked at me. I looked at him. Then I looked at Hopkins, who looked like he wanted me to hurry the hell up.

"I have occasional business dealings with Craig Ryan, and I've had trouble locating him recently. I wonder if you've had the same problem."

Hopkins set his glass on a ceramic coaster. He never got riled, but just held that easy, lazy grin and a demeanor like no one could ever rattle his cage.

"You assume I know Craig Ryan?" he said.

Damn mind games. "We've been informed —"

"But you didn't start by asking 'Do you know Craig Ryan?' You just assumed that you were told the truth by whatever lowlife you asked. I don't think assumptions can get you very far in this business."

I leaned back in the chair, sneaked a peek out the side door into the dining room. The skinhead and a similarly dressed friend stood guard. I knew they could hear every word we spoke and be ready to take us out if we showed signs of trouble. We had arrived unarmed, too, so the goons had twice the advantage.

I said, "Forgive the assumption, sir, but it's important that I find Mr. Ryan. If he is still alive, which I would like to believe, then he owes me a large amount of money. He's good for it. If someone else wanted to eliminate Mr. Ryan for reasons other than my reasons for dealing with him, I certainly don't want to interfere. But I would appreciate my cut."

Hopkins nodded, the grin now more thoughtful than playful, deciding how much he would counteroffer to whatever price I was about to say. Maybe that smug absolutism, him thinking I was so easily bought (and my own shame for believing I had come there just to be bought) caused me to change the game plan and risk everything.

"How much does this Craig Ryan owe you, anyway? Can't be much."

I said, "Four grand weekly."

"How many weeks has he missed?"

"Well, two. But you don't get it. I said 'weekly' meaning next week, and the one after that, and so on. I would like this transaction to continue."

I thought Hopkins might come out of the chair. He started forward, stopped, then stared at me with that grin, those dark eyes.

"Perhaps it's time you and Craig reconsidered your terms."

I shook my head. "It's been going very nicely, I think we'll both agree. And Dole, too, right?"

My friend was looking at me as though he wished to be anywhere else but there, and also wished that I were dead. I ignored him.

Hopkins settled into the chair, covered one hand with the other, and said, "If you really need the money now, I can certainly help with the missed payments, and I'm sure Mr. Ryan can settle with me later."

"So now you admit to knowing him?"

Hopkins didn't answer. Placid and tranquil, his style of intimidation.

I glanced once more into the dining room, then at Dole. Tried being psychic: *Can you take both of them?*

He looked past my shoulder, then moved his eyes just enough. A shrug. Then his own look beamed over: *Might as well.*

I said, "Sorry, Dr. Hopkins. I don't think two weeks makes up for the overall loss." But I thought, *The Audi payment is due next week. Take the money.*

"Well, I wish I could help. I can't afford to put you on the payroll, not sure you'd like that type of job, anyway." He had a small laugh, too damn charming for his own good.

I stood and walked to his chair, stuck out my hand. I hadn't done this before and wasn't sure if it would work. Hopkins looked at me oddly for a moment. I saw Dole in peripheral vision, standing by the door, out of the guards' sights. Hopkins took my hand, gave it a hearty shake. Then I squeezed way too tightly and yanked his arm hard, almost out of socket. He yelped like a teenage girl for a long damn moment. I pulled his body out of the chair, turned, and wrapped my other arm around his throat.

The first guard whisked through the door, gun drawn. Dole grabbed the skinhead's ears and brought his knee up to meet the nose making a loud crack, almost as loud as Hopkins' whimpering. A burst of blood. Dole draped himself with the guard just in time as the other guard began firing. The skinhead took the bullets, and Dole pulled the gun from his dead hand, got off a few shots, one striking the other guard's leg. He started cursing in French. Dole took careful aim and hit the back of the guard's head. The easy out.

I pushed Hopkins to the ground, drove my knee into the middle of his back, pumped from the adrenaline, pretty sure that after this, killing Hopkins was the logical end. If I let him live, he wouldn't let me. But no time to think of that.

"Craig. Where is he?"

"Are you crazy? Do you know I'm going to kill you? You

can't kill me. People *know* me. You'll be getting ass-raped in county lock-up by sunrise if you kill me, and you know it."

Dole dropped Skinhead's body, then took the pistol from the French guard and tossed it to me. I pressed the barrel into Hopkins' neck. I said, "Anyone ever done this to you before?"

He shook his head, groaned.

"I know how to kill people and not get caught. I don't like to, because it's messy and stresses me out. But I've never missed. And you certainly won't be the one I start missing on, got it?"

He cried real heaving tears. I took that as a *Yes.*

After a few moments, he said, "In the garage. Craig's in the garage. He tried to run, but we found him in Bay St. Louis three days ago. He's not dead yet."

"How close was he to being dead when we got here?"

"Maybe two more days."

I felt the muscles relaxing in my body, the rush subsiding and being replaced by fear and relief. I yanked Hopkins up by his shirt and started to push him towards the garage when Dole stepped in front of us, pressed his fingers on Hopkins' chest.

"Um, maybe not a good time to ask," Dole said, "but can I still get some of those coffee beans?"

In the garage, I flipped the lights while Dole held Hopkins with one hand and a sack of coffee in the other. The garage was typical cinder block, but didn't have the smell of oil, mildew, and tools. Too clean, too florescent. A fairly new BMW took up one slot, and Craig took up the other. He was naked and tied face down on a treadmill that had sandpaper glued down the center. It was streaked red, as was Craig's stomach, thighs, everything in between. He had weary eyes, and brown tape circled his head, covering his mouth.

I knelt beside him. "You okay?"

He screamed into the tape, angry. I slapped his back.

"You should be happy to see me, right?" I pretended to reach for the treadmill's ON button, and Craig's fingers wiggled like crazy. I pulled back, went looking for a knife, found one, and then cut the ropes. He couldn't hold up his arms. His skin was raw, torn, bloody. I hoped he would be okay until we could get back to his house, wrap him in gauze or something.

I cut the tape several times and peeled away, but took flecks of skin and hair with it. He was too tired to complain.

"You missed your weekly beating," I said.

"David, man, I wasn't running out on you. Okay? I know I owe you big time. I was going to pay up, I swear."

"What the hell did you do to Hopkins?"

"I thought I could pull enough people into this deal to double the initial investment. I would've given his money back, but he was asking too many questions, had me stumped. I didn't know who I was dealing with."

"Damn right."

I found Craig's clothes and tossed them over, then looked at Dole. He held both of Hopkins' wrists behind his back, no trouble.

"What do you think we should do?" I said.

Dole laughed. "Did you see *me* picking a fight with Hopkins? Shit, no way. Your call on this one."

I scratched my head and thought about what to do. Take down Hopkins in his own home? Explaining the guards would be hard enough already. Let him live and hope he's grateful? Yeah, sure.

I said, "Looks like we'll just have to go back to Craig's and think about it a while."

Hopkins said, "This is where things get cloudy. Are you just going to drag me around with you for the rest of your life?" The grin was back. I walked over to him, lifted his chin with the gun barrel, and said, "Have you ever really been scared?"

"What?"

I shoved the gun under his crotch and fired. The shot missed him by inches. It was like a flash grenade in the garage, and the slug tore a baseball sized hole into the back wall. A dark wet spot spread down Hopkins' jeans.

"If that was the first time, you've got a long night ahead of you."

Back at Craig's, we followed him into the foyer. He saw the dead parrot on the floor and whispered, "Oh, Conan."

"The bird's named Conan?" I said.

Craig nodded. "Poor baby."

I patted his back and said, "Sorry about that. He attacked us."

Dole shoved Hopkins to the side and kept a gun trained on him. Hopkins crossed his arms and kept shifting his weight.

I said, "Craig, how about you get the eight grand you owe, and I'll get out of your way. I'll check on you tomorrow. But you need a doctor to keep out infection."

"I'll be fine," he said. Probably wouldn't listen to the advice. Stubborn spoiled asshole.

"I'll take you to the hospital myself, at gunpoint if necessary."

He laughed.

Hopkins said, "Yeah, protect your investment, Sugar Daddy. And I bet he doesn't even suck your dick. What's the point?"

I nodded to Dole. He slapped Hopkins in the head.

We all heard the noise from the end of the hallway, and we followed Craig towards the kitchen. As we passed the threshold, we saw the open back door, the dirt trail, and a madman in a raincoat standing by the stove. He was caked in dirt. There was a lump of foil in one hand, a muddy shovel in the other. Then I recognized the face, one I hadn't seen since he handed me a check months ago: Mr. Eastman.

"You lying sack of bat shit," he said, stabbing a blistered finger at me. "Said you didn't find anything, and this whole time he's paying you off."

Craig said, *"Jesus!"* and hid behind me. Dole and Hopkins hung back.

"Mr. Eastman, I can assure you, I did all I could. I'm here tonight because of a new lead —"

"Stop it, that's enough. You don't think I know? I've been watching you all this time. I know he pays you enough so that you can afford your fancy convertible. I know your Frankenstein buddy here beats this guy up regularly. See, look, see what I found in the freezer?" Mr. Eastman lifted the foil lump, bounced it in his hand. "You should all burn in hell, you sickos. Worse than Judas, worse than Satan."

He lifted the shovel and lunged at me blade first. I fell out of the way but got off a couple shots, nailed Eastman in the chest. He slumped over and shook until all life was gone, still and bleeding on the marble floor.

Craig breathed hard, fast. I went to the back door, closed it, but saw that Eastman had dug up his daughter, the garbage bags covering her cut away. No use putting her back down.

"Fuck," I said.

"God, I'm glad you were here," Craig said. He hovered close, waiting for me to solve these new problems for him. But it wasn't that easy. With Eastman dead, a lot of the incentive for Craig to keep paying was gone. Who'd believe me if I told? What could the mother do? I glanced at Hopkins, who carried that self-assured grin again.

He said, "Easy choice, isn't it?"

"Shut up."

"All I'm saying is, it should be obvious."

Craig leaned his head forward. "What should be obvious?"

"This," I said. I turned around and shot Craig in the face.

Dole put Hopkins in the trunk and then came back. We tidied the scene, wiped prints, put the gun in Eastman's hand and fired, put the other gun in Craig's hand, fired. We made sure the red herrings looked like the gospel truth. And then we got the hell out of there.

I knew I would have to turn the car in later that week. No way I could afford it anymore. Such a sweet machine, so cool. I gunned it down Highway 90, top down, smelling the salt air, hearing the waves, hoping that Hopkins wouldn't mess up the trunk that much.

After a while, Dole said, "I'm going to miss beating the shit out him. He was good practice. Kept me in shape."

I turned on the radio to shut him up, found a classic rock station.

Later that night, we cut Hopkins into pieces and scattered his parts for miles up and down the beach, buried them deep under the dry sand.

The Sweetness at the Crummy End of Town

Ann Aptaker

Duke Skeetz, hard and thin as a ramrod, walked through the darkness in a rotting neighborhood on a cold, windy, moonless night. The icy damp ate through his gloves, seeped into his cap, bore through his overcoat and chilled the metal of the nine-millimeter hardware holstered under his left arm. Duke shivered, cold to the bone, the price for having overly keen senses. He'd made them that way, worked them over and sharpened them into tools to help him survive as a fixer, the guy people call when they can't call the cops. Duke trusted his senses to get to the truth of things. They never lied. People did.

Duke turned onto Fourth Street, headed for Sam Pitkin's bar in the middle the block. A windowless saloon, it gave no light outside except from a swinging sign above the door — BAR — in flickering red neon letters. The sign swung wildly in the wind, leaving broken red trails in the night mist. None of its glow reached the pavement. Fourth Street, like most of the streets around here, was dark as a grave.

Duke's senses tingled sweet and sour when he walked into Sam's saloon. The odors of hard whiskey and stale tobacco hung over the piney tang of the sawdust Sam spread on the floor to sop up vomit and piss. Weak yellowish light, murky with smoke, hid the raw ugliness of the chipped walls. The room was nearly empty, quiet enough for Duke to hear the drunk at the bar chew the juicy end of his stogie.

The only other patron in the place was a woman sitting in a booth. Duke pegged her the showpiece type, more costume than class. He thought her costume was a pretty good one, though, and he took a little time to wander around the black lace that hugged the woman from her neck down to the deep V of the green satin dress that drew all the light in the room to her tits. His eyes followed a shining line that continued below the table, rounded her ass, slid down a set of calves that had as much in common with flowing gold as with flesh. He took a pleasurable return trip to her face, where her full, purple painted mouth dangled a cigarette as if her lips ached for something better to do. She had big, dark, teary eyes, and black hair that framed her head like a bat's folded wings. Cigarette smoke curled around her. She excited Duke.

He looked away from her to Henry Phipps, a-k-a Phippy, who lay face down on the floor between Duke and the woman, dead. Phippy's fancy white wool coat was blotched with red. His arms stretched out on either side of him, his white coat spread wide. It made him look like an angel, Duke thought, one who'd had a rough landing after Heaven gagged on him and spit him out.

Sam Pitkin stepped out of a room in the back. The limp bar-cloth thrown over his shoulder was old and shriveled, sour, like Sam. He had a voice that sounded like he'd swallowed ground glass: "Duke! Y'got here fast. Good. Good. I called y'right away, the minute Phippy dropped dead. He stumbled in here with a hole in his chest, right through the heart it looked t'me, Duke. He was bleedin' all over my floor. He tried to say somethin' . . . he started to say, *'Tell Volner . . . '* but he never made it t'the end. He was a helluva sight. I gotta tell ya, Duke, between all that blood and his talk of Rudy Volner, he scared my regular boozers right out the door, 'cept for Lou" — Sam cocked his head toward the drunk at the bar — "but he's too close to dyin' hisself to be scared a'much."

Duke nodded towards the booth. He said, "What about her?"

Sam said, "She came in after, went pale as panties when she saw me standin' over the dead body. I wondered why she didn't just turn around and get outta here, but I think she really needed a drink. That's what she said, anyways. I thought she was gonna break down and cry. Lissen, Duke, I didn't call no cops, and I sure as Hell didn't call Volner. The lady over there said maybe I oughta call, y'know, family. Everybody knows you was sorta family to Phippy. So I figured, well, you might wanna just look into things y'self."

"Who's gonna pay me, Sam? You?"

Two words drifted across the room and brushed like feathers against Duke's ear: "I will." They came from the woman in the booth.

Duke looked at her now with the hard, steady gaze that one unfortunate recipient described as a knife Duke used to open someone's mouth. The woman cringed. She opened her mouth, more feathery words flew out: "Oh, I'm Charlotte Deare. Phippy must've mentioned me." Duke sensed fire underneath the breathy delivery.

He stayed on her face. He liked her face, liked its precarious balance of high-boned beauty and smeared mascara. "Why would he mention you?"

Charlotte said, "Phippy and I were going to be married."

Duke smiled, a thin thing that had no warmth, no sorrow. He didn't say that Phippy was a 'round-the-clock liar, or that he was lousy husband material who'd been a cheating heel while he was married to Duke's kid sister, Belle. Belle died in a car wreck six months ago. Drunk driving, the coroner's report said. Sure, Belle was a heavy boozer, so no one was surprised when her car took a dive off that old pier. All Duke said to Charlotte was, "No, Phippy didn't mention you. But I haven't seen him much lately." He took his gloves off, stuffed them into his coat pocket, lit a cigarette and told Sam to bring him a bottle of rye and a glass, along with more of whatever Charlotte was drinking. He left his cap and coat on when he slid into Charlotte's booth.

Sitting across from her was like watching a jungle plant bloom after a rain. Her smeared eyelids and purpled lips had the lure of fleshy flower petals. The scent of her was an exotic floral, too, with a tart undertone that stung Duke's nostrils.

She said, "You're Duke Skeetz. Phippy told me you're his brother-in-law. I'm . . . sorry about what happened to your sister."

Duke said, "Ever hear of Rudy Volner?"

She drew back a little, the jungle flower closing. She looked away from Duke, looked down at her hand while she crushed her cigarette out in the metal ashtray. Her hand was pale, bloodless as ivory, her nails well manicured and painted the same sultry purple as her lips. She spoke so softly it was almost under her breath, but the heat was there: "Volner's a scary guy."

"If you were Phippy's fiancée, then you knew Phippy worked for Volner."

"Sure, I knew. I . . . I was scared plenty about it." She fumbled with a black leather handbag beside her, took out a white hankie and a round gold compact. When she opened the compact it shielded her from Duke's hard gaze while she wiped the mascara away. Now and then she'd move the compact to one side of her face or the other, as if she wanted a better look, but it was really just a teasing peek-a-boo she pretended not to be aware of. When she'd finished and put the compact away, the black smudges of mascara weren't completely gone, giving her eyes a vampirish quality that stirred Duke's soul.

Sam showed up with Duke's bottle of rye and a glass, and a bottle of gin for Charlotte. She wasted no time pouring two fingers of booze. Sam hung around until Duke slapped cash into the old man's open palm.

Charlotte held her glass of gin in front of her face before she drank. She stared at Duke through the clear liquid. It made her eyes glisten. She said slowly, quietly, "I'm really scared, y'know, Mr. Skeetz."

"Duke."

"Duke." She tossed the shot back in one swallow, closed her eyes, couldn't suppress the little smile brought on by the warming effect of the gin. But a deep breath got past the gin's afterglow, erased the smile, replaced it with flaring nostrils. After another deep breath that Duke noticed caused nice things to happen under the plunging black lace and shiny green satin holding her tits, she said, "And I'm right to be scared. I . . . came here to meet Phippy. We were going to have a drink, then take in a movie. Instead . . ." The white hankie went to her cheek again. Then she balled it into her hand, worked it like worry-beads. Then she poured herself another drink.

Duke swallowed a shot of rye. He said nothing, just watched Charlotte swallow her drink, dab her eyes. The scent of her, the sweet and the tart, flowed through him.

She grew restless while Duke's silence crawled all over her. Her only escape was to start talking again: "I was across the street, on my way here, when I saw Phippy. He must've just gotten here, too, 'cause he was about to open the door. I started to call out his name . . . I was so happy t'see him, y'know? But then a car drove up. A big Lincoln. The door on Phippy's side must've opened — I couldn't see from across the street, you understand — but I heard a guy call out to Phippy, and when Phippy turned around he said, 'Hi, Mr. Volner' and then there was gunfire, and . . . and Phippy . . . I couldn't see Phippy until the Lincoln drove off! God I was so scared! I couldn't move! Y'know that kind of scared, Duke? The kind that paralyzes your knees, nails you to your spot?" Everything about her — the way her knuckles turned white when her hands gripped the edge of the table, the way she leaned towards Duke — begged him to reach over and comfort her.

Duke poured himself another rye, drank it, and put the glass down on the table. He wiped his mouth with the back of his hand. His knifelike gaze gave Charlotte another working over.

She escaped it, looked away from him, poured herself another drink, spilling a little booze on the table. It amused Duke to see her put her forefinger to the spill, then bring her fingertip to the tip of her tongue. She closed her eyes, gave her finger a demure lick. When she opened her eyes again, she didn't look at Duke, she looked at nothing; maybe the table. She said, "After the Lincoln drove away, I . . . I ran across the street to help Phippy. He was dragging himself in here. It was horrible. I tried to follow him, but I was nearly knocked over by a bunch of drunks stumbling out. By the time I got inside . . . Phippy was . . . dead." She finally got around to looking at Phippy, stared at him lying on the floor in a pool of his own blood. Her face went blank. Duke knew the look; some people wear it like armor when they deal with death. When Charlotte finally looked back at Duke, there was a fierceness in her he'd figured would seep out sooner or later. She said, "Listen, I want you to get this Volner guy. I can pay you. I can lay my hands on maybe five grand. If that's not enough I can —"

"What d'you mean, *'get'*?"

"Let's go to his place, *now,* confront the murdering bastard."

"And do what? Do him in?"

"If that's what it takes."

The way she said it nearly stripped the flesh from Duke's bones.

He didn't like anything about this whole setup.

No, he liked one thing: the payoff.

Duke liked the payoff so much that when he slid out of the booth he extended a gentlemanly hand to Charlotte. She took it. Her hand was warm, hot, felt like heated cream across Duke's rough skin. Her eyes weren't teary anymore; the glisten in them now was the glassy sheen of anticipation.

She slid from the booth, taking her handbag, a pair of black leather gloves, and her coat from the seat. The coat was silver fox fur. Duke helped her on with it. His hands sensed the life of the animal that now warmed the flesh of the woman. He felt it in the fur's pointy ends prickling his palms.

Duke led Charlotte to the door. Neither of them looked at Phippy.

Before they stepped outside, Sam said, "Y'can't just leave Phippy in here, Duke! Whaddya want me t'do with 'im?"

"Call an undertaker," Duke said. "The one on Ninth. The same guy that buried my sister."

Outside, when they were beneath the red neon bar sign, the stiff wind blew through Charlotte's hair and the bat's wings unfolded. She held her fox fur coat close at her neck. Duke put his gloves on, held his overcoat close, too, one hand at his collar while his other hand held his cap on his head. Together, Duke and Charlotte made their way through the dark neighborhood and the bitter cold. Her high heels clicked fast against the pavement, making the only other sound besides the wind.

Canned disco music thumping through the Joy Club's speakers couldn't drown out the farting, belching and braying of the dozen or so down-and-outs who watched a big redhead with no rhythm grind her goods on a tiny stage. The clientele here didn't care about rhythm. They didn't care about much, wouldn't notice the club's stained walls and stale smell because the fleabags they lived in were just as lousy. Duke knew this was just the kind of dive Rudy Volner wanted, why Volner opened the place in this no-account part of town. The Joy Club was for Volner's own amusement. The redhead — along with whatever blonde or brunette, Anglo, Asian, African or anyone else who had to flaunt flesh for a living — were for his personal use. The pretense of a strip joint, a sleazy but legal enterprise, was a front to provide Volner and his thugs with a paycheck that was strictly legit, right down to the last digits of withholding taxes.

Volner had an office upstairs. Duke and Charlotte went up a narrow stairwell that had a dusty carpet and an overhead fluorescent tube that made the air gritty and green. Duke caught a glimpse of Charlotte's face. The greenish light made her look dead.

The light on the second floor wasn't any kinder. It didn't make the two bruisers in shirtsleeves sitting outside Volner's office door look any too friendly, and it cast a putrid glare on the big pieces of hardware holstered under their arms.

The two brutes stood up as Duke and Charlotte came down the hall. One of the big boys could pass for an ape with a sneer; the other an ape with a scowl. Duke knew the sneering ape. His name was Joe Breunner, but Duke said, "Hello, ham-hocks. Your boss in?"

Breunner's sneer widened into the kind of grin that sends people running for their lives. "Lemme check," he said.

He turned around, knocked on the door.

Duke felt Charlotte against his right arm. She'd drawn away from the other ape, the one with the scowl. Duke noticed a patch of fur twitch on the shoulder of her fox coat; the ape was breathing on her.

From the other side of the door came a thin, "Yeah?" Volner's mousy squeak always turned Duke's stomach.

Breunner opened the door just enough to stick his head inside. He said, "Skeetz is here. You wanna see 'im?"

"He alone?"

Breunner said, "Nah, he's got a set 'a boobs with 'im; y'know, the dame Phippy's been runnin' with."

"Send 'em in."

Duke smiled: Volner's squeak had sounded downright cordial.

Breunner jerked his head for Duke and Charlotte to go in.

It was quiet in Volner's office. The heavy door muffled the noise from the showroom downstairs. It was pretty dark in the office, too. The light of the single lamp on Volner's big steel desk didn't illuminate much more than the surface of the desk and a patch of print carpet in front of it, but it was enough to catch the doughy excesses of Rudy Volner's ugly face. It glared off his heavy glasses. Some of the light even crept up to his blotchy bald head. Too much of the light, in Duke's opinion, made its way to Volner's mustard color sports jacket and maroon shirt, which was open nearly halfway down his chest. Volner's curly black chest hairs stuck out through the open shirt. The sight made Duke itch.

Volner stood up and reached across the desk, offered Duke his hand. Duke saw a reflection of himself and Charlotte in Volner's glasses. Charlotte looked so small.

Duke gave Volner's hand a firm shake. Volner's flesh was soft, too smooth, and had stale traces of a musky scent left by whichever plaything had been up here this evening.

Maybe the big redhead.

Volner said, "I haven't seen you in too long, Duke, not since Belle's funeral." Each squeaky word gnawed at Duke's guts. "I sent a wreath, y'know. A big one. I bet Belle would've liked it."

Duke nodded. Volner was right; Belle would've like it.

Volner said, "Have a seat. I just bought these here guest chairs. Leather. Plenty comfortable. Go on, tell me what you think."

Duke said, "I'll stand. Rudy, this woman is Charlotte Deare. She says she's Phippy's fiancée, or was. Phippy's dead, shot through the chest a little while ago in front of Sam Pitkin's bar over on Fourth Street. She says you did it."

Volner said, "Cigar?" He'd opened a shiny black humidor on his desk, turned it towards Duke. Inside, a layer of pricey cigars sent out a fruity aroma. Duke took a cigar.

Volner took one for himself, rolled it around in his fat fingers before bringing it to his mouth.

Each man lit his own cigar; Duke with a match from a book in his pocket, Volner with a heavy green marble lighter that was part of his desk set. Duke watched the lighter's flame reflect in Volner's glasses. There was a red glow in the center of the flame, the reflected tip of Duke's cigar.

Duke blew smoke, said, "You don't seem too broken up over the death of one of your employees, Rudy."

"You want me to pay for his funeral? Okay, I'll pay for his funeral. He'll get a big wreath, too."

"Don't knock yourself out. That'd be more than Phippy deserves. If I know Phippy, he probably had a bullet comin' for one thing or another. Anyway, Rudy, I know Charlotte's lying."

The reflection in Volner's glasses showed Charlotte even smaller now, and a little to the left behind Duke. He'd heard the whisper of something slide from her handbag. He figured it was a gun. He knew it was pointed at his back, aimed roughly in the area of his kidney, and he knew the gun was tipped with a silencer.

Her voice rose like dust: "One good lie is all it ever takes for a man to play along with me."

Duke said, "Even a bad lie would've won Phippy over, especially from a sweet pair of high heels like you. Isn't that right, Rudy?"

Volner exhaled smoke, smiling. Shadows dug into his face. Duke thought the only way Volner could look any uglier was if he was suddenly hit by sunshine.

Duke said, "You must've been pretty nervous, Rudy. You must've thought Phippy had something on you, something that could damage your operation. Otherwise you wouldn't have bothered to set Phippy up with the hot little assassin standing behind me. She was just his type, and you knew it; the trampy type he ran around with behind my sister's back. You set Charlotte on him to dig out whatever dirt Phippy might've had on you."

Volner put his cigar in the corner of his mouth, puffed it. His tiny voice drilled through a cloud of smoke: "Phippy didn't know shit about my operation, Skeetz. He was nothin' but a two-bit go-fer."

"Yeah. But my sister wanted him to be a three-bit go-fer. She even tried to help him; she kept her ear to the ground, picked up all sorts of odds and ends that might give Phippy an edge with you. Belle was real good at diggin' around for dirt, always was. It's why my mother was scared of her. It's why you were scared of her, too, Rudy. It's why you killed her. What'd you do? Get her real drunk then push her car over the pier yourself, or did you have one of your hired goons do it?"

"I only know what I heard on the news, Skeetz, something about the coroner ruling it a drunk-driving accident. Whatsa matter, Skeetz? Don't you believe our fine city officials?" Volner spread his arms wide, like a slick preacher.

Duke said, "Now you figure to wipe out the last threatening knot in the rope that might hang you, Rudy: me. But that comes later, doesn't it. You've got something on your mind, Rudy, or why the phony play to lure me over here?"

Volner sat down in his great big chair, leaned back, puffed his cigar. Duke enjoyed hating him.

Charlotte said, "Please, Rudy, let's get this over with. I don't like —"

"I don't pay you to *'like'*." Volner squeaked as if his mouse's tail had been stepped on. "I pay you to *'do'* and you'll do what I say or you'll be jiggling your ass again, and this time it'll be for the street-slugs with shit in their pants at the four A.M. show. Now: Skeetz, I had Charlotte waltz you over here because I have a proposition for you."

Duke didn't enjoy Volner's fancy cigar anymore. He took it from his mouth, put it out in the big marble ashtray on Volner's desk. "There's nothing you could offer me that I'd want."

"Your life, Skeetz. I'm offering you your life. I've always liked your talents, and I'm willing to pay for them. Pay good, too. So, come to work for me, and you live. Turn me down, and Charlotte pulls the trigger."

She was nearer now. Duke felt her gun press against him, felt its deadly little circle. He smelled her flowery scent, the tart undertone.

She grunted when Duke's arm flailed behind him, chopped against her wrist. In one movement he spun and caught her thirty-eight revolver, pointed it at Volner's head and fired. The silenced gunfire was no louder than the splat of Volner's brains as he keeled over on his desk.

Duke spun back around, pointed Charlotte's own gun at her. Volner's desk lamp was behind Duke, not much of its light got to Charlotte. She wasn't any more than a shadow.

But Duke could see her outline, hear her breathing fast. He could smell the sweat souring her perfume. She was scared.

Duke said, "I don't know what kind of information you sweet-talked out of Phippy and passed on to Volner, and I don't care."

Her whisper cut through the darkness: "Tell me what you *do* care about, Duke. Tell me. We could be something special, y'know? Think of it. We run on the same juices. We're the same under the skin."

"Don't bet on it. I'd have to take a deep breath every time you walked into a room, sniff the air for the smell of death you carry with you after you've killed. It's how I knew the minute I sat down with you at Sam's that it was you who shot Phippy."

"Smell? That's not a nice thing to say to a lady."

"Your hands, Charlotte. I could smell the cordite residue on your hands. It came up sharp, right through your sweet perfume. Volner's hands didn't have it. His fingers smelled of a different kind of death, the slow kind that he squeezes from his stable of dancing dollies. Then there were the lies you told about seeing Phippy from across the street, and a big Lincoln driving up with Volner inside, gunning Phippy down. Listen, Fourth Street at night is dark as a cemetery. You'd have to be face-to-face with someone to get a straight shot to the heart. The only part of your setup that I liked was the payoff. So far, I've collected half of it."

"And . . . I'm the other half? Why? I didn't kill your sister! It was Volner!"

Duke said, "Yeah, but you killed Phippy. He wasn't much. I never liked him. My sister liked him, though; she *loved* him, right down to his rotten little heart. Killing Phippy was like killing Belle twice over. Volner knew that's how I'd take it. He set you up, too, girlie, in case you don't know."

Charlotte's breathing was fast, loud. Then she laughed, a deep, short laugh: "You're good, Skeetz! Sure, go ahead; the gun's silenced, those dopes outside won't hear it." Her face caught a little more light as she leaned closer to Duke. Her eyes were shining. "By the time those two get the idea to come in here and see what's what, you'll be long gone, won't you. They're too stupid to operate without Volner, so they'll just lay low or get outta town, right, Skeetz? You'll win." The scent of her wasn't sour anymore. All Duke smelled was her sweet perfume. It circled around him as she came nearer. "You're the type of guy who always wins, Skeetz. You're the type of guy I've always tried for. Never had any luck, though. Are you gonna change my luck?" She touched the lapel of Duke's coat, slid her hand up to his face. The fox fur on her sleeve brushed his cheek. He didn't mind.

She said, "Or are you gonna turn me over to the cops? You could, y'know, turn me over to the cops. That's my gun that killed Rudy. The cops would believe you if you said I killed him, that you pulled my gun away afterward. Is that what you're gonna do, Skeetz? Turn me over to the cops? Don't do it, Skeetz. Please. You know what'll happen to me in the lock-up. I'd rather die."

Duke took a deep breath. Sweet.

No More Running

Percy Spurlark Parker

I slid Bob's change across the counter to him as he finished his second beer. He wiped his mouth with the back of his hand, scooped up all but a dollar and said good night. I dropped the bill in the tip jar by the register, headed for the end of the bar. Some guy with a hat clamped tight on his head had come in while I was finishing up with Bob, and had taken the farthest counter stool from the door. If it was a move to isolate himself it seemed a waste. Now that Bob was gone, the guy at the end of the bar was the only customer in the joint.

"What'll it be, mister?"

He looked up from under the brim of his hat. "I'll have a . . ." he started, stopped, smiled.

The damn smile was like a fiery blade slicing a zigzag path into my gut.

"Make it a double bourbon, Lee. So, this is where you disappeared to?"

My tongue felt as if it had gone dry, and it took me a moment to speak. "How's things going, Jake?"

"Much better, now that I've ran into you."

There was a gun under a towel on the second shelf across from the register. But I had as much chance of getting to it as crack has of being legalized. If I made a try for the door he was sure to nail me before I got from behind the counter. Or, he just might decide to have a little fun with me, let me make it to the door thinking I was getting away, when all the time there was someone else waiting for me out there.

I got the bourbon, overshooting the glass as I poured, then made a bigger mess when I tried to wipe it up, bumping into his glass and spilling more booze on the counter. I wished it were earlier in the evening when there were generally more people in the bar. But with Jake and me alone, there was nothing stopping him from killing me right now.

"Take it easy, Lee. You ain't got nothing to worry about from me."

I didn't dare believe him. Jake had been a member of the mob long before I hooked up with them. Heisting cars was his specialty, but he was always available for a little strong-arm work, or whatever else there was that needed to be done.

I finally managed to clean up the mess I'd made, poured him another drink.

"Look, Jake, I know we were never buddy-buddy, but hell, it's been three years now. They got Sam and Mark. Can't they forget about me?"

"They won't forget, Lee, you know that. Not even if they get their money back. Last I heard the price tag on you was a hundred grand. They only got thirty on me."

I heard him but things were happening a mite too fast for it all to sink in.

He shrugged. "We're in the same boat, Lee. I just shook two of their guns back in the last town, Rysville, I think. Had to ditch my wheels and grab some local's heap. Just stopped here for a breather." He raised his glass. "Glad I did."

I took a closer look at him now. He needed a shave; uneven stubble covered his lean jaws. Puffy bags hung under his dark eyes, pointing to a lack of restful sleep. His navy blue suit wasn't dirty, but it hadn't come fresh from the cleaners either. He had the look of a man on the run. The same kind of look I'd had before I'd found this hole to hide in. His shabby appearance would've been an elaborate and unnecessary ploy if he'd come here to kill me.

"The D.A. was pulling me in pretty regularly," Jake said. "One of their investigators came up missing couple months back. I don't know how the boys got the wrong idea, but they must've figured I was giving the D.A. an earful."

I nodded. He could be telling the truth or a partial truth anyway. More than likely Jake was making a deal with the D.A.'s office when the mob got wise.

Jake had gotten into trouble because of his big mouth. My situation had come from knocking over one of the mob's gambling joints. We thought we had it all worked out, we were going to get away clean. But Sam had gotten killed outright, and Mark had stayed alive long enough to give them my name.

I'd gotten away with the money though, almost four hundred thousand. But I really couldn't enjoy it. Fancy penthouses, expensive cars, and glamorous women were out. If I'd tried a high profile lifestyle like that, the mob would've had me in a week. No, all I've been able to use the money for was to keep me hidden.

"Seeing you gives me hope, Lee. Hell, if you've made it this long . . . guess I got a chance."

"It ain't easy."

He nodded. "Yeah, but I got you to help me." He emptied his glass and pushed it forward for a refill.

I poured him another, not spilling any this time. "Keep low and keep moving. That's the only thing that's helped me."

"I could use something more tangible. You couldn't have gotten rid of all that money."

"Advice is all I've got to give."

"You can do better than that, Lee."

"Why should I?"

His thin lips curled into a sneer. "I would think that's obvious."

It was. I either help him, or the mob would get my new address. When I landed in this town I'd made myself a promise that my running days were over. I was here to stay. No more running for me. No more looking over my shoulder every five minutes. And I began spending some of the money to make sure my life would be secure. Buying the tavern was part of it.

Jake emptied his glass again, poured another for himself this time. "They said you got away with over a half a mil."

"They lied."

"Whatever. I'm betting you got a good chunk of it left."

"A little," I said. Actually, I still had more than half of it. "It costs a lot to stay in hiding. There're people to pay."

"There's always people to pay, Lee. Me for one. Way I see it, I can move in here with you, or if you think the town would be too crowded with both of us here . . . throw some of that loot my way and I'm history."

"And naturally you'll forget you ever ran into me?"

"You got my word on it."

Shit. He might as well have said he'd be back every week for an envelope full of crisp bills. "I may be able to dig up a little something for you."

"Dig deep, Lee. The more you give me, the father away I can get." He belched, took a breath, then lifted his glass in a toast.

I'd never killed anyone before, but I could see no other way to rid myself of him. Left on his own, he wouldn't stay away. Or worse, he would try to use me as a bargaining chip to get back in with the mob. So, he had to die. It was just a matter of how.

"I always thought you were a stand up guy, Lee."

"The name's Terry, now," I said, topping off his drink. The slower his reflexes the better. Let's see, there was the gun under the counter, an ice pick in the ice bin, a . . .

"Evening, Terry."

Ron Cetti rested his massive bulk on the stool at the front corner of the bar. The dull shine of his deputy sheriff's badge almost blended in with his khaki uniform.

Jake slouched somewhat on his stool, turning slightly away from Ron. I felt frozen for a moment between the two. I was so engrossed in my thoughts of murder I hadn't heard Ron come in. What was he doing here? Could he tell what I was planning? Could Jake?

"Make it a short one, Terry," Ron said, with his heavy jawed grin. "I promised the little lady I'd start on a diet tonight."

"Ah . . . yeah, sure thing, Ron," I said, going over to the tap and drawing him a beer. The Coor's clock behind the counter read a quarter after ten. Hell, Ron usually stopped in around this time when he was on duty, looking for a beer and some small talk. I really had nothing to worry about from him, but thinking of murder and seeing the uniform had rattled me at first.

"Kindda slow tonight," Ron said, sipping his beer.

I took a deep breath to compose myself. "It'll pick up later in the week."

Ron nodded, dipping in the bowl of peanuts on the counter next to him. "You visiting or passing through, mister?"

Jake stirred some. "Passing through," he said, without looking up.

"Too bad. We've got a nice town here. Quiet. Not too big, not too small. Folks are really friendly. Ain't that right,

Terry?"

"You working for the chamber of commerce now?"

Ron laughed. "Okay, but I'm telling the truth, aren't I? We've got the friendliest town in the whole damn state."

"Sure, the friendliest and the safest," I said. "At least the safest tavern."

Ron's laugh was louder this time, his massive bulk heaving on the barstool. "I caught that, Terry." He finished his beer, stood. "Guess I better get back to my rounds. Give a thought to staying a while, mister. It's really a great town."

"Yeah, I'll think it over," Jake said, waiting for Ron to leave before ordering another drink. "Nice of the deputy to invite me to stay."

"Go move in with him then."

I didn't mean for the bitterness to come out, but it had and Jake responded with a long hard stare. "Changing your mind, Lee?"

"Naw, not at all." I'd made one mistake and couldn't afford another. "It's just taken me some time to get here and I don't want to mess it up." I would have to play him just right. I couldn't let him get wise to what I was planning. "I'll help you, Jake, but you've got to do just as I tell you, or you could blow it for both of us.'

"No problem, Lee. Just name it." There was a slight slur to his speech pattern, the first sign the bourbon was beginning to work.

"How hot is that car you got back in Rysville?"

Jake shrugged. "Not very, I guess. It's parked out front and your deputy didn't say squat about it."

"Well, let's get it out of sight, anyway. There's a place out back where you can stash it until I close. Then we can get over to my place and figure out our next move." I hoped I sounded convincing, although I felt I might've been talking too fast. "Come on," I said, stepping from behind the counter. "I'll show you where you can put the car."

Jake didn't move right away. His eyes shifted about the empty tavern, back to me, then he polished off his drink, gave a hitch to the bulge under his coat and stood.

I headed for the back of the tavern with Jake following me. The washrooms were on my right, the door leading to my storeroom on my left. "I had a hell of a time my first few months," I said, opening the storeroom door, and stepping back so he could go first.

Jake balked at the door jamb. "Kind of dark in there, ain't it?"

"We're just going over to that window," I said, pointing to the shaded window on the back wall. The lights in the alley illuminated the drawn canvas shade. I put my hand on his shoulder and guided him into the room.

With the lights of the tavern spilling in through the open door, the room around us was more a shadowy gray than anything else. "I don't think I stayed in any one place longer than three days," I said, steering him toward the window with one hand, as I felt along the tops of liquor cases with the other. I'd been using a hammer earlier in the day and I was sure I'd left it on top of one of the cases.

"I didn't know where to go," I said. "We hadn't thought anything would go wrong." Where was the hammer? Had I left it somewhere else?

"It was Sam's idea. I was the last to go along." I was going to bungle it, I just knew it. Jake was armed and I didn't like my chances in a wrestling match.

"I think it took me a year before I had my first full night's sleep." Where was that Goddamn hammer? It has to be . . . my hand brushed against its smooth handle.

"At first, anyone who looked at me for more than two seconds I figured knew who I was," I said, keeping the chatter going as I got a firm grip on the hammer.

"Pull the shade back and I'll show you the spot I'm talking about," I coaxed, and at that moment I imagined Jake turning around, catching me with the hammer raised, the gun in his hand jumping as it spat bullets into me.

But that didn't happen. "Where?" he simply asked, as he pulled the shade aside and leaned closer to the window.

I swung. The vibration of the impact ran through my arm, as the blow rammed Jake's head into the windowsill. He let out a short moan as he crumbled to the floor. I didn't hesitate as I knelt down and swung again, then once more just to make sure.

When I stood, I was breathing heavy and I could feel the sweat build up on my forehead and chest. I ran to the washroom, checked myself in the mirror. Surprisingly I hadn't gotten splattered with any blood. Maybe his hat had acted as a shield. Maybe I hadn't broken any skin. I'd heard his skull crack. Felt it. I didn't have to be covered in blood to know I'd killed him.

The front door was next. I flipped the OPEN sign to CLOSED, hit the light switch, then went outside to check on the car Jake had stolen in Rysville.

There was a green Ford I hadn't seen before in the neighborhood parked at the curb. Jake had hot-wired the Ford, disengaging the ignition wires when he'd parked. I got the engine going by twisting the wires back together and drove around into the alley. I turned the lights off but left the engine running, going back into my place through the storeroom.

There was an old quarry just outside of town with a good hundred and fifty-foot drop. Whenever Jake would be found, no one would be able to call it anything but an accident.

I could see the blood now. A small pool had formed on the floor around his head. I propped him up by his shoulders, pulling his coat tail up between us so as not to get any blood on myself and drug him out into the alley . . . into a blinding beam of light, and Deputy Ron Cetti's voice. "Hell of a way to treat new customers, Terry."

Ron slid behind the wheel of the patrol car, sat there a moment before starting the engine. I couldn't see him clearly, but I could tell some of the color had gone out of his face, and there was a stern set to his jaws.

As for myself, the initial jitters had subsided but I could still tell my pulse was going at a good clip.

"Never thought this would involve murder," Ron said.

He'd come back to my tavern to check on the Ford after getting a report that one like it had been stolen in Rysville. He'd seen me drive the car into the alley and followed.

"I didn't have any choice," I said.

"You should've tried something else."

"Not with him, I couldn't. Besides, what are you bitching about? You've finally gotten the chance to earn the money I've been shelling out to you."

"You're paying me to keep your old identity hidden, not to be an accessory to murder."

As I'd said, once landing in this town I'd begun spending some of the money to make my life secure. Ron was a part of that, as were other key people in town.

After explaining to Ron what had happened, we'd loaded Jake into the Ford and he'd followed me in his patrol car out to the quarry.

"I think I need a bonus," Ron said.

"You do, huh?"

"It's only fair," Ron nodded. "I'm thinking ten grand."

"I'm thinking five."

Ron shrugged, thought a bit. "Yeah, okay. I'll expect it tomorrow," he said, throwing the patrol car in gear.

I leaned back, digging my pack of cigarettes out of my pocket. Greed is a funny thing. It always grows. Slowly at times, but it keeps growing. I would need Ron around in case the guys who were on Jake's tail stumble onto me. But after that threat was over, Ron might just be more of a liability to me than an asset.

It was something to think about.

Down Highway 61

Gary R. Bush

I was driving north on Highway 61 toward Hugo, Minnesota. I couldn't help but remember the Bob Dylan song, *Highway 61 Revisited*. Especially the line about Mack the Finger looking to unload forty red, white and blue shoestrings and a thousand telephones that didn't ring. Louis the King tells him to take everything down to Highway 61.

I often wondered if Dylan ever knew Ira Matossian. Ira like to called himself a dealer in lost items, but he was really the biggest fence in the Midwest. If there was money in it, I wouldn't have been surprised if Matossian did deal in shoestrings and telephones that didn't ring.

When a "lost" item of value came Ira's way, an item too hot to fence, he would try to sell it back to the insurer. Some of the insurance companies would rather pay Matossian a "fee" than the full insured value of the item. That's where I came in. Ira couldn't approach the companies himself, he needed a go-between. It wasn't strictly kosher, but to save money, the insurance companies often looked the other way.

On that cold blustery October morning, I had received a call from Ira. Although he tried to hide behind a rough voice, he sounded excited.

"Coppersmith, I have something that may interest you. Come on out as soon as possible." So I left my office in downtown Minneapolis and headed to Highway 61.

Matossian Salvage was straight ahead on the right. It looked liked any other auto parts yard, but it was just a cover for Ira's real business.

I drove through the gate and passed the auto bone yard, then through another gate to the old house that Matossian used as his office.

Cosmo and Basil, Matossian's half German Shepherd Dogs — I was convinced they were half Chinese dragons — were lying outside, seeming impervious to the weather. At night they roamed the yard. I pity the fool who would try to steal anything from the dump when they were on the prowl.

Fortunately the "boys" and I had an understanding. They wagged their tails and barked when they saw me. I tossed them a couple of Milk-Bones, my insurance against a rough welcome.

The barking alerted Matossian, who came out of the house. He thrust his chin, a permanent blue-black shadow, in my face. "Stop feeding my dogs," he growled. "You want to spoil them for their real work?"

I smiled, stepped back and looked up. There was a lot of Ira Matossian to see.

He was dressed in bib overalls and — despite the cold — a loud, short sleeve Hawaiian shirt that showed off arms so muscular and hairy that a momma gorilla would have taken him for her son. A pair of Red Wing work boots covered his size 13 feet.

Matossian looked like an illiterate junk peddler, but I knew he held at least three university degrees.

"I see you're still driving that crappy Trooper, Coppersmith," he said eyeing my ever-rusting SUV. "I've got a nice BMW out in the yard. I think it would be perfect for you."

"Are you sure I wouldn't burn myself on the deal?"

"Max, if you're insinuating that I would sell you a hot car, you cut me to the quick," he said, lighting up a big Havana.

"Right now I'll stick with the crappy Trooper. But you never know when I might need a new ride."

"Suit yourself," he shrugged. "Now come on, we need to talk."

I petted the two monsters disguised as canines and followed Matossian. "There are only a few people who can touch those dogs," he said, looking over his shoulder. "They must recognize their kin. I always said you were a son-of-a-bitch, Coppersmith."

"At least a terrier — once I grab on I don't let go," I replied, as we entered the building.

Surplus metal office furniture took up space in an outer room that served the *legitimate* business. I nodded to the two blondes standing by a row of file cabinets.

Yvette and Yvonne were twin beauties who helped run the business and shared Ira's bed. I could never tell them apart. Ira once told me Yvonne had a small scar on her left buttocks, and that was the only way he could tell which was which. When they had their clothes on he just called them "Ladies." Since they did almost everything in unison, they didn't seem to mind.

Today they were dressed in identical red cashmere sweaters and black slacks so tight that I imagined for a minute that I could make out Yvonne's scar.

"Hello, Max," they both chimed.

"Hello, Ladies," I answered back.

"Ladies, I don't want to be disturbed," Matossian said as we passed through the office.

"Yes, Ira," they sang in stereo.

"How do you do it, Ira?" I asked, motioning with my head toward the twins.

"It's easy," he answered. "I love them."

I nodded. He might look like an ape, but he could be charming as hell, and if he was screwing both sisters it was with their consent.

Matossian's inner sanctum was quite a contrast to the other office and the surrounding junk yard. It was tastefully decorated, but it was the art work on the walls that really caught the eye. Mainly modern stuff — Klee, Picasso and a couple of artists I had never heard of. Ira assured me that they were up and coming and their works would be worth a fortune someday. If asked he could produce a provenance for each piece.

Ira waved me to a comfortable leather chair and sat down behind his desk. "So, Coppersmith, you still the big movie fan? I've come across an original Elmo Lincoln *Tarzan* poster."

"Ira, you didn't bring me all the way out here to sell me a movie poster or a BMW. What's going on?"

"Max, I acquired an item that you may be interested in." He settled back in his chair and took a drag on his cigar.

"You want me to contact an insurance company?"

"No, not yet," he said. "If I remember, some years back, when there was still a Soviet Union, you worked for a clandestine outfit that got Jews out of the 'evil empire.'"

"So?" I asked. Not too many people knew about that part of my life.

"So, Max, this might be right up your alley." He ground out his cigar in a leaded glass ashtray and leaned forward. "I came across a piece of stolen Nazi loot, and I want you to find the heirs of the last rightful owner."

"Nazi loot? What do you mean?"

"About a week ago a house on Bald Eagle Lake was hit and a number of *objets d'art* were taken."

"I read about it. The Grenier estate. Bald Eagle Lake is pretty close to here, Ira. Right down Highway 61. The cops been around?"

"Of course." He gave me a smile that on anyone else I would say was a smirk, but on Ira it was one of sure confidence. "They could go through this place with a wrecking ball and never find my stash.

"Anyway, the Grenier heist. Everything was reported stolen except one item. That item was a work by a late sixteenth, early seventeenth century Dutch figure painter by the name of Joachim Anthoniez Wtewael. Wtewael was a leading exponent of the Mannerist style of painting, and especially adept at small paintings on copper."

"Fascinating," I said. "But does this art history lesson have a point?"

"Yes, the item not reported was a small painting on copper of *Leda and the Swan.* I'm sure you know your mythology."

"Zeus came to Leda in the form of a swan and from that union came Helen and Pollux."

"Right. Anyway, that painting was only eight inches high, but worth a fortune. The last legal owner was a French Jew by the name Joseph Issacshon. Issacshon was sent to Auschwitz in 1942, where he was murdered. His art collection disappeared."

"You have my attention, Ira," I said, sitting straighter in my chair.

"It gets better, Coppersmith," Ira continued. "There was a German art dealer based in Paris, by the name of Gustav Rochlitz. Beginning in 1941, Rochlitz selected looted works in France for shipment to Germany and especially to Hermann Goering. After the war, Rochlitz was arrested and jailed by the French.

"I'm sure the Wtewael was one of Rochlitz's acquisitions. The painting probably ended up at Karinhall, Goering's estate. We know that members of the Allied forces were responsible for removing the stolen art and returning the pieces to their countries of origin. *Leda and the Swan* by Wtewael never turned up — until now."

"So how did it wind up at an estate on Bald Eagle Lake more than a half a century later?"

"A member of the Allies at Karinhall liberated it for himself."

"Well, if that's true, the thief is probably very old right now."

"Actually, he's dead. But his son had the Wtewael."

"His son?" I said. "Andrew Grenier?"

"Andrew Grenier, Jr.," Ira reminded me. "The Greniers are investment bankers with one of the largest private art collections in the U.S. Andrew Senior was a poor art history student when the war broke out. At war's end, he was on the team that searched Germany for the stolen art.

"When he came back to St. Paul in 1947, he suddenly became an investment banker."

"From a poor GI to an investment banker. Interesting," I said.

Ira smiled. "You're ahead of me, aren't you? Yeah, my guess is he sold off some of what he looted to start his business."

"Which made him a little less evil than the Nazis themselves," I said.

"Precisely," Ira answered. "With his stolen goods as a start, he made millions."

"So, tell me Ira, why do you want to return this work to the Issacshon heirs? This painting could bring you a small fortune. And let's face it, you deal in stolen goods all the time. Why is this any different?"

"I don't deal in looted art. Do you remember what Hitler said about the Armenians when he started the Holocaust?"

"Yes, 'Who remembers the Armenians?'" I answered.

"Yeah, the Turks massacred a million Armenians during

World War I, but by the time Hitler came along no one remembered or gave a damn. Well, I'm Armenian and I've never forgotten. I may be a dealer in stolen goods, but I don't handle stuff that was taken from displaced or murdered peoples. That includes Cambodians, Rwandans or even Muslim Albanians."

This was side of Ira I had never seen before. He was a tough deal maker. Never giving an inch in negotiations, hard as nails, probably ready to kill if he had to.

"Don't look so fucking shocked, Coppersmith, even I have some scruples."

"Watch it, Ira, or I'm going to start liking you."

"Don't do me any favors."

"So, you want me to contact some people I know and see if I can find the rightful owner of *Leda and the Swan?"*

"Yeah, I do. But I want more. I want to nail Grenier."

"It was his father that stole the painting, not Junior," I reminded Ira.

"The dickhead knew what he had. Otherwise the Wtewael would have been insured and declared as part of the stolen works of art. And only a small portion of his collection was stolen."

"How do you know that?" I asked.

"Believe me, I'm aware of what Grenier has in his collection. Look, Max, there are bound to be other looted pieces."

"Why? You said Senior sold off the stolen stuff for seed money."

"Because if the Greniers kept the Wtewael, they probably kept a few more pieces. I knew Senior. He was an asshole and thief, but he loved his collection and he loved the Dutch and Flemish painters. Junior is just like his old man."

"And how do you want to go about nailing Grenier?"

"We steal the rest of his collection."

"We? In case you forget, I'm a private investigator licensed by the state of Minnesota. I'm not about to get caught breaking and entering."

"Max, you're talking to me. You've bent, even broken the law before. Hell, dealing with me is not strictly legal.

"And when you went into the old Soviet Union, you weren't going by the book. I know because I helped your organization get the phony papers and passports."

"Well, that was before I ruined my leg on an ore boat on Lake Superior and before I became a PI," I replied, tapping my bum leg with my cane. "What about the thief who took the stuff from Grenier originally? Why don't you use him?"

"No, can't."

"Are you afraid he'll want compensation for the Wtewael?"

"No, that's not a problem. I just don't want anyone else involved."

"Well, I'm not going to break into any home. I'll take the painting of *Leda and the Swan* and see if Issacshon has any heirs."

"I'll settle for that." Ira reached behind his desk and picked up a small package. "Here's the Wtewael."

I took the painting and he walked me out. I said goodbye to the Ladies and patted the dogs as I passed them. If Ira or the Ladies didn't walk a person past them, the dogs would rip that person apart. Even my friendship with the dogs wasn't a guarantee of safety.

When I returned to my office I made a few calls, starting the process of looking for the Issacshon heirs.

It was Sunday afternoon a little more than a week later that I got a call from Yvette. She was crying. "Max, Ira's been killed. Could you come out here, please?"

Driving through a mix of snow and rain, I was at Matossian's in less than an hour. Yvette or Yvonne let me in.

Ira was at his desk, a bullet hole through his head.

Through tears and sobs, Yvette and Yvonne told me what they knew. Sometimes they spoke singly, sometimes in unison.

"Ira had an appointment here this morning. We went to the Mall of America. Ira was supposed to meet us for lunch. When he didn't show we called here and home but there was no answer. Finally we drove out here, found the gates unlocked and Ira dead. His office was tossed but nothing was missing."

"Who was he supposed to meet?" I asked.

"He didn't say, just that he would meet us for lunch."

"Where were the dogs?"

"In the yard."

"Coming in wouldn't be a problem," I said. "Ira would have greeted his visitor and the dogs would have behaved."

"But going out would have been different. If Ira wasn't there to escort the visitor, the dogs would have attacked," Yvonne said. Or maybe it was Yvette.

"OK, who could get past the dogs?"

"Well, there's Wilt and Larry who worked the yard, but they've been with Ira for years. You got along with the dogs," Yvonne continued.

"But at the least they would have held you at bay until they got the command to stand down. Either one of us or Ira would have to have given that command," Yvette said, finishing her sister's thought.

"There had to be someone else," I said.

"Andrew Grenier," Yvette or Yvonne said suddenly.

"What about him?"

"He liked the dogs."

"Back up," I said. "Grenier has been here?"

"Many times," Yvonne answered. "You see, Max, he was

both a customer and supplier for our business. So was his father. He got along with the dogs just fine. In fact, he found them for Ira."

"Grenier found the dogs?"

"Oh yes. His cousin raises guard dogs," Yvette said.

"Grenier could get by the dogs," Yvonne said. "He killed Ira."

"Why?"

"He had to figure Ira had his paintings. He probably threatened Ira with a gun," Yvette said.

"And Ira probably laughed in his face," Yvonne finished.

"And Grenier killed him," they said together, tears now forming in their eyes.

"I want to destroy him," Yvonne said and Yvette nodded.

"I'd like to go back and get the rest of his artwork and expose him for the bastard he is," Yvette said.

"Go back?" I asked. "What do you mean, go back?"

They looked at one another for a moment. "We did it, we pulled the job."

"You?"

"We're master thieves."

I was nonplussed. These two petite blonde beauties, thieves.

"So that's why Ira didn't want you involved again. He worried about you," I said. They both nodded.

"If you were in business with Grenier, why did you rob him?"

"Because he's an asshole," they said in unison.

Then Yvette went on. "He would hit on us every time he came in here. Then one evening he came in here when Ira was away on a business trip. He bought a painting by Cornelis Cornelizoon that we had acquired. He had a flask of what he claimed was a very rare Armagnac. He wanted to close the deal with a toast. We don't remember much after we drank. But we know we were both raped. A few days later we received pictures of ourselves in various obscene positions. We figured he had slipped us Roofies." She was angry and embarrassed at the same time.

"The date-rape drug — Rohypnol," I said.

"Yes. It was then we decided to get the negatives back. Breaking in to his estate was no big deal for us. We found the pictures and the negatives in the safe and while we were there we took a portion of his collection for payback."

"Did you tell Ira what happened?" I asked.

"We didn't dare," Yvette said. "Ira would have killed him."

"He loved us," Yvonne whispered, tears forming in her eyes. "Now I wish he had killed the bastard."

"What did you tell him?"

"That we knocked over Greiner because we didn't like him."

"At first Ira was furious, but once he saw the Wtewael, he recognized it right off. And when Grenier didn't declare it as stolen, that's when he called you."

"And," I said, "Andrew Grenier, figuring Ira had his stuff, came here, confronted him and Ira told him about the Wtewael. Like you said, Grenier probably killed him."

"What are we going to do?" they asked.

"You'll have to notify the police," I said. "I'm sure you have a good lawyer. Call him and let him call the police. Stick to the truth. Ira had a meeting with an unknown person and when he didn't join you, you came here and found him dead. Let them investigate. They're going to be tough. But they can't pin the murder on you. You were at the Mall when Ira was killed. I'm sure people would remember two stunners such as yourselves."

"What's going to happen to the business?" Yvonne asked. "It took Ira years to build it up."

"That's up to you," I told her. "The less I know about

your business, the better for all of us."

"It would be almost impossible to find our vaults," Yvette mused.

"True," Yvonne concurred. "We could . . ."

"That's enough Ladies, I don't want to hear about the business."

"Yes, Max," they answered in unison.

"What about Grenier?" Yvonne asked. I think it was her but without seeing her left buttock I couldn't be sure.

"I'll deal with Grenier. I want you to keep away from him. He might even go after you. I'm going to send someone around to keep an eye on you." A call to an old friend at Fuchs Investigations and Security would ensure the twins received 'round the clock protection until I gave the all-clear.

The cops grilled the twins and the two guys who worked for Ira, but in the end they couldn't break their alibis. Wilt and Larry were in Green Bay watching the Vikings get creamed and more than one person remembered seeing Yvette and Yvonne at the Mall of America.

In the meantime, I received a call from my sources about the Wtewael. Heirs were found in Israel, and a list of other missing pieces from the Issacshon collection was sent to me. It was unlikely that all the art works ended up at Karinhall, but Issacshon had owned another Wtewael. A painting on copper of Perseus slaying Medusa. It had been documented by Goering that he had the Perseus painting in his possession. I wondered if it too was in the Grenier collection. If it was, I was going to get it. But first I planned to nail Junior for murder.

Soon after the call about the Issacshon heirs I heard from Margaret-Elizabeth Graham at Global Mutual Insurance. MEG and I had worked together at Global Mutual for a couple of years, before I had been fired for insubordination.

"Max, how would you like a finder's fee?" MEG's English accent had lost none of its charm, despite her years in the America. "A few weeks ago there was an art robbery up your way. Our investigators thought they had a lead but the fence they were narrowing in on was killed. I know you have some contacts that are — how shall I say this? — rather of dubious character."

"You mean crooked," I said.

"Your choice of words, Max. Now the victim was . . ."

"Andrew Greiner," I finished for her.

"Don't tell me, you read about it in the papers." She laughed.

"That's right."

"Uh-huh," she said, not believing a word of it. "We insured the lot for forty million. The stolen works were paintings by Jan Grossart Mabuse, Caterina Van Hemessen and Cornelis Cornelizoon. All Flemish or Dutch artists. Andrew Grenier has a world-famous collection of Northern European Mannerist works of art."

"Did he have any by Joachim Wtewael?" I asked.

"No, he didn't have a Wtewael insured by us. I'm surprised you would know Wtewael's name, let alone his painting style."

"Princess Flavia" — MEG looked like the English actress Madeline Carroll, who played Flavia in *The Prisoner of Zenda* — "I thought I stopped surprising you a long time ago."

"That's what keeps our friendship fresh. But now you have my curiosity piqued. What do you know?"

"I have to protect my sources. But I can get the paintings back."

"Max, I don't know what's going on in that brain of yours, but knowing you, it must be something sinister, probably dangerous and maybe a bit illegal. Just be careful."

"Flavia," I said in my best Ronald Coleman impersonation, "I would face any danger just to see you happy."

"Max, we are both too young to have seen that picture."

"Television or video, my dear."

"Call me if you recover the lost works. I'll fax you the complete list."

An idea had come to me. Once again I found myself on Highway 61. I reached Matossian Salvage, petted the dogs and confronted the twins.

"Give back the paintings?" Yvette or Yvonne asked. "We can sell them in Japan for more than the insurance company is willing to pay."

"If you want to get Ira's killer, the paintings will have to be returned."

"You have a plan?"

"Yes."

I had a few bones to pick with Andrew Grenier, Jr. One, he held art stolen from Jews during the Holocaust and knew where it came from. Two, he raped the twins and took humiliating photos of them. Three, he probably killed Ira Matossian, and despite Ira's line of work, I liked him.

I left the twins in early evening and drove down Highway 61 to visit Grenier at his home on Bald Eagle Lake. The gated mansion was not far from where the Barker-Karpis gang hid out in 1933, before they kidnapped William Hamm, Jr., the brewing magnate. Times had changed, but crooks were still crooks.

I gave the maid an envelope. In it was a list of the stolen paintings except for the Wtewael. I waited in the foyer. The maid didn't return, but Grenier showed.

He was a tall man, nearing fifty, but the kind of guy who still water-skied on the lake in the summer and snow-skied at Aspen in the winter. His hair was dark without a touch of gray. His face was tanned and smooth with only lines around his mouth and eyes.

"What do you know about my paintings, Mr. . . . ?"

"Coppersmith."

"Coppersmith? My paintings?"

"Is there a private place we can talk?" I asked, looking around the foyer.

He hesitated a moment and then motioned with his head. I followed him into a small gallery and closed the door behind us.

There were a number of paintings on the walls. Most were fifteenth or sixteenth century works, and from my limited knowledge I guessed them to be Dutch and Flemish.

"I see the thieves didn't get all your works," I said, pointing to the walls.

"They didn't even get near this wing," he said as he sat down in an armchair. "What do you know about my stolen paintings?" He hadn't asked me to sit, so I found a Louis XV chair to my liking, dragged it over to him and sat down.

He glanced at the paper I had given to his maid. "This is a list of works of art stolen from me. Do you have them, Mr. Coppersmith?"

"I might be able to get my hands on them, for the right price."

"And that price would be?"

"Shall we say twenty percent of the net value?"

"Shall we say I call the police?"

"Shall we talk about *Leda and the Swan?"*

His face went white. "You know where the Wtewael is?"

"Yes," I smiled. It was on its way to the rightful owners, but I didn't let this bastard know.

"I want it back." He stood up and so did I.

"You can have it," I paused. "For a price."

He nodded and walked to a small Georgian writing desk. But instead of a checkbook he pulled a revolver. "Don't play with me, Coppersmith. I want the Wtewael. I am prepared to kill to get it back."

“Stupid, Mr. Grenier. If I’m dead you won’t see your Wtewael or your other works again.”

“I’m willing to beat it out of you if I have to.” He was a big man and athletic, but he didn’t come from the same streets I had. He was just out of reach of my hands, but not out of reach of my cane. I swung it and smacked his wrist. The pistol dropped and Grenier screamed in pain.

“You son-of-a-bitch, you broke my wrist.”

“A friend of mine made this cane. Hollow Kevlar with liquid mercury in a titanium tube,” I said as I held the cane straight up, let the mercury fill back into the tube, and pressed the recess in the cane that opened the valve and locked it in place.

I picked up his revolver. It was Ruger .32 H&R magnum, an unusual caliber. It was also the same caliber as the gun that killed Ira. I emptied the gun and placed on the desk.

“Now, let’s talk. You want your paintings. I want your money. A very simple deal.”

“How do we do the transaction?” he asked, his good hand clinging to his wrist.

“I’ll have the paintings at Matossian Salvage at eight P.M. the day after tomorrow.”

“Matossian’s dead,” he told me.

“Is that a fact. Just be there if you want your paintings.”

“Those twin blonde bitches, they have my stuff.” That’s when I reached across the desk, grabbed his shirtfront and pulled him to me.

“They aren’t in the picture anymore, you fuck. I’m the man. You deal with me and only me. Clear?” I smacked him around a couple of times to emphasize my point.

“Clear,” he whimpered. Big man, when he has a gun and big man when he dopes and rapes women.

“Good,” I said, throwing him back across his desk. “I’ll see you at eight the day after tomorrow.”

I walked out of the gallery and tossed the bullets into a

Chinese urn. "That urn's priceless," I heard Grenier say, as I found my way to the front door.

Two nights later, Grenier showed up at Matossian's. I heard him enter the outer office.

"In here," I called. I was sitting behind Ira's desk, my cane laying on top of the desk. "Right on time, I see."

"Where are my paintings?" Grenier demanded. I noticed his right wrist was bandaged and his eye black from when I punched him.

"What paintings?" I asked, smiling.

"What do you mean? Stop playing games," he demanded.

"Tell me what paintings you want," I said, still smiling.

"My Caterina Van Hemessen," he said quietly. "My Jan Grossart Mabuse," a little louder. "My Cornelis Cornelizoon," louder still. "My Joachim Wtewael!" he screamed.

"Would that Wtewael be a painting on copper of *Leda and the Swan?*" I asked.

"Don't fuck with me, Coppersmith. You know damn well it's *Leda and the Swan.*" He was acting a lot tougher then the last time I saw him.

"The only painting of *Leda and the Swan* by Joachim Wtewael that I know of was stolen by Herman Goering, then stolen from Karinhall after the war. Perhaps stolen by someone with the Allies? Someone whose job it was to return the art works to the rightful owners? Someone like your old man. But he kept the Wtewael because he was a thief."

"The Jew was dead."

"He had heirs."

"Fuck them and fuck you, Coppersmith." He pulled his revolver from his waistband with his left hand. "Give me my paintings."

"Or what — you'll shoot me? You killed Ira Matossian

and didn't get your paintings. Now you want to kill me? You'll still end up empty."

"Ira, that cheap crook. He stole from me. The stuff I bought from him, the money I paid him over the years, and he steals from me."

"Not before you raped the twins."

"Yeah," he crowed. "I fucked those women."

"After you slipped them Rohypnol," I interrupted.

"Yes." He gave me a dirty smile. "And I told Matossian I screwed his bitches. Maybe I should have waited, because he went for me and I had to kill him. I thought I'd never recover the paintings, but then you showed up.

"Now, tell me where my painting are or I'll kill you too," he demanded.

"You'll kill me anyhow," I said, letting my hands rest on the desk.

"Keep your hands off that stick," he said gesturing with his revolver. "I'm not going to give you a second chance to hit me with a loaded cane. But I'm going to use it on you. I'll start by breaking your arms. I'm going make you wish you were dead." He reached for my cane with his bad right hand.

"How about this?" I asked, picking up a silver dog whistle.

"Go ahead and blow," he said. "The dogs will obey me," he added, smiling. He raised the cane.

"OK," I said and blew the whistle.

The dogs came charging in. One leaped and his jaws clamped down on Grenier's wrist, the one holding the gun. The other dog seized the bad wrist, the one with my cane. Grenier's scream could probably been heard ten miles in either direction on Highway 61.

I retrieved Grenier's pistol and my cane. I let the dogs maul him a little before I called them off. They let go but stood ready to attack if Grenier made another move.

His wrists must have been in agony. I had broken the

right one and it was now torn and bleeding. The left one was shredded as well.

I gave Grenier first aid and he finally noticed the dogs. "Those aren't Cosmo and Basil," he whined.

"Nope. I rented them from a friend in the security business. Actually they're Dutch Shepherd Dogs. I hope the irony isn't lost on you."

"You'll never prove anything," he said, his bravado returning.

"My friend Jack Bannon, the same guy who made my cane, also installed a video camera above the desk. I've got your confession on tape."

Grenier eventually got his Dutch and Flemish paintings back, except, of course, for the Wtewael. But a lot of good it did him in prison. I still got my finder's fee. And to add insult to injury, while Grenier was confronting me with his demands, Yvette and Yvonne knocked over the rest of his collection. The other stolen Wtewael and a dozen other looted works were returned to the rightful heirs. The remaining paintings and pieces were fenced by the lovely twins.

And yes, Yvonne does have a small scar on her left buttocks.

Next time you see me, I'll be driving down Highway 61 in my "new" BMW.

Hauser Rules

Dan A. Sproul

Nick Hauser began to drink too much after his wife dumped him. His ex-wife, Ellen, moved a bit north of Miami, up near Hallandale, with their two kids and her new husband, a stockbroker. She told Nick it was because of his job. He kept rotten hours, cavorted with immoral women and was rarely home except to sleep — common complaints for the wife of a vice detective.

A few years later, Nick embarked on a drunken weekend excursion in a Miami Metro squad car to Jacksonville to visit a girlfriend. Nick's years of experience as a detective in homicide and vice couldn't save him, nor could his reputation as the toughest cop in the department. He was cashiered out without benefit of pension.

On the street, he got work with a private security firm but it didn't last. With the few dollars he was able to save, Hauser obtained a Private Investigator's license and rented inexpensive office space in Miami Springs. Money was tight. He was forced to sell insurance on the side to meet expenses.

Hauser wasn't much of a salesman. It didn't take long for him to mishandle some cash and lose his insurance license. Unable to pay the rent on his tiny office, he slept in his car. Not long after, his car, parked outside the Bandoleer Bar, was repossessed along with everything he still owned.

Hauser spent some of his vice squad days in the Bandoleer Bar, a strip and clip joint. The girls did separate bits — stage dancing, lap dancing for cash and finally conning patrons into buying them drinks: ice tea highballs at five bucks a shot. Business at the Bandoleer was good.

The Bandoleer owner always sprung for free drinks when Nick showed up. Nick Hauser, obligingly, had always looked the other way at the goings on. A kinship evolved. So it was that Hauser was allowed to sleep in the Bandoleer storeroom at night to keep an eye on the place for a few drinks and a few dollars a week. Sometimes Nick helped the bouncer with an unruly customer if he was sober enough.

For a time, visiting police buddies kept Hauser in booze and filled his otherwise empty days. Nick favored the corner stool at the far end of the bar. That particular spot commanded an excellent view of the entrance and a panoramic spread of the patrons seated along the bar. After a few months, his buddies didn't seem to be coming around as much anymore. Then, on a tranquil Sunday morning in August . . .

Ellen stood just inside the doorway waiting for her eyes to adjust. The club was dark after coming in from the afternoon Miami sun. The only real illumination in the Bandoleer was a few lights over the inlaid wooden stage where later in the day bare breasted young woman would gyrate around a metal pole to suggestive music. Ellen hadn't seen Nick in almost four years so had difficulty spotting him right away.

Hauser didn't notice her or bother to look up until she slid onto the stool next to him. He stared at her for a long few seconds before he was sure.

"Ellen?"

"Nick, God you look like hell. You must have lost thirty

pounds. I didn't recognize you at first. Dave said . . ."

Nick rubbed his eyes. "I must have the D.T's? Is that you Ellen?"

"Of course it's me. Dave told me you might be here."

"Dave?"

"Dave Lang. Your old partner in Homicide. Christ, are you drunk?"

"Maybe. What you doin' here? That is, if you really are here."

"Goddamn it Nick, why are you drinking so much? I need to talk to you."

Nick responded with a half hearted shrug. "I have to drink to celebrate the little things, like Thursday. We only have one of them a week, you know."

"Today's Sunday," Ellen pointed out.

"I meant Sunday."

"Can you get coffee in this place?" she asked.

Nick accepted the coffee, grimacing with each sip as Ellen laid out her story. She told him that she had witnessed a bank robbery — two men wearing rubber masks. One of the masked men said something profane to one of the customers waiting in line at a teller window.

"What did he say?" Nick broke in.

"Why does that matter?"

Nick shrugged. "Just curious."

"He said, 'Get your lard ass out of the way, you fat fuck,'" she quoted, then continued on. "Stupidly, the customer swung on the bank robber. Hit him in the face. The blow broke the rubber band holding the mask. It fell to the floor. Almost at the same time, the robber shot the customer in the stomach. Then he . . . he looked right at me and ran out of the bank."

Ellen paused to look at her hands twisting nervously in her lap. "I saw his face," she said in a trembling voice. "I was standing in line behind the fat customer. I was the only one that could identify him. I picked him from a line up. The police arrested him along with his brother. They think his brother was the other robber."

"I don't see the problem . . ."

"They're trying to kill me."

"I thought the police arrested them," said Nick puzzled.

"They had to let them go . . . ," she said, with voice still shaky. "I refused to testify."

"I see," said Nick. "What's the rest of it?"

"Nick, I know things were difficult when we divorced. I just felt that since Ed adopted the children and you didn't have to pay support it wasn't a good idea for you to spend a lot of time — I mean . . . that's why I . . ."

Nick didn't feel up to hearing her spiel of why she didn't think it a good idea for him to see his kids. "Finish your story," he interrupted, impatiently.

"It started with phone calls," she began again. "Somebody called almost every day. First they threatened the children if I testified. One day a stranger tried to pick Caroline up from school, but she'd already taken the bus. Her teacher called. And they did other things. They smashed the windows in my car . . . threw rocks through the windows in the house. And always the calls, everyday."

"So you told the police that you wouldn't testify?"

"No . . . not then. The police watched the house for a week. During that week two hoodlums grabbed Ed leaving work and beat him severely. They bruised a rib."

"So how's old Ed doin'?"

"Goddamit, it's not funny Nick. You don't know Ed. He was terrified. He left town for a few days. Went to his brother's place in Key Largo. It was then that I told the police I wouldn't testify. They had to release the Chavez brothers. I thought it would stop then. But now it's worse. The police won't guard the house anymore. A pickup truck rammed my car yesterday morning and ran me off the road into a canal.

The driver was wearing one of those rubber masks. He jumped out of the truck and fired two bullets into the back window of my car. He'd have finished the job if a car hadn't stopped to help. It scared the killer off."

Nick slid the coffee cup away from him. He felt he was as sober as he needed to be. It appeared to him that the Chavez boys had some stooges do the preliminary work to scare her into not testifying. Now the first team was out. They obviously wanted to make sure she never testified. "Where are the girls?" he asked.

Ellen motioned for the bartender. "I put them on a plane to my sister in Atlanta." Turning to the barman, she confessed that she needed a drink.

"What exactly do you expect me to do?"

In truth, she didn't know what she expected. Coming to Nick was hard. Her options were gone. She had no one else to turn to. The house was all there was and she was afraid to go home. She couldn't bring herself to abandon everything and just run. The police were no help. Nick, in her experience, had never been a cruel man. But she knew he wasn't soft either. And she had heard stories — stories from other cops that worked with him. Nick Hauser didn't back down from anybody. Nick Hauser could be one mean bastard, or so they said.

The gravity of her situation overcame her. She broke down into hitching sobs. "I just . . . I just want to go home. I want to be safe."

Nick was silent as he watched her crying softly next to him. He might not have been worth a frog's fart as an insurance salesman. But he was a good cop. Through the years he'd immersed himself in the scum of the earth on a daily basis. He'd seen pretty much everything. God knows, he didn't owe Ellen anything. Still, he decided to help her. There were his two girls. But that wasn't it. He decided to help her because he could. And because nobody else would.

"You have any firearms in your house?" he asked.

She wiped a trickle of tear away with a sleeve. "You'll help me?"

"Didn't Dave tell you that I've got a Private Investigator's license?"

"He said you lost your office."

"Yeah, but I didn't lose the license. It'll cost you three hundred retainer up front, and three hundred a day plus expenses."

"Isn't that . . . you know . . . a little steep?"

"Your problem is a little steep."

Ellen dug around in her purse. "I'll write you a check . . . if I can find . . ."

"You'll have to make it cash. My bank isn't talking to me anymore."

During the ride to the bank in Ellen's rental Mercury Cougar, she told him that Ed kept no guns in the house because of the girls. That posed a small problem. Nick determined that it wouldn't be safe for her to return home just yet. Not until he had done a few things. He would need a weapon. And the Chavez brothers, he would have to find them and have a meaningful discussion.

He picked up Ellen's cell phone off the dash and punched in the number to the department. It took several minutes to wade through the "Nick how you doin's" to get Dave Lang on the phone.

"I need the sheet on the Chavez brothers. The ones involved in the bank heist Ellen witnessed. Known associates and whereabouts."

"I know the case," Lang acknowledged."I don't have to pull the file. I got it here on my desk. I figured there was chance you might call."

Raul and Rudolfo Chavez and close associate Jesus Prado last lived in one side of a duplex apartment attached to the back end of Montoya's Garage on 135th street in

Hialeah. They were suspected of two additional bank jobs with the same M.O. as the Cypress Grove heist that Ellen had witnessed. Dave mentioned that no one had ever gotten hurt before in any of the previous jobs. Nick just finished the call as Ellen slid back into the driver's side.

She counted the three hundred into his outstretched hand. "What do we do next?"

"You can't go home," he told her, grabbing up the cell phone once more. "We need to put you in a motel. And I'll need your car." He punched a number into the phone and was silent for several seconds.

"What are you going to do?" Ellen asked.

"And I'll need your cell phone," Nick said, ignoring her question. Someone picked up on the other end of the phone. "Hello, let me talk to Maurice." A few seconds passed. "Maurice, I need to do some business . . . it's Nick Hauser. That's right, I'm not a cop anymore . . . this is a private deal . . . yeah, well you're one too . . . Okay, in twenty minutes."

He put the phone back on the dash. "Have you been home since you rented this car?" he asked her. She indicated that she had not. "That's good. Chavez and associates won't recognize it."

He dropped her in room number six of the Tropic Breeze Motel and headed the Mercury toward Cooper City to meet with Maurice Washington — or Nubby as he was more often called. Maurice had lost his left hand years past for the cavalier handling of mob bag money when he worked as a pickup man. Nubby, always the entrepreneur, had branched out over the years into paid snitching and the peddling of stolen credit cards. Nick had also pinched Maurice at least once for the casual sale of untraceable weapons kept in the trunk of his ten year old Cadillac.

Nick pulled the Cougar in behind Maurice's Cadillac parked in an alley at the rear of a liquor carry out. Nubby lounged against the trunk of the Cadillac, waiting with arm and stump folded across his weasel thin body. He gave the Mercury a long look. “Word is that you is tanked out. What you be doin’ wid dat fancy car?”

“Skip the chit chat. What have you got in the way of handguns?”

“What you want?”

“How about a nine millimeter Beretta. And two clips . . .”

“Shoot . . . I ain’t got dat,” said Nubby impatiently.

“What have you got?”

Nubby unlocked the trunk and unveiled his merchandise. There was but a single revolver laying on a white cloth. “Dis be all I’s got right now.”

“What is it?”

“Dat der is a Ruger twenty two caliber revolver — almost brand new.”

“That wouldn’t knock a hummingbird off a rose bush. I need something with some stopping power.”

Nubby shrugged his skinny body. “Dat’s it. Take it or leave it.”

Nick reasoned that he wasn’t blessed with the time to run all over the city looking for just the right piece. “How much?”

“Two hundred fifty.”

“That piece is probably hotter than a Guatemalan roofer in July. I’ll give you a hundred. And I need ammunition.”

“Oh no,” Nubby sputtered, “Dat’s da price — two fifty. You ain’t no cop no more.”

“Maybe so,” said Nick. “But I got a lot of friends on the force. One call and you’re busted.”

“Hundred do seem like a fair price.”

Montoya’s garage sported two trash strewn bays with

a relatively new tire changer and an air compressor caged at the rear. The grease smeared owner, buried in the hood of a seventy three Chevy, told Nick that Raul Chavez was down the sidewalk to the back of the building in apartment B.

With a broken air conditioner, the Chavez brothers liked to keep the front door and windows open. Open orifices along with the ceiling fan allowed enough air circulation to keep the dump, if not comfortable, at least not sweltering. The trade off was that it let in flies and an occasional unwanted visitor.

Nick Hauser entered with the Ruger out front. Raul, Rudolfo, and Jesus were all poised with a cold beer at the lips, in the hand, or on the table. Their six eyeballs locked on the small caliber pistol.

"Hi, boys," said Nick. "Line up over here, please." He kicked a folding chair out of the way and motioned to an uncluttered wall.

Raul was the older brother and leader of the small band. "What is this?" he asked, as they moved to line up at the wall. "Are you a cop?"

"Private," said Nick. "I've come to ask your help in a matter. Turn around, hands on the wall — spread 'em. Legs farther back . . . really lean."

As they leaned on the wall, Nick did a quick pat search of each then circled the room peering into cupboards, opening drawers. "I came to ask you boys to stop bothering Mrs. Wheeler. Stop throwing rocks through her windows and most important stop making attempts on her life." He felt down between the cushions on the couch and pulled out a Colt .45 caliber automatic, fully loaded. He stuffed it in his belt. The .38 caliber Smith & Wesson he found in the next cushion, he stuffed into his pocket. Nubby would give him a hundred bucks for it. "Well, what's your answer?"

Jesus Prado, at the end of the line, spoke first: "Who's Mrs. Wheeler?" He then inquired as to whether Mrs.

Wheeler had certain sexual proclivities.

Nick fired one round from the Ruger into Jesus' foot. Jesus fell to the floor screaming. "Yeeeow . . . you motherfucker, you shot my foot . . ."

Nick prodded the moaning Jesus with his shoe. "Since you're on the floor, spread out face down. And try to keep quiet." Nick moved to Rudolfo. "How 'bout you? You ever hear of Mrs. Wheeler?"

"I don't have to tell you nothin'," said Rudolfo. "You're not a cop." Nick pulled the hammer back on the Ruger. There was a barely audible click, click.

"Eh . . . just a minute. You mean the lady in the bank?"

"That's right."

"We all called her on the phone," Rudolfo admitted. "And Jesus threw some rocks through the windows in her house. That's all I know."

"What about the windows in her car?" Nick asked.

Rudolfo shrugged.

"Yeah . . . ," Jesus groaned from the floor. "I did that."

"Who beat up her husband and tried to pick up her kid from school?" asked Nick. "You do that too?"

"Goddamn . . . I need a doctor," Jesus announced.

Nick nudged Jesus softly in the ribs with his shoe. "Hey, what you need is to know that this is as nice as I get. You don't start cooperating — things could turn nasty. You'll all be hoppin' around here on one foot — or worse."

"Tell him," Raul ordered from over his shoulder.

"Me and Gonzales followed her old man to work," said Jesus grimacing in pain. "We went back in the afternoon and waited by his car in the parking lot. Gonzales held him. I smacked him a couple times. Told him that if his wife testified we'd come back again. I think Gonzales kicked him when he was on the ground."

"And trying to kidnap the little girl?" Nick prompted.

"That wasn't nothin'," said Jesus. "We waited for all the

buses to leave before I went in the school. I knew she wasn't there. Shit, I didn't even know her name. I just asked for the Wheeler kid. I staged it so the teacher would call. It worked didn't it?"

"Yeah," Nick confirmed, "but it puzzles me. Once she agreed not to testify, why try to kill her? You could have done that at the beginning without all the chicken-shit rock throwing and the rest of it." He put the barrel of the Ruger at the base of Raul's skull. "It was you, wasn't it? When you got loose you wanted to make sure she didn't change her mind."

"No man," said Raul. "Nobody bothered her after the cops let us loose. It's true, all of us called her on the phone. I told Jesus to scare her, but I don't kill people."

"What about the guy in the bank? I suppose you didn't pop him?"

"The fat ass swung on me," Raul said. "The gun went off accidentally when he hit me in the face. Anyway, he's not dead. He's going to make it. Look, I admit we wanted to scare her — but that's as far as it went."

"No, I ain't buyin' it." said Nick. "You think I just fell off a Christmas tree? Which one of you drives a white pick-up truck?"

Jesus groaned from the floor. "Nobody owns a truck. I got an eighty nine Camero."

"Ninety Four Mustang," said Rudolfo.

"Ninety Seven Thunderbird," Raul contributed.

"And I suppose you can account for your time yesterday morning?" Nick asked. The inquiry was met with silence. "Well," he prompted. "Speak up. Where were you? How about you Raul?"

"I ain't sayin'," Raul answered.

"I'll give you a break," said Nick. "I'll let you take your shoe off now. That way they won't have to cut it off later. That's very painful."

"Look," said Raul, "I'm telling the truth — we didn't

try to kill that woman."

"Okay, so where were you yesterday morning?"

"You're not a cop right?"

Nick assured him that he was not a cop.

"All right," said Raul. "We was in West Palm Beach, robbin' the Palm Pioneer Bank — all three of us."

The plan for Nick had been a simple one. Scare the brothers until they shit on their shoes or, if necessary, put them in the hospital. And if that didn't work . . . well whatever it took to stop the attempts on Ellen's life. But now, there was an element of doubt. It was just possible he was shooting at the wrong feet.

"You don't know who I am," Nick told them. "But I know you assholes. I can find you anytime I want. Remember that. And, oh, yeah, I've cleaned out the sofa. Don't be running out the door after me. You could lose more than a couple toes."

Montoya, of Montoya's garage was dead. Nick was enlightened to this fact when he questioned Montoya's brother-in-law, Rameriez; who, cussing in Spanish, still toiled on the battered seventy three Chevy. No, Nick was told. The Chavez brothers didn't have any white truck. Rameriez had never seen them with a white truck. He indicated that Jesus Prado's Camero was in the adjacent bay. Rameriez then volunteered that the Camero was a rolling piece of shit. Nick ambled over and took a quick look. The interior was splattered with some kind of orange paint, covering the dash, the console and the ceiling.

Nick stopped at a convenience store on Red Road. He bought a can of beer to go and headed for the Tropic Breeze Motel. Raul had claimed that he was in West Palm Beach — easy to check. Nick put the question to Dave Lang and gave him the number to call back. Ellen's cell phone rang as he pulled into the slot in front of Tropic Breeze number six. Dave reported the Pioneer Bank had been hit — three guys in rubber masks at about eleven in the morning yesterday. The get away car was an older Chevy Camero. A passerby reported that the money exploded in the car in an orange cloud as it passed by him.

Nick mused that as bank robbers the Chavez gang was a bumbling catastrophe . . . two jobs in a row they blew. But if all three were indeed in West Palm . . .

After announcing himself outside number six, Nick strode through the doorway with the small paper bagged Budweiser in his hand. Ellen pounced immediately.

"How can you get drunk at a time like this?"

"What the hell you talkin' about? It's only a beer."

"Get rid of it!" she ordered.

"You can kiss my ass . . ."

Without warning she slapped the beer out of his hand. It sloshed onto the number six carpet. He rushed to the regurgitating beer can to salvage what he could. But only dregs remained.

"That's one of the reasons I divorced you," she said in a shrill voice — tears welling in her eyes. "You can't be serious about anything."

Nick nodded. "Yeah, well now I remember why it didn't bother me to see you go."

"Nick, can't you understand? They want to kill me."

Nick said nothing. He pulled the Ruger and the Colt from his belt and laid them on the night table between the beds. He took the .38 from his pants pocket and emptied the cartridges into his hand. He dumped the ammunition into a waste basket by the writing desk.

"What are you doing?" Ellen asked.

"Hauser's rule number twenty three," Nick replied, "Never sell a loaded gun to a stranger."

"God, I wish Ed were here," Ellen remarked. "He's sober, reliable. You can depend on him."

"If good old Ed's so dependable what's he doing hiding

under a rock in Key Largo?"

"He's not hiding under a rock. He's just gone for the weekend to see his brother. He'll be back Monday or Tuesday. He goes down there every couple weeks or so."

"What if I told you that the Chavez brothers didn't try to kill you?" Nick said.

Ellen offered him a puzzled expression. "What are you talking about? Have you been drinking all morning?"

"Not all morning. Just until about nine thirty when you pulled me off my stool. Tell me, how's the marriage working out? You and Ed getting along all right? Is the stockbroker business booming?"

"What are you implying?"

"Well, I don't think the Chavez boys made the attempt on your life. You take them away as a suspect, there ain't much left but Ed. I admit though, Ed's got an almost perfect plan. Once he kills you, there is no way that one or all of the Chavez bunch could escape being charged and probably convicted. Hell — it's almost a perfect murder. It's what one might call seizing a golden opportunity."

Ellen got to her feet. "Listen to what you're saying. You think Ed is trying to kill me?"

"Yeah, that's what I think."

"You're crazy."

"Think about it," said Nick. "Has he got any insurance on you?"

"Yes . . . but."

"A large amount?"

"A million dollars . . . it's a joint policy," she spoke barely above a whisper, looking thoughtfully at Nick.

Nick noticed her expression. "What is it?"

"Ed . . . Ed says they are laying people off at the brokerage firm. It's because of the electronic trading on the internet — and the recent bad market conditions. He was arranging to sell the house before all this started. He told me that he needed the money to invest."

"So, what kind of car does Ed drive? I assume it's not a white pickup truck."

Ellen shook her head. "No, he has a Lincoln Town Car. But I can't believe . . ."

"Maybe there's a way we can find out," Nick told her.

Nick drove. They cruised the blocks around the Wheeler home in Hallandale. It looked calm, no sign of a Lincoln Town car or a white pickup truck. Ten minutes later, he took the Miramar exit off the turnpike and headed down the coast to Key Largo, the first in the chain of keys that led down to Key West.

Ellen was convinced that Ed was not a killer. She tried to impress this fact upon Hauser as the miles peeled away. He stubbornly pointed out that nothing else made any sense — nobody else had anything to gain from her death.

"And then there's Hauser's rule number fourteen," Nick told her. "If you can't eliminate the husband as a suspect — you can be pretty sure he did it."

"I'm tired of your stupid rules. I can't understand how you can be so sure it wasn't those Chavez people."

"Instinct and orange dye," Nick assured her.

Ellen confessed that she had only visited twice to the house of Ed's brother. They didn't get along. Jules, Ed's brother, was a loud mouthed atheist among other things. Beside that, Jules had once projectile vomited on her head from the back seat when they were all returning from a neighborhood bar in Ed's car.

"Don't sound like he's all bad," said Nick. This observation was received coolly as Ellen pointed to a small bungalow just ahead on the Gulf side of the street.

"I think that's the place," said Ellen, unconsciously patting around the top of her head.

Only a screen door closed off the living room. Ellen shouted through the screen. "Hello, anybody here?"

She backed up quickly as the screen door flew open. Jules was just over six foot, maybe a couple inches shorter than Hauser. But he was much heavier. Fat thighs threatened to burst the legs from his shorts. Rolls of flesh cascaded over his stretch waistband. "Hey Ellen, come on in and have a drink."

"No thanks," said Ellen. "We just stopped by to talk with Ed."

"She doesn't speak for me," Nick said. "Got any bourbon?"

"We won't be staying that long," Ellen said frostily.

"Or rum is okay," said Nick.

"How about a daiquiri?" Jules inquired.

"Fine." Nick hastily accepted.

"Come on Ellen, have a drink," Jules persisted. "You won't go to hell."

"A small one, maybe," she relented.

"That's the spirit," said Jules. He turned his attention to Hauser. "You aren't a Christian by any chance, are you? We don't serve Christians here unless they're family . . . or unless it's Sunday," he added jovial, exposing crooked teeth.

"That's between me and my lawyer," Nick answered.

"It's okay!" said Jules. "Just kiddin' around — it gets Ellen's goat."

The daiquiri was cold, wet and strong — one of the best Nick had ever tasted.

"Damn, this is good," he told Jules.

"We grow our own limes on a tree out in back," said Jules, implying that it made all the difference. "We haven't been introduced. I'm Jules, Ed's brother." He extended his hand.

Nick took the extended hand. "Nick Hauser, ex-husband."

"So you're the famous cop. What you doin' down here? I didn't know you and Ellen were still . . . you know . . .

communicating."

"It's temporary," said Nick.

Ellen took only a small sip of her daiquiri before setting it on a table. "We need to talk to Ed. Where is he anyway?"

"I think he went over to visit with Warren, my neighbor. They do a lot of fishing together. He lives another block down, just around a little back water inlet. You can't miss it. There'll be a white pickup truck parked in the driveway."

Five minutes later, Hauser spotted the white pickup in the driveway of a red tile roofed Mediterranean style beauty. Brother Jules' bungalow seemed a shack by comparison. Nick stopped a hundred yards up the street from the driveway.

"What are we doing now?" Ellen asked. "Shouldn't we confront him?"

"Hauser's rule number six," said Nick. "Never stand in front of a suspected felon's door, hit it with your fist and shout police."

"Enough with your half-witted rules. What should we do?"

Nick put the Ruger under the seat. He got out of the Cougar and placed the Colt .45 in his back waistband. He pulled his shirt out to hang down over and conceal it. Together they sneaked along a chain link fence down the side of the house until the backyard came into view. Warren and Ed were there, standing in front of a smoking brick barbecue pit. Ellen and Nick watched the pair in silence for more than fifteen seconds. They went unnoticed. Finally, Ellen was forced to speak.

"What are they doing?" she asked.

"I'm no expert," said Nick. "But it looks like Warren is giving Ed a big wet kiss on the mouth. What do you think he's doing?"

"Ed!" she shouted out. "What the hell are you doing?"

Ed and Warren jumped to break their embrace. A startled Ed stumbled backward over a lawn chair and hit the ground rump first. He scrambled quickly to his feet.

"Warren had something in his eye," he sputtered. "I had to get up close . . . you know I couldn't see it . . ."

"Shut up, Ed," Warren ordered. "They know what we were doing." Warren then addressed his uninvited guests. "What do you want here? You're trespassing."

Ignoring his protest, Hauser, followed by Ellen, went through a small gate in the side of the chain link fence. "I won't take up too much of your time," Nick announced to the assemblage. "I'm just here to make a citizen's arrest — attempted murder." He spoke to Ellen without looking in her direction, but loud enough for all to hear. "Now that I see the lay of the land, I guess you were right, Ellen. Ed probably didn't try to kill you. I bet it was Warren here in the white truck wearing the rubber mask. I doubt if Ed's got the stomach for it. That right Ed?"

"I told you it wouldn't work, Warren," Ed contributed. To Nick he said: "I tried to talk him out of it — but he wouldn't listen. I just wanted to sell the house and take off with the money. He said it was for us — for our future."

Ellen lunged forward to take a wild swung at Ed. Warren moved quickly. He grabbed her, got a fist full of hair and pulled her head back. Before Nick could move, Warren had a large barbecue fork pressed to Ellen's neck.

"Don't move or she dies," he warned Nick. "Put your hands behind your head. Ed, search him. See if he's armed."

At arm's length, wary of Nick's repute, Ed timidly performed a pat search finally discovering the bulge in Hauser's right front pocket. Carefully, he withdrew the .38 Smith & Wesson butt first.

"Here . . . I got it . . . I got it," he said excitedly, delivering the revolver to Warren.

Warren threw down the barbecue fork and grabbed the revolver. He shoved Ellen away in Nick's direction.

"What are we going to do with them?" asked Ed.

"Get some rope from the dock," Warren ordered. "We'll tie them up . . . the tough guy we take out about three miles and drop over the side. We'll have to dump her alongside the road up in Dade County along with her car. We can make it look like the Chavez brothers caught up with her."

"Ed how can you can do this?" Ellen pleaded. "It's murder. What about our years together?"

"He doesn't have any choice," Warren told her. "His firm is busted. Most of his customers are busted. He borrowed from his client's accounts for this property . . . the hundred and forty thousand for that Chris Craft at the dock is from Mrs. Biddleman's trust account. We need that million from the insurance to square up. Only now we have to kill both of you."

"I'm really sorry, Ellen," Ed said. He sounded sincere.

Nick dropped his hands to his side. "I had about enough of this horseshit. You ain't going to kill me. People a hell of a lot tougher then you butt-fuckers have tried it."

"And what is going to stop me?" Warren asked smugly.

Nick casually pulled the .45 from his back waistband and jacked a round into the breach. Warren began to frantically pull the trigger on the empty .38.

Click, click, click, click, click.

Nick instructed them in a soft, cold voice. "You twinkles got three seconds to get face down on the ground or I'll blow your balls through the back screen door."

The details were sorted out at the Monroe County Sheriff's office. Nick enlisted the aid of Dave Lang at Miami Metro. It was almost unnecessary. Ed, with little prompting, broke down and confessed, implicating Warren as the shooter.

Nick mentally added a new rule to his list; namely, never point a gun at a bad ass and threaten him unless you're sure the gun is loaded. It would be rule one twenty six. He solicited and received an additional hundred dollars from Ellen to replace the expense money he'd laid out for the Ruger. With Ed in the lockup, he took the spare bedroom in Ellen's house, wore clean shirts, ate good food and charged her a total of twelve hundred to keep the Chavez boys and associates away until after she testified at the trial.

Nick sold the Ruger back to Nubby along with the Smith & Wesson and netted an additional three hundred. He kept the Colt automatic. With his windfall, Nick bought two new shirts and rented office space over the Bandoleer Bar. It was time to start again. This private detective business, he decided, was a piece of cake.

Reunion

Justin Gustainis

Conroy never had much trouble putting a crew together. People were always willing to work with him — professionals were, anyway, and Conroy never worked with amateurs.

He wasn't any kind of legend in the business, like Willie Sutton, say, or Dillinger. That was all right; in fact, Conroy preferred it that way. Legends often attract the wrong kind of attention, and they have a tendency to die young.

But Conroy did have a reputation for doing solid, reliable work. He was a good planner, for one thing — he never went into a bank, or a jewelry store, or a private home without knowing exactly where the loot was, how best to get at it, and how much time he could afford to spend there before the law was likely to take an interest.

He had good control, too, Conroy did. No matter how long you've been in the business, taking down a score produces one hell of an adrenaline rush — kind of like bungee-jumping, but the jazzed-up feeling lasts longer. People with that much juice pounding through their veins tend to be excitable. Combine that with the firearms that are tools of the heist artist's trade, and sometimes the result is unnecessary casualties among the civilians.

But Conroy never "lost it" while working, and he always tried hard to steer those on his crew away from needless bloodshed. He knew that the cops look for you longer and harder when you leave dead citizens behind after a score.

One good thing about the plan for taking down the armored car company was that very few civilians were going to be around when Conroy's crew made their hit. Only a couple of guards were assigned to the night shift, and they could be handled without much trouble. It was a maxim in the business: the fewer people involved in a score, on both sides, the less that can go wrong.

It was 2:50 A.M. when they stashed two of their cars in the parking lot of an all-night supermarket and piled into the gray mini-van that they had stolen from behind an appliance store. Seven minutes later, Conroy brought the van to a quiet halt behind the shopping plaza that contained the armored car company.

It went the way it was supposed to, at first. Everhart was one of the best lock men in the business, and he bypassed the alarm on the back door, spotted the backup alarm, bypassed that, and had the lock itself open within four minutes. As soon as he heard Everhart whisper "Got it," Conroy stepped into the nearby alley and used his flashlight to signal Gitner, who was standing at the alley's other end — which put him just around the corner from the armored car company's front door. Seeing the three flashes, Gitner pulled the brim of his blue "Notre Dame Fighting Irish" cap a little lower over his eyes and picked up the pizza box that he'd fished out of a Dumpster earlier in the evening. The box now contained nothing but a few crumbs, a stale piece of mushroom and a Browning .380 automatic with a silencer attached. Gitner walked about twenty feet along the face of the building, which brought him directly in front of the thick metal door that said BRAXTON SECURITY, INC. Standing in full view of the surveillance camera mounted above the door, he pushed the button under the sign that read, RING FOR ADMITTANCE. Gitner kept the pizza box in plain view and let the hat brim darken his face with shadow.

Inside, a man wearing the blue-and-gray Braxton Security uniform heard the door buzzer, put down his thermos and looked at the monitor mounted in the wall above him. It showed him a sharp black and white image of the figure with the pizza box standing patiently at the front entrance. There was no monitor to give a similar view of the rear, since Braxton Security's home office was too cheap to install a camera back there. Instead, company regulations stated that no employee was to unlock the back door without first looking through its fisheye lens to establish the identity of the person desiring entrance.

The man in the Braxton uniform, who was slightly overweight and more than slightly balding, stared at the monitor for a moment, his brow furrowed. Then he turned his head and yelled through an open doorway, "Hey, Carter!"

A couple of moments later, another man in blue and gray appeared in the doorway — a slim, medium-sized black man with very short hair and a thin mustache. "What's up?" he asked.

The heavyset guard, whose name was Porterfield, gestured toward the monitor with his chin. "Guy at the door with a pizza," he said. "Did you order something?"

The black man's voice held just a touch of contempt. "I been back there most of the last hour, workin' on the audit, right? You sittin' next to the only phone in the place. Did you see me order up some pizza?"

"All right, all right," Porterfield said. "I was just askin'." He watched Carter go back into the other room, made a face, then pressed the button that worked the intercom connected to the front door. "What d'you want, buddy? Nobody in here called for anything."

"Just a second," Gitner told the camera, managing not to give it a clear shot of his face. He fished a slip of paper out of his shirt pocket and peered at it. "It says 'Braxton Security, Southgate Plaza,'" he announced. "That's you guys, right? Says so right on the door here."

Porterfield made an annoyed sound and pushed the "Speaker" button again. "Yeah, I know this is Braxton Security, but nobody in here sent out for any —" That was as far as he got, because suddenly three men in baseball caps and sunglasses were standing in the office doorway, and they all had pistols, and all three of those guns were pointed right at Porterfield's face.

Porterfield sat very still, moving nothing but his eyelids, which were blinking rapidly. After a long moment, one of the men held a finger to his lips to reinforce Porterfield's silence, then made a summoning motion. Porterfield, not quick at the best of times, just sat there until the man repeated the motion, this time with his other hand, which was holding a Colt Python .357 magnum. Gestures made with such a cannon tend to get people's attention, which was the main reason Conroy carried it. Porterfield slid off his stool and hesitantly walked to the door, like a small boy approaching the principal's office.

Conroy got the guard turned around so that he was facing back the way he'd come. He pulled the automatic from the guard's holster and handed it to Paglia, the fourth member of the crew. Like the others, Paglia wore big sunglasses and a baseball cap; his particular headgear extolled the Minnesota Timberwolves. He took the guard's pistol from Conroy and stuck it in the back of his jeans to get it out of the way. Then he headed off to unlock the front door and let Gitner in.

Conroy was standing right behind the guard now, murmuring in his ear. He knew that terrified people sometimes lose their ability to think rationally. They forget to act in their own self-interest, and that makes them dangerous. Conroy wanted the guard scared enough to do as he was told, but not so frightened that he'd try something dumb.

"We're only here for the money," Conroy said quietly. "We're professionals, not psychos. We don't kill people for no reason. Nobody gets stupid, nobody gets hurt. Understand?"

The guard's double chin wiggled as he nodded several times.

"That's good," Conroy said. "Now, where's the other one, the black guy? In the back room?"

More nodding from the guard.

"All right, fine. Call him out here. And listen —" It was time to balance reassurance with threat. Conroy let the barrel of his pistol gently touch the guard's spine as he continued, "— don't even *think* of trying anything cute, like calling him by the wrong name, or something. If he comes out shooting, the first guy who gets shot is going to be you. Understand me?"

Porterfield nodded again, more vigorously this time.

"Okay, then. Call him."

The guard drew in a breath. "Carter! C'mere a second, will you?" Porterfield's voice was a little quavery, but Conway thought it sounded good enough. He hoped, for everyone's sake, that the other guard's name really *was* Carter.

From the other room there was the sound of a chair scraping along linoleum. A second or two later, the black man came through the doorway, looking annoyed. He was saying, "Hey, I already told you that I didn't —" but stopped as his brain registered what his eyes were showing him. Carter froze for a long moment, then slowly raised his hands, palms outward, to the middle of his chest. "Easy now," he said, as if confronting a growling Doberman. "Let's everybody just take it easy."

"We will if you will," Conroy told him, speaking in a normal volume now. "We're just here for the money. Nobody has to get hurt."

The black man nodded solemnly. "That works for me."

Conroy handed the white guard over to Everhart, then said to Carter, "That's fine. Why don't you keep your hands like they are and walk on over here. No sudden moves, right?"

"Yeah, sure. Whatever you want." The guard walked up to Conroy, who turned him around, relieved him of his pistol and told him to put his hands behind his back. Conroy took from his jacket pocket one of those plastic restraint cords that cops sometimes use in place of handcuffs. He was securing the black guard's wrists when the man said, "Listen, I don't want you guys gettin' pissed off, or surprised, or whatever, so you oughta know that there's somebody —"

At that instant, Conroy heard, coming from the back room, the utterly unexpected sound of another chair being pushed back, followed by footsteps. Damn it, there were only supposed to be two of them working this shift! He got his pistol leveled at the doorway just in time to see a woman appear there, a tall woman with blonde hair, wearing glasses, a dress of gray jersey, and a pencil behind her right ear. Conroy's surprise at her presence was nothing compared to the shock that grabbed him an instant later when he realized that he was looking at *Amanda Westlake*. There was no chance that he was wrong — when you have loved a woman the way he had loved Amanda, and then lost her, her face isn't something you forget in only four years.

You couldn't fault Amanda's memory, either, even if her discretion needed work. She stared at the big man with the pistol, aviator sunglasses, and "Toledo Mudhens" cap, frowned, narrowed her eyes, then said, in a loud, clear voice:

"Roger! What the hell are *you* doing here?"

Conroy broke the grip of mental paralysis quickly and forcefully, the way a *judoka* will escape a choke hold. To Amanda he growled, "Stay where you are and shut up!" He handed the black guard over to Gitner, saying, "Get him trussed up and into the garage with the other one. Check the armored cars, find out which one's got the money in it. I'll be with you in a minute." He pretended not to notice the way Gitner, who had his own shades on now, was staring at him.

He walked toward Amanda and gestured with the barrel of the Colt Python. "Back where you came from, lady, let's go," he said harshly. "And keep your mouth shut." He could see from Amanda's face that she was frightened now, and trying hard not to let it show. But to Conroy, who knew her face well enough to dream about it, the terror was all too clear.

He followed her into the room she had just come from. It was some kind of office, with shelves full of manuals, charts and plaques and framed group photos all over the walls, and a long table with several metal folding chairs pulled up to it. On the table were computer printouts, a fancy calculator and a number of ledgers, one of which was open to reveal lined columns filled with numbers. Conroy remembered that Amanda had been preparing for the C.P.A. exam back when they'd been together.

Conroy used the pistol to gesture toward one of the chairs. "Sit down," he said, more gently now. When she had complied, he stepped closer and said, "Now put your hands behind you."

Instead of obeying, Amanda turned to look at him over her shoulder and said sharply, "Damn it, Roger, I want an explanation for this." Conroy didn't take the protest literally. She knew exactly what he and the others were doing; the words were just a way of giving vent to her fear.

He bent forward, so that he could speak softly and not be heard outside the room. "Amanda, listen to me: we've got ourselves a serious situation here, more serious than you probably realize. So play along with me, all right? I've got to tie your hands like we did with the two guards, or those three guys with me are going to start wondering whose side I'm on. And we do *not* want that to happen. Now, put your hands back here."

She did as he asked. As he tied her wrists with another one of the cords, he said softly, "We can talk if we do it quietly, but we haven't got a lot of time. I'm a thief, Amanda. It's what I do. I've been doing it for twelve years."

After a second or two she nodded slowly. "So that's what you would never tell me, back when we were . . . I knew you were lying about part of your life, that's why I finally left. But I thought that it was another woman. I never imagined . . ."

"Better get used to it fast," he advised. "Now tell me what you're doing here, and at three o'clock in the damn morning, besides."

"I'm an accountant, a C.P.A. I have my own business, working freelance. Braxton's management thinks someone's been skimming from the cash that passes through this place, so they wanted a surprise audit. Using an outside firm like mine is part of the 'surprise.' So is doing it at this ungodly hour."

Conroy nodded glumly. "Yeah, it's a surprise, all right. So, tonight's the first time you've been in here?"

"That's right. A vice president of the company hired me last week, at my office downtown. He set everything up for me to come in this evening. Gave me a letter of authorization, and everything."

That was why none of Conroy's crew had spotted her in the three nights that they'd kept the place under surveillance. She hadn't been there — until tonight.

He was about to ask another question when his attention was caught by the sound of footsteps approaching. A moment later, Gitner was at the office door. He looked at Conway, then at Amanda, and back at Conroy again. Gitner's face behind his sunglasses was impassive. "We found the right truck," he told Conroy. "We're unloadin' the money bags now. Looks to be about as much as we figured, maybe even a little more."

Conroy nodded. "Okay, I'll be right there." This was meant as a dismissal, but Gitner stayed where he was. He continued looking at Conroy for another couple of seconds, then made a gesture with his head toward the corridor behind him. "Talk to you a minute?"

Conroy knew that refusal was not an option. "Yeah, all right," he said, and walked toward the door. Gitner backed up four or five steps until they were both standing in the short hallway a few yards away from the door to the office. Gitner lifted his cap and scratched his head with two fingers of the same hand. The silenced automatic remained in his other hand, its barrel pointing at the floor.

"Bad break," Gitner said softly. "I mean, running into somebody who knows you, an' all."

"Yeah," Conroy said. "Bad break. Just one of those freaky things that happen sometimes."

Gitner nodded, replaced the cap, then used his free hand to remove his sunglasses. His gaze never left Conroy's face, but he didn't look especially agitated. Gitner had been in the business for a while, himself. His face was calm, and the gray eyes were devoid of any emotion, including pity. After a moment, he said to Conroy, "Is it true what I heard, that you never done time? Never even took a bust?"

Conroy shrugged. "I was busted once, when I was just out of my teens. Nothing serious, though. I ripped off some typewriters from a college, and got caught when I tried to sell 'em. They kicked me out of the school, but dropped the charges. It was a long time ago."

"Yeah, okay, that's good," Gitner replied. "I guess that means them two guards can live, then."

Conroy narrowed his eyes. "What do you mean?"

"They heard her call you 'Roger,' remember?" Gitner spoke as if explaining things to a child. "The kinds of computers they got these days, it won't be hard for the cops to bring up mug shots of all the guys named 'Roger' who are known for doin' this kind of score. Can't be a whole lot of guys, right? So maybe your picture would be in there, if you'd been busted before for this kind of thing, and maybe one of them jerks we got tied up, or even both of them, points to your picture, even with the shades and the hat you got on. And could be you get pulled in for questioning, and maybe one of the guards picks you out of a lineup, and then, maybe you decide to deal yourself a reduced sentence by giving them Paglia's name, and Everhart's name, and my name, too. Know what I mean?"

Conroy said, evenly, "Some people might call that pretty fuckin' paranoid, man."

Gitner shrugged. "Don't matter what you call it, since it don't apply here, looks like. If you never been picked up for this kind of thing, then you ain't in the big FBI computer. So it makes no difference, them two Braxton guys hearing her call you by your first name, and all." Gitner nodded with satisfaction. "That's good, 'cause I pretty much agree with what you been sayin' all week, about how dead bodies mean more heat from the law. So, all right, them guards can live. No point making this mess any worse than we got to."

Gitner replaced his sunglasses, the pistol in his right hand still pointing downward, but Conroy noticed that the silenced barrel was gently tapping against Gitner's leg, like a dog's tail wagging in anticipation of a treat. "But that don't apply to the woman, though — she's got to go. You know that, right?"

What Conroy knew was that it was absolutely essential to maintain his credibility as a professional. If he failed at that, then either he or Gitner was going to die in the next few seconds. "Yeah, I know that," he said. "I was just trying to find out what she was doing here, and how we could've missed seeing her the last three nights."

"I been thinkin' on that myself. How *did* we miss her?"

"Tonight's her first night. It's some kind of surprise audit. She's an accountant, brought in from outside. The company thinks somebody's skimming."

Gitner just shook his head. "Shit, don't that beat all? Just one of them weird things that happens, like you said." The pistol barrel was tapping, tapping. "Listen, I don't know how well you and this lady know each other. You and her must've been pretty tight, I guess, the way she recognized you so quick." Gitner looked away for an instant, as if suddenly embarrassed, like a man about to confess to a leather fetish. "What I'm sayin' is, if you don't want to do it yourself, it's okay, you know? I'll take care of it. All you got to do is say so." Conroy could not see Gitner's eyes through the sunglasses, could not see there the eagerness that was plain in the man's voice. But the silencer on Gitner's automatic continued to tap his leg, the rhythm a little faster now.

"Thanks for the offer, man," Conroy said, his voice showing nothing but polite gratitude. "But it's okay — I'll take her out myself." He made a nasty smirk appear on his face, and said, "It'll give me some payback for the way she dumped me four years ago, the cunt."

Gitner grinned at that. "Payback is a bitch, like the man says." Then he was serious again. "Don't be too long, huh? We got to get moving on out of here."

"I know," Conroy replied. "I'll catch up with you in the garage."

"All right, then," Gitner said, and turned away.

Conway went back into the office, knelt next to

Amanda's chair, and took a small leather case from an inside pocket of his jacket. His hands trembled a little.

"What was that about?" Amanda asked. She tried to sound calm, but her control was starting to break up, the way ice on a pond cracks if you put enough weight on it.

"My associate there was offering to kill you, just in case I lacked the guts to do it myself."

"Roger, listen to me, you don't have to do this," Amanda said, a thin note of hysteria rising in her voice. "I won't turn you in, why would I? It would just cast suspicion on me, make it look like an inside job, or something. I swear to you, Roger, on my mother's grave, I would never —"

"Save it, Amanda," he said quietly, removing a hypodermic needle from the case, along with a small plastic ampoule of a yellowish fluid.

"No, listen, I've been sitting here thinking — there's no reason why we can't get back together again, I've never really stopped thinking about you, wishing I knew where you were, how to get in touch with you. I mean it, Roger, we had something special between us, and we could make it work this time, if only —"

Conway realized that any resentment he felt toward Amanda, any desire to punish, was not standing up very well in the face of her growing desperation. He placed his index finger across her lips, a gesture he had used sometimes in the old days to help her calm down. "I said 'save it,' because I'm not going to kill you, or let anybody else do it, either. So try to relax a little, and listen, all right?"

She looked at him, some of the apprehension fading from her face, and nodded.

"The thing is, we have to make the other guys *think* I killed you. And we have to make it work, Amanda. We have to pull off a trick that would make Houdini proud, otherwise they'll probably whack us both. Understand?"

She nodded again, eagerly. "Tell me what you want me

to do," she whispered. "Whatever it takes, anything you say."

"Your part of it doesn't really involve a lot," Conroy said, "except lying on the floor and being unconscious for a while." He lifted the hypo and showed it to her. "I carry this thing when I'm working, in case I need to put anybody to sleep, like I'm going to do with those two rent-a-cops in the other room. Each one of these capsules holds 120 ccs of liquid phenylbarbitol — a guaranteed three-hour nap, and it's safer than hitting people on the head; skulls fracture easier than you'd think, then you have a corpse to worry about."

She was staring at the hypo. "So you want to inject me with that, and knock me unconscious?"

"That's the idea. Then I'll lay you out on the floor in a way that'll seem convincing, mess up your hair and clothes to make it look like you struggled, and tell the others that I killed you with my hands." His hand touched the Colt Python, which was resting on the table. "I've got no silencer for this thing, and you can't silence a revolver, anyway." He smiled at her from one side of his mouth. "Just as well, under the circumstances, huh? It'd be pretty hard to fake gunshot wounds."

She nodded, but there were frown lines between her eyes. "If that's the best way to do this, then okay. But, Roger, if I'm unconscious, I won't be able to hold my breath if one of them comes in and looks closely to see if I'm dead."

"True, but you won't be breathing very deeply with this stuff, anyway, and I'll lay you out so that some of the furniture is between you and the doorway. The good thing is, the four of us have to book out of here pretty soon. With any luck, none of the other guys is going to take time for a real close inspection of your 'corpse'."

Amanda Westlake looked at Conroy for what seemed a long time to both of them, but was only six or seven seconds. Then she took in a breath and let it out loudly. "All right, then," she said quietly. "Let's do it."

A few seconds later, she watched, wincing, as Conroy depressed the hypo's plunger, injecting the amber liquid into her arm. As he withdrew the needle, she asked, "How long will it take?"

He was putting the hypo back in its case. "You'll probably start to feel it in a minute or so, and you'll be out cold in three or four minutes."

"Roger?"

"What?"

"I meant what I said, before. I imagine there's going to be a big fuss over this robbery, but after the dust settles, I think we ought to consider a reunion." Her smile was rueful. "A better one than this, I mean."

Conroy was fussing with the hypo case and did not look at her. "You think so? Really?"

"Yes, I do — really. Look, my briefcase is on that chair over there. It's got a compartment in the lid where I keep my business cards. Why don't you take one, and get in touch when it's safe? Six weeks, six months, whatever you think is wise."

Conroy's smile was patient and a little sad. "Amanda, it might not be too cool if your business card falls out of my pocket in front of those three guys, especially after I explain to them in gory detail how I just killed you, you know?"

"Oh."

"Listen, you live in this town now, right?"

"Well, in the suburbs."

"And you're in the phone book, right?"

"Sure, there's a listing for both the business and my home."

"I'll call you, Amanda. When it's safe."

"All right, I'll be waiting. Oh, wow, I'm starting to feel woozy already. This drug of yours works fast."

"It's meant to. Don't worry, it's perfectly safe."

"I'm not worried. Not now."

"Amanda?"

"Ummm?"

"I never stopped loving you, the whole time, every day of the last four years. Did you know that? Amanda?"

As she started to slide out of the metal chair, Conroy caught her and eased her limp form to the floor. A glance into one of her eyeballs assured him that she was unconscious.

He moved quickly to finish the rest of it.

Six minutes later, Conroy slipped behind the wheel of the stolen van and started the engine by touching together the ends of two ignition wires he'd torn loose earlier. Paglia climbed in next to him while Everhart was slamming the van's rear door on the last of the money bags. As Everhart slipped into the rear seat, Conroy said, "Where the hell is Gitner?" His hand was reaching for the door handle when Paglia said, "Here he comes."

As Gitner took his place in the other rear seat, Conroy said, "All right, last check before we go. Let's be sure we've got everything we went in there with." He went through his checklist out loud with them, and if any of the men thought it was a waste of time, he didn't say so. They all knew that the prisons are full of thieves who got careless and left something behind that later ended up as People's Exhibit A. Less than a minute later, they were done. Conroy announced, "Okay, we're out of here," and put the van in gear.

As they made the turn into the street, Conroy said over his shoulder to Gitner, "What were you doing in there, man? I thought you were in a big sweat to get going."

Conroy could see Gitner's shrug in the mirror. "I just wanted to be sure them two Braxton Security clowns were really out from that happy juice you shot 'em up with. Don't want one of 'em getting to a phone for a while, you know?"

Conroy was looking hard in the mirror now. "Gitner."

The blond man stifled a post-tension yawn with his hand. "What?"

"You didn't snuff those two guards, did you?"

"No, man, I already told you we didn't need to do that. No way they can give the cops anything to ID any of us. What am I, some kind of psycho?"

Conroy decided to act as if he hadn't heard the question.

After a moment, Paglia said to Conroy, "Too bad about that blonde chick, man. She looked pretty hot. Was she really your girlfriend or something, once?"

Conroy nodded a single time. "Or something," he said quietly. "Years ago."

Everhart leaned forward from his seat right behind Conroy. "I didn't hear any shots from that artillery piece you're carrying, so how'd you do her?"

"Why, you fixing to write an article for *True Detective,* or something?" The snarl in Conroy's voice surprised all of them, Conroy included.

Everhart sat back quickly. "Just wonderin', all right? I didn't mean nothin' by it."

There was silence in the van for several seconds. Finally, Conroy said "Look, she meant something to me once, okay? So I led her down the garden path a little." The snarl was gone now; Conroy's voice just sounded tired. "I said that I couldn't stand to kill her, blah, blah, but that one of you guys would do it for sure — unless it looked like she was already dead. So I told her that I was going to give her a shot of the phenylbarb, then lay her out in a way that would make her seem dead to somebody who didn't look close. I mean, once she figured out the situation, what with her blabbing my name and all, she was terrified. Who wouldn't be? But she was doing a lot better by the time I put that needle in her arm."

There was a red light ahead. Conroy slowed the van, then began to speed up again as the red changed to green. "So I gave her the shot, and it went pretty much the way that you saw with those two guards. She was in dreamland in about three minutes."

A big dog was sniffing its way across the street ahead of them, and Conroy swerved deftly to avoid hitting it. He was fond of animals, especially dogs.

"Then," he said, "once I was sure she was out all the way, I strangled her."

After a little while, Paglia said, "That was pretty righteous, the way you fooled her like that, man. I mean, you did what you had to do, but you showed compassion, too. Way to go."

From behind Conroy, Everhart said, "Yeah, it was just bad luck, her being there and all, but you handled it real classy, you know?" Everhart didn't actually have any feelings about the woman one way or the other, but he wanted to make it up to Conroy for getting him mad in the first place.

Another block went by before Gitner said, "I'm sorry I had any doubts about you, dude. I should've known you were gonna do the right thing." Gitner shifted in his seat a little, then said, "Listen, uh, you'll probably see it in the papers later, so I oughta tell you now. I mean, I'm big enough to admit it when I make a mistake, and it don't really matter none, anyway."

Conroy's eyes were back in the mirror now. They blinked twice before he asked, "Admit what?"

Gitner shrugged uncomfortably. "That I was wrong about you, okay? And that I wanted some insurance, just in case you'd gone all soft and mushy over that broad. No offense, all right? I wouldn't even mention it, except it'll probably be in the news when they talk about the score, and most likely you'll see it someplace."

Conroy did not raise his voice, and none of them ever knew what it cost him to ask, in an almost normal tone, "What's going to be in the news, Gitner?"

Gitner shifted position again, and he was looking out the window as he said, "About the broad being found with two bullets in the back of her head."

After that, no one spoke for a while. Then Paglia suddenly said to Conroy, "You all right, man?"

"Yeah, fine."

"Okay, good," Paglia said. "For a minute there I kinda thought maybe you were —"

"It's just my fucking allergies kicking up again. There's a lot of pollen around, this time of year." Conroy sounded all right, so after another moment Paglia looked away. He never thought to wonder what kind of pollen was adrift in the air during October.

Conroy drove the van carefully, skillfully. He kept within the speed limit, stayed in his lane, and stopped for all red and yellow lights. He did nothing that might encourage the attention of a cruising cop on the prowl for drunk drivers.

Conroy had been in the business a long time. He had not planned it that way, but the years had a way of accumulating, one day after another, and every day you were in seemed to make it that much harder to get out. Conway knew, deep down, that he was going to keep on taking down scores until he was busted, or burned out, or dead. But he was a professional, and in this he took a certain pride.

When things don't work out as planned, a professional accepts the twists of fate, and moves on. A professional does whatever it takes to make the score go down right and to fade away clean when it's over. He never loses perspective, never gives up control, never lets personal concerns get in the way of his work.

A professional never cries.

Web of Vengeance

Brian Evankovich

She had a spider tattoo on her inner left thigh about an inch from her vagina and I couldn't imagine why anybody would want somebody else poking around up there with a hot needle and ink. I'd said as much when she showed me "her little critter" fifteen years ago. But it didn't matter anymore. She was dead.

Nick called me when he saw the tattoo, remembering a story I'd told about Sara and her spiders.

A sick job, yeah. But the killer had turned her once pretty face into mush with a trio of slugs.

"Where, Nick?" I said. Very quiet. My whisper loud in the morgue's cool examining room.

"The alley on Neil Street, near Hap's Bar and the Indian Deli. Last night."

"Sex assault, Doctor?" I said to the ME.

"No. No sign of anything like that," he said, on the opposite side of the table. "Just the two slugs in the face and the third in the head."

I pulled the sheet back over the lifeless body that had once been Sara Gage. An old girlfriend from fifteen years ago. The kind you remember with a smile and a "Where is she now" moment when going through dusty high school yearbooks and only then because you're clearing out space in the garage.

"You go through her clothes?" I said. The pile of dirty clothes sat on the tray at the head of the examining table. Pink shirt, jeans, underwear. Her shirt had a spider on it, too, in the center. She'd had a thing for spiders. I couldn't remember why.

We'd called her the Spider-Girl back in school. Teased her about dating Spider-Man. She'd have other clothes with spiders in her closet, diagrams framed on her wall, a shelf full of books about the creepy crawlers. Sara was the only woman I knew who didn't freak out when she saw one crawling on the kitchen floor or coming down from the ceiling on a string of web.

"Nothing. No ID, house keys, anything," Nick said. "But now we have a place to start."

I needed a drink. Nick decided the hell with police regulations and joined me. We hit Jack's All-Star Kitchen and ordered a couple of beers.

"I can't believe how long it's been," I said. Tipped back the Miller and looked out the window.

"You dated her back in high school?"

"We broke off just before I left for the army."

"Ever serious about her?"

"No. I didn't know what the hell I wanted back then. But I had a girl and some money in my pocket so we had a ball while we could," I said. "She sent me a few letters during my first few months in the service. I think her last said she was leaving Las Palmas to get a job in Seattle and would write when she got settled, but she never did. And then fifteen years went by. And now this."

"Anything else we can use?" Nick said.

I shook my head.

"I'll let you know what we come up with."

"I'd like that."

I stared out the window. Made circles with my beer bottle on the table. "Maybe you can try Sara's parents. I think they still live around here."

Nick took out his notebook. I gave their names but held back on the address. I still remembered. And wanted to get there first.

We finished our beers and he took me back to the police station where my car waited.

I hit the road and headed across town.

The Gages lived in the Uptown Hills area, where houses started at one million and a good fixer-upper half that. I turned the car up a steep hill and scanned the addresses. Lots of green in this neighborhood. Trees, yards, all well taken care of. Like they had a full-time crew working every day to keep 'em up.

No kids out playing, but plenty of his-and-hers Mercedes and expensive SUVs in driveways. A few hot rods and hand-me-down cars on the curbs.

I parked a few doors down from Sara's folks.

I stood by the mailbox a while looking at the house. Not much had changed. The chimes under the porch were new, and it looked like they'd had the place repainted.

Going up to the front felt funny, like the first time I picked Sara up to take her to a movie. Wasn't sure if she or her father would answer and breathed a sigh of relief when she opened the door wearing her favorite pink sweater and blue jeans with the black shoes and her hair tied back. On the way out she remembered I liked to watch her hair bounce on her shoulders so she took out the pony tail and let it hang.

I rang the bell, waited, rang again. Finally the lock clicked back and the door opened.

"Yes?"

She seemed shorter, her hair gray, but the sharp eyes that had given me such a thorough going over when I started dating her daughter were still there.

"Hi, Mrs. Gage."

"Johnny?"

I smiled.

"I haven't seen you in years! What are you doing here? Did Sara call you?"

"I need to talk to you, Mrs. Gage."

The smile vanished, her face softened.

"Sara hasn't come home . . ." She put a hand to her mouth and choked out a sob.

I went inside. Gave it to her straight. She didn't take it well and cried on my shoulder for a few minutes. She told me she'd hoped things were going to calm down with Sara's return. Her husband had died two years before — cancer — and she'd been awfully lonely. When Sara said she was moving back, she'd been excited to have somebody around the house again.

I let Lorna talk and ask questions. I answered what I could without giving too much detail. Later she could learn that it would be a closed-casket funeral because there was no face left to look at.

"Why are you here?" she said. "Why not the police?"

"They'll be here soon. My friend Nick Shepherd, most likely. I got here first because he has to look your address up."

"Sara didn't call you?"

"I had no idea she was back."

"She got back two weeks ago. She was laid off."

"Had she been in Seattle all this time?"

Lorna nodded.

"She hadn't been too happy the past few years," she said. "She said she wanted to get another job around here. She was going to call you. I saw your name in the paper once."

She smiled a little. "I told her she should . . . you know. See if you'd settled down yet." She started crying some more. "Why would anybody do this?"

She cried on my shoulder some more. When she stopped, I said, "What had Sara been doing?"

Lorna shrugged. "Seeing friends, catching up."

"Who?"

Lorna shrugged.

"I need a list, Lorna. I need a place to start."

She looked at me a long moment. Nodded. Got up and went into the other room.

It took a few minutes, but she gave me a short list of names of people Sara knew. I didn't recognize any of them. I said I needed to go. She opened the door and we both stopped as Nick came up the walk. I said good-bye to Lorna and walked out. Nick's eyes bored into me.

"Hi, Nick."

"Damn it, John," he said.

"See you, Nick," I said over my shoulder.

I returned to my office.

Leanna, my secretary, sat behind her desk typing away as I shut the door behind me. I parked myself on the edge of her desk. She looked up as I took out the piece of paper Lorna had given me. "Three names," I said. "I need addresses and phone numbers."

She snatched the slip out of my hand. "Got it."

Leanna was a whiz with the Internet and reverse directories. As a former journalist, she knew reporters and had contacts all over the place that came in handy. She'd quit working for the papers when she realized she could make more money as a receptionist and have better hours. Working for me, she had the best of both worlds.

I went into my office, eased into the chair behind my desk, and stared out the window. It seemed like yesterday when I saw Sara last. I couldn't believe so much time had gone by. I stopped and turned to the paperwork on my desk before I became too upset, but it was too late. I wasn't upset enough to cry, exactly, but I felt a heavy weight in my chest. Coupled with the rage boiling in my gut. I just wanted to stop and hole up for a while.

So I told Leanna I'd be back and drove to a favorite quiet place of mine, up in the hills east of Las Palmas, where a few farmers had ranches and where cattle roamed chomping grass. I pulled over to the shoulder of an overpass overlooking one of the freeways and just sat there watching the cars, staring off in the distance.

Nick would be pissed at me for seeing Lorna. He'd know I was dealing myself in. He'd know I'd want Sara's killer at the end of my gun. He'd know the only way to stop me was to arrest me. He could make the charges stick, too. California law says private investigators can't touch homicides.

But nothing would stop me from tracking down Sara's killer and turning his face into mush same as he'd done to her.

I sat in the car watching the freeway. How was I supposed to feel about somebody I hadn't seen in fifteen years? I'd put Sara behind me a long time ago. If she'd dropped by for a visit we'd have a few beers and a nice chat and then say good-bye. But this was different. Nobody deserved what happened to her.

About an hour went by. I fired up the car and drove back to the office.

Leanna had the addresses and phone numbers of the names I'd given her by the time I returned.

I started with Jayne Hansen and found her behind the counter at the flower shop she owned. She handed a large bouquet of something or other to a young man who glanced away from me as he went out. I stepped up to the counter.

"Can I help you?"

"I'm John Coburn." I showed her my private shield. "You and I had a mutual friend. Sara Gage."

Her eyes widened a bit. "The police told me not to say anything to you."

"Great." I put my shield away.

"You were a friend of Sara's?"

"We dated once. A long time ago."

She watched me.

"Do you know anything she may have been into, something that can make sense of what happened?"

She opened her mouth to say something, then shut it and shrugged. "I can't tell you."

The front door opened and two chatty women entered. Jayne went to help them select a set of roses, which they asked to have delivered to a party the next day. I waited, glancing around at the wall-to-wall flowers, and when the ladies left Jayne looked back at me.

"I don't know anything. Sara had only called me the night she came home."

"What did she say?"

"Just that she'd decided to move home and was having her stuff delivered later. She got tired of Seattle. I think she broke up with somebody and decided to start fresh back home."

"Who?"

"I don't know. She was with this guy a while."

"Did you talk to her often?" I said.

"Now and then. You know, birthdays and Christmas."

"She tell you his name?"

"I probably have it somewhere."

I waited.

"But I promised the police."

"How long was she with this guy?"

"Twelve years, I think."

"And they broke up."

"Yeah."

"And she came home to start fresh."

"She didn't say that exactly, but that's the impression I got."

I thanked her and got back in the car. As I drove through traffic, I called Sara's mother, but she said she wasn't allowed to talk to me either. I asked who Sara had been dating in Seattle, but no matter what I said to get her to help, she refused. I told her I understood and hung up.

Called Nick next. "Having a little trouble, Johnny?"

"I'm just trying to find out what happened to her."

"Read it in the papers. We've got some good leads we're checking on."

"Let me in."

"No. And don't waste time talking to anybody Mrs. Gage told you about. I've already seem them."

He hung up.

I let out a curse and tossed the cell phone on the seat beside me.

Leanna tracked me as I entered the office, went straight to my desk and slumped down in the chair.

"John?" she said from the doorway.

I told her about Nick, and she shook her head. "You know how he gets whenever you get involved."

"I know."

"Can't you let this one go? Let the police handle it?"

I stared at the wall. Leanna went back to her desk.

I went through the motions the rest of the day and told Leanna to quit early. I sat around for a bit, then locked up.

I headed over to my friend Suzi's diner and found a spot at the bar. Suzi came over with a smile. "You don't look so good."

"Bad day." And I told her about it, keeping my voice low. She nodded, ignoring looks from other waitresses and customers. She owned the place, she could do what she wanted.

When I finished, she said, "I'm sorry about all that, John. It's terrible." She squeezed my hand.

After she took my order, I sat and turned a napkin in circles, ignoring the rising commotion around me as the dinner crowd showed up. Suzi went back and forth filling coffee cups and delivering plates of food. Every now and then she gave me a hopeful smile but I didn't feel like responding.

She brought my steak and fries and salad. I sipped my Coke and started eating. I really didn't taste anything but it filled the hole in my gut. The other hole.

On a normal day I'd linger over dinner, wait for the crowd to die down, and have coffee and dessert with Suzi. Tonight I just paid and waved good-bye. She gave me another smile but that was all.

Pulling the car into the garage, I hit the button that closed the door and went inside. Hung up my jacket and shoulder holster on the coat rack by the front door.

I didn't find anything on TV so I just stared at the Weather Channel and started to wonder if I should go to bed when somebody knocked on my back patio door.

Curtains covered the door, drapes covered the windows, and I had no lights on in the back. I went to the front, grabbed my Colt Government Model .45 and slipped out the door to the gate alongside the house. The gate creaked open but I didn't think the guy in back could hear. Walked slow down the path along the side of the house, stepping around my lawn mower and garbage cans, pieces of yard equipment. Around the corner of the house, the .45 out in front of me, I set the front site on a young guy about 18 who snapped his head around at the sound of my grunt and dropped his jaw at the sight of my gun.

"Wrong door, bub," I said.

He sank against the wall, his legs giving out. His back scraped along the wall as he lowered himself and I kept the .45 right in his face.

"What gives, kid?"

"Don't kill me!" It came out a hoarse whisper.

"What are you doing here?"

"I know Sara."

"You *knew* Sara." I lowered my gun, stepped back. "Get up."

He stood on shaky legs.

"Who are you?"

"Todd. Todd Willis."

"How did you know Sara?"

"She knows my aunt."

"Who's your aunt?"

"Trudy Willis."

I nodded. "I remember Trudy."

The kid looked me up and down, his eyes stopping on the .45 in my hand. His bottom lip quivered, he started to cry. I put an arm around his shoulders and led him away.

"Let's go inside."

He couldn't stop sobbing, and his shoulders were rocking by the time I sat him down on the couch. I got him some water, but he didn't notice. His hands covered his face.

It took a few minutes, but he stopped. His eyes bleary red, his body shaking, he looked at me with wide eyes.

"I dumped her body," he said. "Sara's body. I dumped it in the alley."

I grabbed a fistful of his shirt and gave him a face full of .45. He screamed.

"I'll be dumping your body if you don't start talking,

kid."

He started sucking wind in short, sharp gasps and tried to talk but swallowed his tongue. It took a lot not to break him in half. I swallowed my rage. Let go of his shirt and put the gun away.

We stared at each other for a long time. He caught his breath but I never took my eyes away from his.

"I didn't kill her," he said.

"Start from the beginning."

He told a hell of a story.

Then we got in the car.

"Is this the alley?" I said, slowing the car.

"Yeah."

I got out. Not much vehicle or foot traffic tonight. I stepped into the alley and shined a flashlight around. There was nothing to see. The crime scene boys had picked it clean.

We drove on and I said, "Why?"

"Aunt Trudy has a lot of money."

I shook my head. "It would never work."

I stopped for a light and tapped my fingers on the steering wheel. I should deliver the kid to Nick, I thought. Then again, there were a lot of things I *should* do.

"Have you seen your uncle or father since the murder?"

"Not really. I've been hiding out."

"Where does your father work?"

"He runs a car shop. 5th and Westfall. Mort's Automotive."

"Your uncle?"

"Software guy. I can't remember the company."

I drove on.

I spotted Todd's father Morty the next day as he showed up for work and unlocked the front door of his auto shop. His neighbors were other mechanics or body shops. The lot was packed with cars. Morty opened the garage door and looked around, then turned and went inside.

I sat there all day, watching cars go in and out, customers come and go. All the shops were busy. At noon Mort took off for lunch. I sat across the restaurant from him while he ate his sandwich and I picked at mine. Back to work afterwards.

I followed him home, almost losing him in traffic. Todd had given me the address so if I did lose him I could pick him up again.

Todd came home from work a few minutes after his Dad. I saw his mother, April, come out front and water the plants. Wondered if she knew about the plot, as Todd did.

I took off and headed over to Todd's Uncle Roger and his Aunt Trudy's place. No cars in the driveway. No lights on inside. I went up to the door and rang the bell. Nobody answered.

I waited in the car. Other cars came down the street but passed without stopping. A dark sedan turned in and I cursed, sliding down in the seat. The sedan stopped in front of the Willis house and Nick climbed out. Went to the door, rang the bell, waited, went back to the car. He drove away from the curb and rolled toward me, pulled the car to a stop and rolled his window down. I turned on my car's power and hit the switch to lower mine.

"Working tonight?" he said.

"Stakeout. Split."

"Not watching the house I just left, are you?"

"What gives you that idea?"

"Just curious. I'm a curious guy."

"I'm working," I said.

He gave me a grin but nodded. "Watch your back, Johnny." He drove away.

I rolled my window up and sat for another two hours. Nobody at the Willis house came home. I still had a couple of days. At least I hoped so.

I went to Suzi's for steak and fries and a little chitchat. She said my mood was better than the day before. Just a little.

Up early the next morning. Nothing on the radio about a murder. In the car by five-thirty. In front of the Willis house — Roger and Trudy's — by six-fifteen. Waiting. Waiting some more. Roger left first, driving a Mitsubishi sports car. Trudy left second in a mini-van. I followed the mini-van to an office complex. Trudy hopped out wearing a suit. I couldn't help but grin. Older, like all of us, but still pretty; that suit didn't come off the rack at Sears so she still made sure she had nice outfits.

I wondered just what kind of insane nut job her husband was for wanting to knock her off with his brother's help. And kill Sara because she found out. And make his nephew dump the body.

I rolled down the window to let the air in and sat back to wait.

I trailed Trudy and a few friends to lunch and then back to the office where I sat in the car some more. And more. At five o'clock she left with another trio of ladies in her van, and drove to a Mexican restaurant where they laughed and chitchatted their way through the front door.

I sat and watched from the parking lot. The place had windows all around and I saw them near the front.

I figured I had some time so I hustled across the street to a Shell station and grabbed a sandwich and Coke. The sandwich was good but was three days from its expiration date. It sat in my stomach like a rock and made me want to go back for Alka-Seltzer.

Trudy and her friends left after eating and climbed back in the van. I followed them back to the office where the others girls took off in their own cars. I stayed with Trudy through town to a 24-hour grocery store.

I hung around near the front while she was inside. People came and went while I scanned the parking lot. I had the .45 under my left arm and spare magazines in my pocket.

Nobody else hanging around except teens staying out late, talking loud, a few on skateboards.

Trudy came out with a full grocery bag and headed back to the van. She walked with her head up and shoulders back. I looked over at her mini-van and saw another car coming down the lot toward it.

When the car stopped I took out my .45, clicked off the safety and held it against my leg as I moved toward Trudy.

The bitch of it was I couldn't do a thing until I was sure and when I was sure she might be dead.

I cut in front of a guy on a motorcycle ready to shout a warning to Trudy because the driver's side window of the car was rolling down, a man leaning out, extending his arm, the steel in his hand glinting in the parking lot light.

I dashed to a tree, the gun in both hands as I braced myself against the trunk. "Trudy!" And she spun her head around and the man in the car fired. She screamed and fell to the ground, the groceries spilling. I emptied the .45 into the car, laying a pattern through the windshield and driver's window. The man behind the wheel let out his own scream and his arm dropped and the gun clattered to the ground.

More screaming, people scattering. I rushed over to Trudy who started to get up as I knelt down. She saw my gun and screamed again, backing up against the bumper of her van.

"It's okay! It's okay!"

She looked at the car with the dead man in it, back to me, back to the car, to me again, gasping for breath. I grabbed her hand and she started to kick and scream and everybody watched us with wide eyes and terror as I dragged her over to my car, stuffed her inside, and sped away leaving behind a trail of rubber and smoke.

Trudy stopped shouting and trying to get away when she realized who I was. She didn't relax, though; leaning against the car door and staring at me like a cornered animal. Asked me what the hell was going on, and I told her to just stay quiet and take it easy. She kept asking, so I finally told her that her husband had just tried to have her killed and that shut her up real good.

I pulled into a motel and checked in. Trudy couldn't walk very well after my news so I half carried her into the room. She stood in the middle of the room while I locked the door and checked the windows. At the table I slapped a new magazine into the .45 and set it and the other spare clips on the writing table.

I turned to Trudy, but before I could say anything she put a hand to her stomach and rushed to the bathroom where she threw up dinner and probably lunch, too.

I sat at the writing table with my hand resting on the .45 and listened to her wash her face. She came out, resting against the wall. Her legs still shook like Jell-O.

"Why don't you lie down," I said.

She nodded and stretched out on one of the beds. Arms at her sides, staring up at the ceiling.

"Tell me about Sara," I said.

She sat up and looked at me. "Does all this have to do with — my God!" She gasped and put a hand to her mouth. "Did Sara . . . I mean, was she . . . did she . . ."

"Your nephew Todd dumped her body in the alley after

your brother-in-law killed her," I said. "Todd came to see me last night, told me about it. He was scared to go to the cops because of what he did. He heard Sara and you talking about me so he came to me."

Trudy nodded. "Yeah, we talked about you. I told her you'd made the papers a few times."

"Having problems at home?"

She nodded.

"They can't be so bad Roger wants you dead, can they?"

"Roger isn't well. Hasn't been well for a long time."

"And his brother?"

"Always does what Roger tells him," Trudy said.

"Sara was at the house late one night and heard Roger and Morty talking in the garage, about when to do the job. She confronted them. Morty shot her."

She stared at me with eyes like saucers.

I held up the .45. "You know how to use one of these?"

She kept staring and said nothing. I asked again and she blinked a few times before nodding.

I stood up and left the .45 on the table. "Stay here until I come back. Anybody but me comes through that door, you shoot. Got it?"

She nodded.

I pulled the door shut behind me and stood outside until the lock slammed home.

I thought it over as I drove back to Trudy's house. I had enough to hand over to Nick but I wasn't going to stop until I confronted the man responsible and dealt with him my own way. Roger would be home, waiting for a phone call from his brother saying the hit had gone as planned. He'd get something else instead.

Without my gun, there was no way Nick could get me for murdering Roger Willis. Shooting Morty was justifiable;

after all, he was about to cause death or grave bodily injury to another. I could tell Nick I went over to apprehend Roger and left my gun with Trudy so I wouldn't be tempted to kill him.

I could tell Nick a lot of things if Willis forced me to defend myself.

I drove up and down the street twice, looking for signs of cops on a stakeout, before parking in front of the house on the curb. From the glove box I took out a pair of black gloves and pulled them on tight.

It hit me as I walked up the path to the front door. Sara and her spiders. I'd always gotten a kick out of how quietly spiders could sneak up on you. Spin a web, hide in a corner. Wait for their prey to get stuck, move in and strike. *Bang,* just like that. Wrap a bug up in a web cocoon in thirty seconds flat. No escape.

I was about to trap my own prey in a web he'd never get out of. Roger Willis thought his plans had been successful. He'd never expect me. Never see me coming. And by the time I struck it would be too late.

I opened the front screen door of the Willis house. Knocked twice.

No answer. I knocked again, pounded several times. The porch light snapped on, the door opened, and Roger stuck his head out. I bashed him square in the nose. He fell backward and hit the floor hard.

I stepped inside, shut the door. Roger held his bloody nose as he pushed himself to his feet. He cocked his fist and I slammed my foot into his balls before he could swing. He hit the floor again and curled up. I dragged him from the entryway into the living room and shoved him onto the couch.

"Nice try, Roger, but your brother is dead, your wife is safe, and your nephew is ready to spill everything."

"I didn't —"

I punched him again. And again, splitting his face open. He got up to swing but I slipped behind him and shoved him to the floor. I slammed a foot into his gut. I brought my foot up to stomp on his face but only hit the carpet because he was rolling, rolling, rolling away from me and —

That's when I saw the butt of a pistol sticking out of his waistband behind his back.

Roger Willis got to his knees and drew the gun in one swift motion. I lunged forward and grabbed his wrist, twisting hard as his finger tightened around the trigger, turning his arm back and giving him an eyeful of his own gun. I slipped my finger through the trigger guard right along with his and gave him two seconds to think about it before I jerked my finger back and let the gun go *bang!*

When the cops showed up I was sitting on the couch watching Roger's blood soak into the carpet. They frisked me, put the cuffs on me, and sat me in a corner. The older of the two, a sergeant who knew me, listened to my story. He called Nick, and when he showed up, they took the cuffs off and Nick and I stood in the kitchen and talked.

While I told him everything the forensics and homicide crews showed up. I didn't even hear their racket. Nick asked the other cops if any of them had found a .45; none had. He searched my car. Frisked me. I kept telling him Trudy Willis had my gun and we jumped in his car and went to the motel.

She told the rest of the story and Nick saw my gun and softened up a bit.

It wasn't that easy, of course. The DA wanted a full investigation, grand jury, everything. I stressed I'd gone to Roger's house to confront him and bring him to Nick, and left my gun with Trudy on purpose so I wouldn't be tempted to take the law into my own hands. They bought it. It took a few weeks, but they didn't file any charges and the papers made me look like a hero. Which didn't hurt business a bit.

We buried Sara during the grand jury probe on a sunny day, her grave shaded by an oak she would have loved. Suzi held my hand during the whole thing and I held Mrs. Gage against my shoulder. Didn't even hear the minister. Just stared at the casket.

I finally realized something I'd tried to deny from the beginning. Sara wasn't something I'd left behind 15 years ago. She'd been as much a part of me as anybody else.

After the service I took Suzi and Mrs. Gage home, then returned to the cemetery, watched the attendants shovel dirt into the grave, and said good-bye to my Spider-Girl.

The Butcher

Robert D. Hughes

The summer the Butcher began slicing up young women like sides of beef made the record books as one of the hottest in Chicago history. In fact, those were the top two subjects of conversation around water coolers and coffee pots that season — the weather and The Butcher.

The latter's name was coined by an enterprising young reporter at the local CBS affiliate, a baby-faced blonde named Alma Lambert. At the outset of the series of macabre killings, Ms. Lambert had the pleasure (and it obviously was, for her) of breathlessly intoning on-camera that a young woman's severely mutilated body had been found "arranged in a ghastly display in a North Side alley, the victim of a horrifying butcher."

The Town Hall cops who got the squeal found Terri Dunbar in seventeen pieces of varying size, neatly laid out on a long two-by-ten pine board set up on the edges of a couple of adjacent nearly-full Dumpsters behind a bar in the shadow of Wrigley Field. Certain of the victim's internal organs were missing — the heart, liver and kidneys were mentioned by the press. The head anchored one end of the board, its sightless eyes staring into the night.

How do I know so much about this? Simple — I represented the parceled up victim's parents, who hired me to find the killer when Chicago's finest didn't. Me, I'm Dennis Malone, private investigator usually employed by insurance companies to expose fraudulent claims or by worried parents to find brats who've run away yet again.

The Butcher case began on a Monday morning between three and four A.M. in an alley behind a Clark Street drinking establishment after a Cubs night game. Most of the drunks had cleared out to their respective suburbs, and the atmosphere in the bar was approaching mellow as four o'clock closing time drew near. The bartender, one Keith Brooks, went out back for a quick breath of air after locking the front door and the register. When he spotted the victim in the form of various cuts — tenderloin, T-bone, rib steak, etc. — on open-air display, he hurled his dinner, then rang 911.

The homicide bulls came up empty. No prints, no fibers, no bodily fluids, nothing to point any fingers at. The killer had worn gloves and used clean cutting equipment. He'd made no unusual noises nor been spotted as he set up his alleyway display. They figured the carving had been done elsewhere. It wouldn't have taken long to drop off the grisly partages.

A month went by and a second victim, Angie Briggs, turned up in a nearby alley in the same circumstances. Four weeks later, a kid with the moniker Tiffany Webber surfaced in another Wrigleyville alley, same deal as Briggs.

Theories abounded regarding the Butcher's motive. The local TV crime beat guys and gals marveled at the precision of the surgical technique and the retail-style display employed by the sanguinary slicer. The parcels were arranged symmetrically and far enough above ground level to be out of easy reach of neighborhood dogs and cats. Great significance was seen in the missing organs of the victims — one late-night expert raised the specter of a hometown Hannibal Lecter. Was the Butcher a cannibal? Was he selling the body parts on eBay? Surgeons and actual butchers immediately went to the top of the media's list of prospective suspects. Boy, were they wrong.

As summer waned, it was still hotter than the hinges on the door to hell, and those who could afford to, hightailed it to cooler climes, typically the beaches around the bend of the lake, up in Southwestern Michigan.

Nearly three months after her death, the first victim's parents faced me across the scarred oak desk my aging personal computer calls home. Paul Dunbar, a stocky bird with a gray crew cut, looked like one of those retired generals CNN likes to have on to explain the progress of the current war — it was terrorism that year. His younger wife Heather might have been beautiful before she'd ballooned to one-eighty. After hearing a glowing account of their late twenty-year-old daughter's model childhood and youth, I lobbed a few questions their way.

"Any enemies you know of?"

"No," they replied in unison.

"Did she date anyone in particular?"

They exchanged meaningful glances. Paul nodded, and Heather spoke up. "Terri had what you'd call a contemporary life-style," she said.

"What do you mean?" I asked.

Both Dunbars squirmed for a moment, then Heather said, "She dated a number of men."

"And didn't exercise the best judgment," Paul added.

"Got any names?"

They both shook their heads.

"And her employer was. . . ?"

"The Ecstasy Theater. She worked the box office," Paul murmured.

It went on that way for another twenty minutes. Nothing remarkable about Terri. Sounded like any perfectly normal promiscuous kid who worked in a porn movie house and hung around bars. The Dunbars said they'd raised her in Des Moines and moved to Chicago only four years ago. Terri had taken a one-bedroom apartment in the Lake View neighborhood after graduation from high school, and gone a little "wild" on her own. She'd walked to Jeremy's the night before the barkeep stumbled on her cleaved carcass, and hadn't been seen since.

I asked the Dunbars about their daughter's previous employment history. They ran down a list of short-lived gigs in retail shops, a stint with a bicycle messenger service, a few months with a notorious personal injury law firm as a paralegal. The last item had me raising my eyebrows to myself, since I'd heard a bit about the firm's principals over the years. I pressed for details.

"Oh yes, Terri did very well working at Slade and Garcia. Mr. Slade even had her to dinner at his country place." This from Heather.

I duly took notes, ran through a few more queries, extracted a retainer and sent the Dunbars on their way with traces of hope on their faces. After an Internet search and a consultation with the Yellow Pages, I was armed with enough to start detecting.

A call to my old college roommate Joe Skrepenak seemed like a good place to start. The profanity-prone former all-Big Ten lineman had joined the Chicago Police Department as a patrolman twenty years earlier, risen swiftly through the ranks and now held the title Deputy Chief of Detectives, Homicide.

Once I'd identified myself, he said, "The fuck you want now, Malone?"

I tried to sound offended. "Thought you guys would appreciate hearing from me, especially after I solved the Golden Voice case for you, using my superior sleuthing skills."

"Bullshit. You were just in the right place at the right fucking time. Pure luck. But it ended up okay," he conceded.

"And now, I've been retained to close up the infamous Butcher case."

Dead silence from the phone.

"Seriously, Joe, the first victim's parents hired me."

"And you want to pump me and use my department's resources to give yourself something to pick at. Am I right?"

"As always. When can I stop by?"

"Can't show you the file. This one's too hot. The fucking mayor's even involved."

"What — he confessed?"

"Listen, wiseass, I'll let you buy me a drink. Five-thirty at Billy Goat's." The line went dead.

Billy Goat's Tavern is Chicago's most recognized and overpublicized bar. The joint on Lower Wacker Drive was the thinly-disguised inspiration for the old *Saturday Night Live* skits in the seventies, where John Belushi yelled "Cheeseborger, Cheeseborger, No Coke, Pepsi." It's said the Cubs were permanently hexed when the proprietor, Sam Sianis, brought his pet goat to Wrigley Field in 1945 for a World Series game. The ushers wouldn't let Sam bring the malodorous mammal into the park, though he'd bought a ticket for it. The Cubs lost the Series and haven't been in one since.

I spotted Joe Skrepenak at a little table with his Armani-clad, baked ham arms crossed on his chest. French cuffs with brushed gold links in the shape of .45 automatics added a chic touch. Joe's a clothes-horse, not uncommon among Chicago homicide detectives. In fact, it's an expected part of the image, not that he minds. As I took a rickety chair, he pointedly eyed his chunky Rolex and growled, "'Bout fucking time, Malone."

"Traffic," I said. The all-purpose Chicago excuse.

Joe drained his draft and waved at Sam Junior to bring two more. I scanned our surroundings. At the next table, a fat man, elbows on the table, clutched a huge burger in his fists. As he chomped into the mass of bun and beef, rivulets of grease streamed between his fingers and flowed onto his thick wrists. It brought to mind other, raw cuts of meat, and it was all I could do to keep from losing my lunch. I took in a deep breath and turned my attention to the homicide chief.

"Joe, what can you tell me that the media haven't?"

"One thing, the guy doin' this shit ain't a fucking surgeon. And he ain't a fucking butcher either."

"Why not?"

"Those guys don't use serrated-edge knives."

"The uh, incidents were a month apart. Any significance?"

"Not a coincidence, ya ask me. Matter of fact, the asshole's due again."

"Exact same modus for all three?"

"Yep, all of 'em in alleys behind bars within a block of the ballpark. Home games each date. None of the vics were umpires, so it's probably not a player getting revenge for a bad call."

"Any witnesses?"

"Thought we had one, but it turned to shit. A guy's taking a leak against a phone pole, sees a dark-colored SUV idling nearby, thinks nothing of it until he finds the smorgasbord that was this Webber kid set up like a Fourth of July special. The wit goes over to see what's on the board, and the SUV peels away. No description of the driver, no fucking plate. People don't pay attention."

"Were all three sliced up the same way?"

Joe nodded. "Pretty much. Everything there but some of the vial organs — heart, liver and so on. Fucking liver. The wife makes it with onions." He grimaced.

"Anything happen when your guys canvassed, interviewed family, friends, co-workers, all that stuff."

Joe frowned. "Nothing jumped out and bit us on the ass. I'll tell you one thing. Whoever this guy is, he's smart . . . and stone cold."

"How's he lure these girls, you suppose?"

"How'd Ted Bundy do it? Prob'ly got a smooth line of bullshit. Might have looks, maybe a flashy car, lots of dough. See, these kids have all been sorta down-home — didn't have a lot of street smarts."

"What about the law firm Terri Dunbar worked at?"

Joe shrugged. "My man Roberts questioned the head ambulance-chaser there, guy name of Slade. Said the kid did a decent job, didn't volunteer a whole lot. Roberts had the impression she was a fuckup and the guy didn't want to say anything bad."

"This Slade — what's your take?"

Joe barked a nasty laugh. "Guy's a contingency puke, what can I say?" He shrugged his big shoulders expansively. "Those fuckers are oilier than a crankcase, but ain't no law against it. There was, half the city council'd be in the slammer. Hey, I gotta split. Meeting the wife for dinner, not that I'm hungry."

"Speaking of dinner, what do you say to a friendly wager, me versus you guys, whoever cracks the case gets a freebie."

"You're fucking on," Joe growled as he departed.

I thought about Joe's remarks on the way to my apartment. The Butcher apparently took the victims somewhere the night before their bodies turned up. It would take a while to cut them up. Probably a smooth operator with the ability to persuade impressionable young women to accompany him someplace. Someplace private, where screams and struggling wouldn't be heard. The word "cold" had rung a bell somewhere inside me. Why? I decided to sleep on it and start fresh the next morning.

Morning dawned humid and still. I'd ruminated about

the case off and on during a largely sleepless night. I felt a pressing need to find this butcher creep before he killed again. I couldn't let the Dunbars down. It was hard to imagine what they must have felt when they got the news about Terri. It was obvious I couldn't compete with the homicide division of the CPD in terms of manpower. Joe's investigators were good and thorough. They'd have already knocked on doors and questioned anyone remotely connected with the victims. My best bet was to find an edge somehow, a small lever to pry open the door. I decided to play a hunch. A few minutes later, I got on the horn to Jimbo Spain at the Illinois Secretary of State's main office.

"Dennie, how they hangin'?"

"Free and easy, Jimbo. What's new in the bureaucracy? Still selling licenses to truckers?"

"Nah, we hadda stop last year when the shit hit the fan. Too bad, I kinda miss the extra income." He sounded genuinely put out.

It went on like that for a few minutes — I've learned you can't rush Spain. Finally, I asked, "Jim, can you tell me what kind of rigs Jeffrey P. Slade and Horatio T. Garcia of our fair city drive?"

"Yeah, but it's gonna cost ya big-time. Just a sec."

A few minutes later, Spain returned. "Slade's got himself a couple — brand new Caddy Escalade, black, and a Mercedes S500, silver. Garcia drives a Lexus LS430, gray, also this year's. I suppose you want the plates, too."

I did, and he gave them to me. I rang off after promising suitable recompense, box seats to the Bears opener.

The rest of the day, I made other, less productive phone calls, drove by the sites where the bodies had been found, interviewed Terri Dunbar's landlord, read the newspapers, took a catnap. That evening, I went to the last place Terri had been seen alive, Jeremy's on North Clark. The popular sports bar occupied a choice spot just a long foul ball from

Wrigley Field. A game with the Cardinals was in progress, so a sizeable throng was on hand. Most of the customers were lustily cheering for or jeering at the Cubs, who'd blown a seven-run early lead and were trailing by one in the sixth. I caught the attention of the husky bartender as he lit a cigarette and inhaled greedily.

I placed a twenty on the bar top. "You're Keith Brooks?"

"Yeah. What'll ya have?"

"An Old Style and some information."

Brooks eyed the bill on the bar as he drew a draft and slid it over. "What kinda information?"

"I understand you were the one who found Terri Dunbar in the alley. I'm a detective working for her parents. Was she a regular in here?"

The bartender hesitated, glanced toward the rear exit that gave onto the alley. "How 'bout some ID."

I opened my wallet and flashed the Cook County Sheriff's Benevolent Association card I carry for just such occasions.

Brooks seemed satisfied. He braced sinewy forearms on the bar and leaned toward me. In a conspiratorial voice he said, "Yeah, she came in sometimes."

"Did she hang out with anybody in particular?"

"Not really. But she was friendly with a lot of people." He raised his head and scanned the room. "Don't see any of 'em right now. Not that I'd know their names. Just the faces, ya know."

"She with a boyfriend?"

"She, ah, played the field. Lot of times, she'd leave with a guy, different one each time."

"Was she a pro?"

Brooks looked affronted. He pivoted to stub out his smoke in an ashtray on the back bar. Turning back, he said, "Hell no. Seemed like a decent kid. Kinda small-town, know what I'm saying? What's the word . . . like a farm girl in the big city."

"Naïve?"

"Yeah, that's it. Probl'y too damn trusting for her own good."

"What about the night before she —"

"Cops asked me the same thing. She spent time with some big dude in a suit. Didn't notice if they left together. Only time I seen the guy in here."

"Got a description?"

"Rich guy. Kept flashing a fancy watch and he had that look like somebody makes tons of dough, like a commodity trader or a developer, ya know. Tipped me damn good. Gray hair, forties."

I asked a few more questions but Brooks was tapped out. I told him to keep the twenty, and he tucked it away without hesitation. Since I had nothing better to do, I nursed another beer and watched the rest of the game on the big-screen. The Cubs tanked in eleven.

The next afternoon, I swung my restored midnight blue 1967 Mustang into a parking structure across the street from the Loop skyscraper housing the law offices of Messrs. Slade and Garcia. Spaces were at a premium, and I ended up on the seventh level. Each floor had a musical theme, to irritate parkers into remembering where they'd left their cars when they returned. A life-size image of Tammy Wynette flanked the elevator door and *Stand by Your Man,* cranked to ear-bleed, poured out of hidden speakers above it.

In the Sears Tower, I ascended to the forty-first floor — about a third of the way to the top. I checked the directory and found the Slade & Garcia digs down a plush-carpeted hallway. A fashion model buffing glossy purple fingernails paused in her work long enough to listen to my pitch about needing a good lawyer. She failed to return my smile, announced my name into an intercom, said Slade would see me momentarily and had me take a seat in the reception area. After holding down a visitor's chair and paging through old issues of *Country Living* and *Yachting* for thirty-five minutes, I was ushered into Slade's corner office.

The lawyer looked like the eager image in his late-night TV ads — as ready to pounce as a cheetah with red pepper up his rectum. He had an oversized pumpkin of a head, draped with a luxuriant thatch of silver hair. A white telephone was wedged between chin and shoulder as he tilted back in his massive black leather executive's chair. He looked up at me for a nanosecond and gestured impatiently to an uncomfortable-looking perch across the desk. I scoped out the office while I waited. Abstract art on the walls. No family photos or mementos on the desk. A Hugh Johnson wine book on the credenza.

I returned my attention to the lawyer as he wrapped up his call. The guy looked familiar, and not just from the TV ads. Had he been an entertainer years ago? A musician?

Slade pegged the phone and said, "Burt Bacharach."

"Huh?"

"You were trying to remember his name. Happens all the time. I look just like him . . . or is it the other way around?"

He was right, but then, they say everybody on earth has a double somewhere.

He arched his eyebrows expectantly. "How may I help, Mr., uh, Maloney?" Right to business — understandable, if, on the average, you pocket a pair of Ben Franklins every time the big hand makes a circuit. I slid a business card across the desk. He regarded it briefly but left it untouched.

"It's Malone. Anyway, Terri Dunbar worked here last summer. Could you give me your impression of her?"

Slade looked puzzled. "I don't seem to recall the name."

"How many paralegals do you guys employ at a time, anyway?"

"One or two, but there's a lot of turnover."

"Well, far as I know, Dunbar's the only one diced up by the Butcher."

That caught his attention. The bushy eyebrows knotted in concern. "Oh, yes. Most unfortunate. Okay, I remember Terri now. A very nice kid, very hard worker, ideal employee. I don't have that much contact with the staff. My partner, Horatio Garcia, supervises them. He's out of town, though."

"Do you have a number where I can reach him?"

"He's visiting relatives somewhere in Montana." He raised his hands palms-up, indicating the hopelessness of pursuing that avenue.

I hit him with a few more queries, to which he provided curt answers. Finally, he glanced at the slim gold watch on his tanned wrist. Four o'clock on a warm Friday afternoon. Perfect time to make a getaway for the weekend. "I've got an important meeting in a few minutes, Mr. Malone. Is there anything else?"

"Yeah. Have you seen Terri Dunbar since her employment here ended?"

"No, of course not. Why would I?" he said, a little too quickly. Another peek at the watch. "You'll have to excuse me," he said, getting to his feet. He stood about six-three and kept in shape.

"Sure. Thanks for your time."

On the way past the reception desk, I said to the model, "Have a nice weekend."

She looked up and might have nodded before returning her full attention to packing her nail maintenance supplies into a canvas bag. Knocking off after another hard day in the trenches.

Ten minutes later, I was lounging in the Mustang across the street from the main entrance of the melodic parking garage. The muscle car's twin pipes burbled reassuringly, though the engine was always a trifle twitchy at idle. I'd cranked up the AC, but sweat still rimmed my collar. I noticed the sign on a greasy spoon on the corner: "Coldest beer in tawn," which got me thinking about the growing literacy problem among sign painters.

Then it came to me. "Cold," Joe had said. I'd done investigative work for the city's most successful and flamboyant personal injury lawyer a few times, a second-generation Irishman named Patrick Conway. He'd once referred to his competitors, Slade and Garcia, as cold-hearted sons of the devil. "Especially that Slade fella," Patrick had said. "He'd take a torn blanket from a freezing Eskimo."

I spotted my quarry. A dark-hued Cadillac Escalade exited the parking structure deliberately, like the Edmund Fitzgerald pulling away from that Lake Superior dock for the last time. The driver had an oversized globular noggin and the rear license plate read SUPRLWR. I was mildly surprised to not see the purple-nailed manicurist in the passenger's seat. Maybe Slade already had a date lined up. I fell in behind the black behemoth as it rumbled south to Adams, then east to Lakeshore Drive.

Slade moved into the right-hand lane and proceeded south as slowly as molasses flowing uphill. I reined in my spirited Boss 302 and hovered a few cars behind. The lawyer was apparently occupied with a handheld cell phone, as evidenced by his vehicle's abruptly speeding up, slowing again and weaving back and forth like a chicken on acid. We trundled south to I-94, got on and rolled east. A half hour later, the Escalade crossed the Michigan line and headed north on 94. I was pretty sure by now he'd exit the interstate somewhere along the strip of upscale beach towns strung out along the southeastern shore of Lake Michigan like beads in a lamp chain.

In summer, the multimillion-dollar homes perched atop precipitous sand dunes among the towns of southwest Michigan's "Harbor Country" are populated by the economic and political muckamucks of Chicago. The breezes off the lake are always cooler on the Michigan side and the water never really warms up, no matter how stifling the heat. My expectations were met, as Slade took the off-ramp at the resort village of New Buffalo. He stopped at a hardware store and went in. I followed with my face casually averted. Slade bought a coil of bright yellow rope and a roll of silver duct tape. Then he hopped back in his truck and tooled along on two-lane blacktop up the shoreline, through Union Pier and into Lakeside.

On the far side of the little town, the paved road gave way to gravel and continued north, hugging the shoreline. The houses and lots became progressively larger. I passed two or three bed-and-breakfasts, high-tariff joints I'd seen advertised in *Chicago* magazine. In fact, I'd once spent a memorable weekend in one called the Boulder House, with a girl named Michelle. That had been a hell of a lot more fun than this trip. I didn't realize then how exciting things would get for me before the night was out.

As we crawled up the narrow coast road, I caught occasional glimpses of Lake Michigan between pine trees and residences to the west. A little while later, Slade's brake lights came on and he hung a left at a sandy driveway leading toward the lake. I stayed back until he vanished, then crept the Mustang forward to the turnoff. I opened the side window and peered into the lane where Slade had disappeared. The rustic drive twisted through dense woods of pine, oaks and maples. A small patch of gray two-story house was visible through the trees, with the pale glimmer of water in the background. The sky had clouded and the light dimmed as thick-bodied clouds scudded in. I checked the time — six-thirty. It would be light for over three hours this time of year on the western edge of the Eastern Time zone.

I U-turned and motored back to Lakeside to wait for darkness. I topped up the Mustang's bottomless tank at a mini-mart and then found a restaurant with a sign in the window touting Polish sausage on a bun, Italian beef sandwiches and gyros. Inside, I claimed a window booth. A sixtyish waitress in a peach-colored uniform sauntered over and set a tall glass of ice water on the table in front of me. She pulled a pencil from behind an ear and an order book from a pocket. The name badge on her ample bosom read POLYXENA.

"What're ya havin'?" she asked.

I opted for the gyros plate with yogurt sauce. "Know anything about a lawyer named Jeffrey Slade, has a place up the shore?"

"Guy with the black Cadillac lake freighter. Yeah he comes in once in a while. Tips big, probably why I remember him."

"Ever see his girlfriend, good-looking blonde about thirty, purple nails?" I was shooting in the dark.

The waitress gave me a funny look, like she wondered if I were pulling her leg. She scribbled my order on the pad and turned for the kitchen. After a couple of steps she stopped and said, "Times I've seen him, he was with young girls." Then, deadpan, "Like last night, for example."

The gyros were excellent. I had a piece of fresh blueberry pie for dessert, washed down with a couple mugs of black high-test coffee. I wanted to stay alert. After strolling the beach for a mile to kick-start the digestive process, I pointed the Mustang north again. By this time, the sun was a gauzy orange ball sinking fast toward the lake. It would be dark soon.

I parked near the entrance to Slade's drive, checked the clip in my shoulder-holstered Colt .380 and moved in on foot. The wind had died but the temperature remained in the eighties. Kamikaze mosquitoes swarmed my bare head and neck. After swatting a few, I gave it up and resigned myself to being eaten alive. Which reminded me of the need to be cautious as I approached the house. I navigated the pathway by moonlight — the moon was full and only partially-cloaked by backlit clouds. I reflected that it had been exactly a month since the Butcher had taken a victim. He was, as Skrepenak had said, due.

The sound of waves cascading into the sandy shore masked the little noise I made schlepping to the head of the driveway, where a three-car garage loomed. To my left lay a bulky two-story house clad in gray wood with white shutters and a peaked roof. Lights shined in several windows. A large barn sat in an open area about fifty yards past the house. Slade's lot covered at least five acres — a sizeable buffer zone between him and the nearest neighbor. I crept to the house, found a side window and cautiously peered in. A large den with a wall of windows facing the lake was deserted except for a complete set of resort furniture from the Crate and Barrel catalogue. No sign of habitation. All was quiet. I was about to move on to the next window when I heard a high-pitched wail like a cat dropped on a griddle.

I could have gone back to the Mustang, snared the cell phone and summoned the Michigan State Police. It would have been the easy thing to do. But, as Ike and Tina sang in *Proud Mary,* I nevuh evuh do nuthin' nice and easy.

I bolted to the front entrance of the house, no longer trying to conceal my presence. A large door painted dark green was illuminated in the pale glow of a black coachlamp. Moths circled the pebbled glass fixture like commercial jets over O'Hare on a Friday evening. I pressed an ear to the door, heard nothing. I tried the knob and it turned easily in my hand.

I opened the door and stepped into a large vestibule. Now, I was officially into the felony zone — b & e. What if Slade were innocent? Ah hell, in for a penny, in for a buck. The adjoining living room was empty, as was the next room, the den I'd studied from the side window. There were four empty beer bottles on a coffee table between a tobacco-brown leather couch and a high-definition TV. I explored every room in the sprawling two-story structure, along with the garage, where Slade's oversized vehicular status symbol lurked in one of the spaces; the other two were vacant.

The high wooden barn glowed phosphorescent in the moonlight as I approached. I'd wasted a good ten minutes on the house and garage since hearing the scream — the lack of any subsequent sounds didn't bode well for the health of the screamer. The wide sliding door at the end of the building stood open a crack, emitting a beam of bright light. A steady metallic rasping sound came from the barn's interior, punctuated by piteous whimpering. I quickstepped to the narrow opening and peered in.

It took a moment for my eyes to adjust to the sudden brightness inside the cavernous space. A row of floodlights suspended from rafters twenty feet overhead cast harsh light on a gruesome scene. A pretty young blonde of perhaps eighteen dangled upside down with her head inches above a metal bucket strategically positioned below her on the wooden floor. She wore nothing but a gag duct-taped over her twisting mouth. Yellow ropes around her ankles ran up to pulleys attached to a stout overhead beam. The ropes had been tied off to side supports about three feet apart, effectively splaying her legs wide so her body formed a Y. The scene reminded me of my brother's deer-hunting cabin in northern Wisconsin. He has a hoist rigged up outside where he dresses out whitetail carcasses. The captive's hands were bound behind her back. She struggled and jittered like a trout on a stringer.

A few feet from the hoist, Jeffrey Slade stood at a square wooden butcher's block with tapered legs. He wore a smile on his round face and a pair of latex gloves on his hands as he swiped a long serrated knife blade against a sharpening stone in rhythmic strokes. A blood-stained butcher's apron protected his clothing. An array of knives of various sizes, a hacksaw and a massive cleaver were set out on the thick end-grain block in front of him, like a surgeon's instruments readied for an operation. A dark red slick of a partially-congealed substance covered the floor in a circle around the carving table. Slade was watching the poor struggling girl so intently as he worked, he didn't notice me entering.

"Freeze!" I yelled.

Slade never flinched. After a quick glance in my direction, he stared down at the cutlery before him and said, "Oh, it's you, shitheel."

I drew the Colt and trained it on Slade. He turned and looked at me full-face for the first time.

"You wouldn't dare use that," he said.

"Wrong," I replied. I let one go at the table in front of the lawyer. The .38 slug crashed into a knife, breaking the haft from the blade and sending them in opposite directions. Slade grabbed a long-bladed knife from the table and darted away. He disappeared behind a stack of wooden boxes as I gave chase.

As I drew abreast of the boxes, they suddenly tipped forward, then toppled in a jumble all over me. I cursed myself for not anticipating this tactic as I fell to the floor, losing the Colt in the process. Heavy boxes pinned the right side of my body, including the arm and leg, to the floor. Whatever was in them, it wasn't cotton candy. I could feel a lump rising on top of my head, like bread in an oven. I listened for Slade, but all I could hear was pathetic puling coming from the young kid strung up like a deer about to be bled. She might have managed, "Help me" from beneath the gag fastened over her mouth with duct tape.

"Looking for me?" Slade strode into view with the wicked-looking knife held chin-high, point forward. His face was sweaty, and he was breathing hard.

"Yeah. How about dropping the knife and help get some

of these boxes off me? We'll work something out."

Slade's laugh was rich and long, but I thought it sounded a tad desperate. "What the fuck do you think this is?" he said. "Some James Bond movie?" He shook his head. "Actually, know what I'm going to do? I'm going to add you to the next display. Sort of a two-for-one special." He waved the knife in my face.

"By the way, that serrated blade is the sign of a damn amateur," I said as I finally levered my trapped leg free from captivity.

"Amateur? I'll show you amateur," Slade yelled. And then he made the mistake most guys who aren't familiar with knife-fighting make — he launched a telegraphed roundhouse overhand stab toward my head. By the time the knife had gained forward momentum, my foot was in the air on an intercept trajectory. The sole of my size-ten boot connected squarely with Slade's wrist and the knife did an end-over-end past my shoulder and into the gloom away from the lights.

I managed to shrug off the last wooden box and lurched to my feet as Slade lunged at the butcher's block and snatched another knife in a long-fingered paw. I stood my ground, ready to make a defensive move as he started deliberately toward me, the knife extended in a clenched fist. But Slade never made it to me. As he edged by the butcher's block, his right foot slipped on the gelatinous mess on the floor, and he cartwheeled spasmodically before hitting the deck face-first.

A brief moment of dead quiet passed. Slade lay prone, still as a tomb in a buried city. The young woman strung up on the meat hoist resumed sobbing and moaning quietly. I went to the fallen lawyer and flipped him over. Whether by accident or of his own volition, Slade's right hand had somehow curled inward as he landed. The result: the razor-sharp knife clutched in his fingers had perforated his chest, slid between ribs and lodged deep in flesh. Fresh blood leaked out of his breast to join the viscous pool on the floor next to the butchering table. I did the obligatory check for a neck pulse, detected a weak flutter, then nothing.

I grabbed the one remaining knife from the butcher's block and stepped to the meat hanger. Two quick thrusts, and the poor soul who'd been hanging by her heels slipped to the floor. She lay crying and gasping for breath as the reddish hue of her blood-engorged head slowly dissipated. When I cut the gag from her face, she fainted. I found a blanket and wrapped her in it before calling the police.

A week later, the heat wave finally broke, and with it went the collective sour spirits of the city. I'd just hung up the phone after a conversation with an insurance exec about stolen cases of Kentucky bourbon I'd helped recover, when the instrument chirred again.

"Okay Malone, I'm beating you to the punch here." Joe Skrepenak's wheels-on-gravel baritone.

"Ah, Mr. Skrepenak. You must be calling to enlist the services of a trained professional investigator."

"Horseshit. I got enough fucking investigators around here already. The feebs are crawling up my ass. You want the skinny on that fucking perv, Slade?"

"Is the Pope a geriatric Catholic?"

"Listen, wiseass, you might learn something. DNA in that barn matched the victims. And Slade had a condo a block from the ballpark. We tossed the place and found souvenirs from the three kids — fingers, toes, whatever."

"What do suppose drives a guy to do stuff like that?"

"Here, let me read you what our in-house shrink says: 'A truly deviant individual, the subject's normal fantasies of interpersonal adventure were infused with abnormal desires to humiliate, dominate and destroy others. An intelligent individual, he believed the authorities would not be able to catch him.'"

"Jesus, sounds like a politician."

"Similar. And the fucker prob'ly ate the missing parts — just thinking about it damn near scrags my appetite."

"Which reminds me . . ."

"Okay, okay. I'll admit I owe you one. Dinner, that is." Like a kid reluctantly fessing up that it's his turn to take out the trash.

"Oh yeah, I'd forgotten our little wager," I lied. "Let's see, what's good? Maybe that new steak house on Huron Street."

Long pause. Then, "Y'know, the wife's been after me to cut down on the fucking red meat. And I kinda think she's onto something. There's this vegetarian joint near the station . . ."

Good Father

Tom Sweeney

"Are you doing homework?"

Startled, I reached for my gun and jumped erect, sending my chair clattering to the back of the guard shack. Before my hand reached my holster, though, my brain registered the thin, reedy voice as belonging to Eddie Walker, friend and playmate to my employer's ten-year old son.

I stepped out of the guard shack and scanned the gateway and sunlit macadam pad in front of the Conway estate before looking down at Eddie. "How'd you get in here?"

"Through the gate."

I glanced at the heavy gate hung on stone-ish looking concrete pillars that formed part of the estate wall.

"It's locked," I said.

"Not through the gate, silly. *Through* the gate."

Eddie, like Old Man Conway's son Brandon, couldn't have weighed more than sixty pounds and looked like scarecrow-boy with Dumbo ears. Brandon sported roughly the same build, which explained the rich boy, poor boy friendship, the boys probably finding comfort in each other's appearance.

Still, the bars on the gate were barely six inches apart. "You squeezed between the bars?" I asked.

"Sure. It's part of my training. The hardest part's the ears. You gotta do your head first. Otherwise you panic with your body in and your head out. It's easy."

Great. Now I needed to worry about the two of them sneaking out while I studied. I'd garnered no job offers since my layoff and this might be my only chance at fulfilling my boyhood dream of being a cop. Minimum job requirements these days included an associate's degree in criminology. I was doing fine in night school, but between classes, another job flipping burgers and spending as much time as possible — never enough — with my son, I needed to study during the dead time of this security guard job. There'd be no dead time if Eddie and Brandon started playing trick-the-security-guard.

"From now on use the buzzer, okay?"

"Sure. This was just a practice gate for me anyway."

Eddie's a Saturday morning regular, and I knew he was on the daily sheet. "Go on up to the house," I said. "And whatever you do, don't try to sneak by me on the way out."

The momentary collapse of his smile told me he'd planned just that. Cripes! That's all I'd need. Have him and Brandon get off the grounds and get lost on my watch. If I thought I had trouble now — a thirty-year-old with no law enforcement experience trying to get a job with the police department — just wait until my resume included getting fired from a security guard position for incompetence.

I squatted down to talk to Eddie at eye level. A number of possible warnings crossed my mind, but really, he wasn't so different from my own son Darren. In the end I just chucked him on the butt with my clipboard. "Get going," I said. He was off and running on the instant. "And have a good time today," I called after him.

I picked up my criminology book from where it had

fallen behind the fire extinguisher and checked my watch. Nine o'clock. Three hours left on my shift. Then shower and change, pick up Darren from The Witch, and off to Fenway Park for the Red Sox Annual Father-Son Day. Haven't missed one yet and divorce isn't going to stop me. Even The Witch said it would be good to keep some traditions. For Darren's sake, she'd amended, so I'd know she wasn't thinking about me.

Saturday is a day of routines, at least in the morning. Same people, same times, every week. Dead quiet from four o'clock until nine when Eddie walks in. Mrs. Conway and Cindy out in the silver Lexus around ten. Reynolds the music teacher in at quarter to eleven in his beat-up truck, a dirty white Chevy S10 with one dark green front fender.

Sometimes Reynolds and I talk — he's in the same boat as I am. Divorced, in debt, and steadily sinking under heavy child support payments. Like me, he's looking for a better job and, also like me, having no luck. Today, though, he didn't stop to talk. He showed up fifteen minutes late and sped away toward the house as soon as I cleared him. He looked upset and I don't blame him. Old Man Conway pays well, but he's tough to work for and prone to firing people for minor indiscretions.

Twelve o'clock came, and along with it Mo Abrams, my relief. Mo's a retired cop, and I've been pumping him for tips on getting onto the force. I thought about telling him about the trick Eddie and maybe Brandon could do, but what would that accomplish besides pointing out that I didn't see Eddie sneak through the gate. While I stood there, the phone rang. The round institutional clock in the guard shack showed two minutes past twelve, so I let Mo pick it up. I turned to leave when the words, "Nope, haven't seen them" froze me in my tracks.

I turned back and listened to Mo's side of the conversation: "Yes . . . No . . . Yes, sir . . . Right . . . Uh-huh . . . I'll watch for them, sir."

When he hung up, I raised my eyebrows in question. "Oh, just Brandon and that kid who takes piano lessons with him," Mo said. "They didn't come back in the house after their break." He made a face. "Piano lessons — ugh. Can't blame them for hiding out."

I knew I should tell about Eddie's new trick, but didn't know how to open the subject. Or was afraid to. Either way, I breathed a sigh of relief when Mo buzzed the gate open for me. On the way out to my car, I stopped twice, each time almost going back to tell Mo what I knew.

But what did I really know? That Eddie could slip between the bars of the gate? That he and Brandon might have slipped by me and were now roaming about in the city? Even with my attention partially on my Justice and Society text, I would have caught them if they'd tried.

Yeah, Eddie surprised me this morning, but I hadn't known about his trick then. Besides, he came from the outside in. I would have noticed if he'd already been inside and had to walk past the guard shack.

That last part I believed in my heart. He couldn't have gotten by me. To hint to Conway that Brandon might have slipped through the gate, to call attention to myself in such a negative manner: No, that would accomplish nothing except to screw up my chances for a job with the Barrington Police Department. I had an in with Mandy Wilford, chief of detectives, from my temp job filing last summer. He knew me, knew my ambitions. And my abilities. He'd recommended me for this security guard job, in fact. No need to have Old Man Conway talk bad about me to him.

The moment for talking about Eddie seemed to have passed. I started my car and drove off, leaving the estate in Mo's hands.

The Conway Estate dominated the east side of Barrington. Built before income taxes took down the Godlike stature of industrialists, the Estate once sat a mile from the nearest building. Barrington had grown up around it, though, surrounding it with two-acre lots selling for twice what I've earned during my entire life on this planet. The two-hundred-odd acres of the Estate were surrounded by a twelve-foot wall and intense security. No one in the Conway family had ever been robbed, attacked, or kidnapped, and Old Man Conway meant to keep it that way.

The Main Gate faced east, so I drove half-way around the estate to get back to town. I turned right onto Anderson Road, driving between an unending row of four-bedroom homes on the left and the equally unending high wall of the estate sliding along the right side.

The estate wall ran another half mile, all the way to the river, but the houses ended where an abandoned set of railroad tracks paralleled the main road heading left into town. The tracks once carried the original Conway into town in his private railroad car. Beyond this point only scruffy woods faced the estate wall.

I rumbled across the tracks and turned left at the blinking light marking the T-intersection where the old train gate fronted onto the tracks and the road to town.

This road struggled again with transition. Once a virtually uninhabited country road, in the early twenties one of the first of the Conways built a row of factories here. The factories boomed in the twenties, went bust during the depression and boomed again during World War II. Cheap Asian labor in the sixties apparently put them to rest permanently. Recently, however, a smart set of developers, possibly teamed with Conway, began systematically converting them into high-priced condos.

If I hadn't screwed up my marriage, maybe I'd be living here myself, spending every night with Darren, watching TV and playing cards, telling him to stay away from the river and stay out of the abandoned buildings not yet condo-ized —

all the things real fathers did with their sons.

Carpe diem. At least I had the ball game today, and I hoped Darren looked forward to it as much as I did. A quick shower and change of clothes, pick him up and off for Fenway.

Father for a few hours.

I know a real father would be spending more than weekend afternoons with his son, but this was the best I could manage right now. I hoped twenty years from now I wouldn't regret working two jobs to pay child support, rather than taking my chances at being labeled a deadbeat dad but spending more time with Darren.

I pushed that thought away as self-destructive and focused on driving. The railroad tracks crossed the road on an overpass and swung closer to the river. Something about the tracks made me look in the rear view mirror and the bottom fell out of my chest. Way back down the road, barely visible at the end and framed by the overpass, stood the unused former main gate to the Conway estate. The railroad entrance had been blocked over, and the vehicular gates welded shut. Razor wire and intrusion detectors mounted on the top of the gates integrated with the same protections covering the entire wall.

As far as I knew, though, the intrusion detectors did not cover the gate itself with its close-set bars. No need. No one could squeeze between bars mere inches apart, right?

I checked my watch. Twelve-fifteen. I was already running late. If I went back and told what I knew about the boys squeezing through the gate, I wouldn't get Darren to the game on time. I drove on. If it were any other game, any other day . . .

Crap! I slammed on the brakes and made a squealing U-turn. How could I enjoy a ball game with Darren not knowing if Eddie and Brandon were okay? I sped back the way I'd come, a heavy feeling telling me that as bad as things had been for me and Darren lately, things were about to get much worse.

Mo heard me out before responding. He sat for a moment, then reached for the phone. His finger paused at the keypad, but before punching a number, he said, "Go up to the house and see Conway. I'll tell him you're coming and why."

My car was parked outside the gate, as required, so I jogged up the road that wound through trees for a quarter mile before reaching the main house. At the first bend, I turned to look back at the guard shack. Mo hunched over the phone, speaking urgently. I turned and ran the rest of the way to the house.

The control center was in the old servants' quarters at the rear of the building, and stood testimony to Conway wealth and paranoia. One wall of the control center comprised a bank of a dozen monitors, each receiving a feed from a different surveillance camera. Two men stared at the array of monitors, heads moving slightly as they tried to watch all twelve simultaneously. The monitors showed what surveillance cameras usually show: lots of scenery with very little activity. A larger knot of men surrounded a workstation to the right. Here tapes could be reviewed.

Conway stood in the front, arms folded and amazingly calm, much calmer than I'd be if Darren turned up missing. I started to fill him in with what I knew but he cut me off with a sharp wave of his hand. "I know. We're getting the tape now — Yeah, look!" he said, pointing to one of the monitors. "See, they got flashlights."

I studied the monitor he indicated, barely making out the boys on the screen, saw nothing in their hands. I was about to ask him to rewind the tape when I realized he hadn't been speaking to me.

I moved back a couple steps and Reynolds the music teacher slid over to my side. Reynold's face was pasty white and his eyes darted about the room. He looked like a man who wished he was somewhere else, and I knew exactly how he felt.

I nodded to him. "What's going on?" I asked.

"Evidently Brandon and Eddie left the house and went into the woods beyond the tennis courts. No sign of them coming back, but there are a lot of cameras around the house and they're double-checking each one."

For a moment nothing happened, then someone burst into the room behind me. I recognized him as Manny, a hard-faced, enforcer-type I'd seen pass through the gates many times, always carrying one of Conway's red let-me-in passes.

Manny handed a tape to someone at the console. "Here it is," he said.

Reynolds tugged at my sleeve. "What tape is this?" he asked.

"Probably from the old railroad gate," I said, "The one facing Barrington. Eddie slipped through the bars of the main gate this morning, and told me it was only a practice gate — are you okay?"

Reynolds backed toward the door. "I just remembered — I have an appointment. I don't want to be late."

Late! The father-son ball game. I should be picking Darren up right now. I needed to call him. Immediately. Several phones lay about the work center. I reached for one, then pulled my hand back and looked to Conway for permission. He stared at a monitor, where a tape fuzzed on the screen and then began to roll. "Anyone mind if I use a phone?" I asked.

No one answered; no one even turned around. I hated to break in, but Darren . . . A phone on the live console to my left caught my eye. I hurried over. The two men staring at the twenty screens never looked up.

"Okay to use this phone?"

One of the men waved a hand at the phone without taking his eyes off the panel of monitors. I grabbed the phone and dialed, praying that Darren and not his mother would pick up.

No such luck.

"Don't tell me you're going to be late," she said as soon as she recognized my voice. I told her I might not make it at all.

"Why not?" She yelled. "You always do this to me, you know that? I had plans, you know. Why can't you pick him up?"

I don't think Old Man Conway would appreciate my talking about his son, and I sure didn't want The Witch to get the idea that I couldn't protect a stranger's kid, never mind my own. "I can't tell you," I said.

"Oh, right. I just change my plans because you don't want to see your son. Fine."

Before I could answer, a movement on one of the screens caught my eye. A white pickup with a dark front fender sped by the old gate. I looked around the room. Reynolds was not in sight.

I let the hand holding the phone fall to my side and pointed to the screen with my other hand. One of the watchers flicked a glance my way. "Did you see that?" I asked.

"What? he asked.

"That truck. This is the old main gate, right?" I tapped the monitor.

He pushed my hand out of the way. "It was a damn truck on the road," he said. "Don't bother me."

As I watched the monitor, a cop car and a dark sedan pulled up to the gate and half a dozen men got out of both vehicles. "Cops showed up," the man called over his shoulder.

The Witch's voice demanded my attention. I held the

phone a good two feet from my ear and I could still hear her. I put the phone to my lips. "Gotta go," I said. I breathed a silent prayer that Darren would understand and hung up.

"Mr. Conway," I called. No one responded so I stepped closer, and said, more loudly, "Excuse me? Mr. Conway?" This time everyone turned to face me. "I . . . um . . . Reynolds just drove past the old main gate." Stares. "He was acting oddly. I mean, he . . ."

Conway turned back to the monitor without speaking. "Rewind that back to where it was before we were interrupted," he said. All eyes went back to the monitor.

I stood for a minute, standing awkwardly like the big dope I was. "I don't think the kids are on the property," I said, "I think they're being held for ransom."

No one looked up, which was just as well, because I realized I couldn't explain my feeling. How could I explain that the man I believed responsible for "kidnapping" the boys was in the house while the kids left on their own?

But I knew kids. If Reynolds turned it into a game, swore them to secrecy and promised adventure and fun . . . Yeah, they'd sneak out on their own and wait for him to pick them up.

Unnoticed, I left the command center. Once outside I ran back to the gate. I'd get my car and find where Reynolds went. He hadn't turned at the gate; only River Road lay in the direction he'd taken.

"Mo, open the gate."

Mo turned to me. He held the phone next to his ear, his face wearing that vacant look one gets when on hold. He put a hand over the mouthpiece and said, "What?"

"Did Reynolds just leave here?"

"Yeah, couple minutes ago. Why?"

"He just drove past the old gate. It looked like he was going pretty fast. I think he knows where the boys are."

Mo shook his head. "He told me he went home for an

appointment."

"He lives the other way. Do you have the main house on the line? They wouldn't listen to me."

Mo shook his head again. "So maybe Reynolds's appointment wasn't at home."

"He went down River Road — what appointment would he have down there? There's nothing but abandoned tenements and old mill buildings."

Flashlights! Old buildings. "Mo, I know where the boys are. They —"

Mo held up a hand to stop me. He turned his back to me and spoke into the phone. I couldn't make out everything he said, but caught bits of it, " . . . there were? Good . . . both kids, you figure? . . . oh, yeah, one of them did it at this gate . . . I know."

He must be talking to the cops at the railroad gate. I wrote "Reynolds kidnapped the kids" on Mo's clipboard, reached around him and pressed the gate button. I half expected him to object, but he paid no attention. As soon as the gate opened enough for me to slip through, I ran for my car.

Two minutes later I sped along Anderson Road coming up on the railroad gate and the two cop cars parked there. I glanced beyond the cars to see what was happening, wondering if I should stop and try to convince them to hunt for Reynolds, and in the two short seconds my eyes were off the road, a kid on a bicycle shot out across the intersection toward the gate. I yanked the wheel left and stood on the brakes. I missed the kid easily — it wasn't as close as it seemed at first glance — but all the cops turned to stare, including Mandy Wilford, Chief of Detectives. Great. I could only hope he was nearsighted and didn't recognize me, and I dropped all thoughts of stopping to talk to the cops. I drove on toward River Road at discomforting speed, eyes looking for kids on bikes and sweaty palms ready to jerk the wheel to the side. For the first time I understood what Mo meant when he said the part of the job he disliked most was high speed chases.

I chanced a look in the rear view mirror. Mandy must have recognized me back there. I'm screwed. Conway will fire me. I'll never get a job with the cops. I'll have to work three shifts a day at Burger Hell to meet The Witch's child support demands, and I'll see Darren twice a year, on Columbus Day and Arbor Day.

If I'm lucky.

I reached River Road and paused for a moment. To the right, there was nothing but a river embankment and the Conway Estate for half a mile, and then country for a few more miles. To the left sprawled abandoned tenements of former mill workers and a few shanties sprinkled along the road. I turned left.

I went less than a mile before I saw Reynolds's truck parked by a brush pile in the garbage-filled yard of a dilapidated tenement.

I slid my car to a gravel-crunching stop next to the truck. I jumped out of my car and ran to the front porch of the tenement. Before I got halfway there, Reynolds came out with a squirming Brandon Conway held under one arm. Reynolds reached back into the house, then turned and took the porch steps two at a time, Brandon bouncing along next to him.

Before he reached the bottom, the first floor of the tenement exploded into flames with a tremendous whomp. Plywood panels covering the front windows blew off and flames shot out. Reynolds never looked back, just lowered his head and ran for his truck.

I moved into his path to stop him. He half-spun and put the heel of his foot into my stomach. I had time for one brief thought — a music teacher who knows karate! — before my vision tunneled down to pinpricks of light and I fell over backwards gasping for breath.

I fought hard not to black out and barely managed to maintain consciousness, but I couldn't move, not even to save Brandon, who still struggled with Reynolds.

Long ago, I told Darren he should fight fair, but sometimes he shouldn't. I told him never to fight fair when someone attempted to force him into a car. Then he was to do anything — *anything* — to stay out of that car. Brandon must have gotten the same lesson, because he had his legs spread and Reynolds couldn't get him into the truck.

I sucked some more wind and managed to stand up. Brandon flailed his arms and caught Reynolds in the neck with a bony elbow. Reynolds slapped him, hard, and Brandon howled and squirmed frantically. I took a clumsy step toward them and then another as my wind returned. I picked a three-foot-long broken tree limb off the ground and half ran, half fell the rest of the way to Reynolds. He turned just in time to catch the branch on the top of his head. He stopped moving, standing stock still and staring at me. I was about to hit him again when he kind of melted to the ground.

Woozy, I almost did the same when a roar behind me made me turn around. Flames shot up and the entire front of the building was on fire — I put my hands up to protect my face from the sudden heat.

Brandon squirted by me. I reached out and barely got hold of his arm. He spun around. "Lemme go, mister. My father will kill you!"

"Whoa, Brandon, it's me. The guy who knocked out Reynolds." He stopped struggling but his eyes were wide open and wild. "Where's Eddie?" I asked.

Brandon looked past me. "In the house."

"Is he okay?"

"Mr. Reynolds hit him. I think he's dead."

A loud crackle came from the house and the porch deck buckled in flames. I had to believe that Eddie was still alive, but if someone didn't get him out of there, he wouldn't be alive for long. Even as I watched, the right side of the house grew streamers of red flames, hot tongues licking out from behind the plywood-boarded windows. Sirens wailed from the direction of Barrington, but they'd be too late to save Eddie.

I started toward the back of the tenement, but Brandon followed me, darting a glance back to where Reynolds lay unconscious. I knelt down and smiled to reassure the boy. "Run across the street and wait for the fire engines. Tell them Eddie's inside." He looked doubtful but trotted off, giving Reynolds's body a wide berth.

I hoped I was doing the right thing leaving Brandon alone outside. Reynolds was still out, but if he came to before help came, he could still kidnap Brandon. And my job after all was to protect Bandon — Conway's son.

Another crackle and blast of heat from the house decided me. I couldn't turn my back on anyone's son trapped in a burning building.

I waved a reassurance to Brandon and ran around to the back of the tenement. Windows and doors here were boarded up, too, but one board looked loose. I grabbed a free edge and pulled. The plywood popped off and thick gray smoke billowed out.

The plywood had been nailed to a pair of two-by-fours nailed vertically onto the window frame, less than a foot apart. Too close for me to squeeze through.

"Help!" The voice came from inside. I tugged at the bars, but they were nailed too securely. "Eddie!" I yelled. "Are you okay?"

"I can't breathe. It's smoky."

"Get down on the floor. Crawl toward my voice. I'll help you out."

"I can't. I can't walk. Help me."

I looked around, desperately seeking help, then ran to

the brush pile and grabbed a long stout branch. I tried to wedge it between the two-by-fours, but there wasn't any way to get good leverage. The boards creaked but held. I pushed on the branch and the end broke off.

"Help. It's hot."

"I'm coming, Eddie."

I grabbed the bars and shook them frantically. Solid, solid, solid. No way. I couldn't break them and I was too big to fit between the bars.

But Eddie and Brandon were too big to fit through the gate, too. "It's easy," Eddie had said. "Just don't panic."

A barrel lay on its side a few feet away. I dragged it over and stood it upright under the window.

The two-by-fours were too close together. I'd never fit.

The plywood over a window ten feet away burst into flames.

"I'm coming, Eddie. Stay where you are."

"I can't move."

I wanted to go in feet first, but remembered what Eddie told me and stuck my head in. No problem there, but my chest was just too wide to fit in. I exhaled all my breath and still couldn't get in. I used my arms on the two-by-fours to drag myself in another inch. I pushed off hard with my feet, but without warning the barrel flew out from under me.

My weight pulled my chest free, but I spread my arms against the two-by-fours and didn't fall all the way out of the window. I pulled myself back in, but once again my chest kept me from going all the way.

I swung my arms to either side and my hands smacked into something wooden. It felt sturdy — a built-in counter or something — and I grabbed it with both hands. I pushed the remaining air out of my chest and pulled with everything I had in me. My shirt ripped, my skin ripped and suddenly I hung halfway inside.

I scrambled the rest of the way. The room was hot as

hell and smoky to boot. I scrabbled on my hands and knees to the doorway. "Eddie?"

A pair of racking coughs sounded almost next to me. "Here," he said. Thank God. I reached through the smoke and felt a body.

"Let's get out of here, Eddie," I said.

He sobbed. "I can't move my legs. Mr. Reynolds kicked me."

That bastard. "Here, Eddie, where's your shoulders?" I felt around, managed to get both hands under his shoulders and started pulling him back through the doorway into the room I had come in by.

Dragging him made me crawl a little higher off the floor into the smoke, or the smoke had thickened, because it got into my lungs and I started coughing uncontrollably. While I wheezed, one of the walls of the room must have caught fire because the smoke turned orange.

I heard voices. By the window? It wasn't the direction I had been pulling Eddie but I couldn't see anything through the smoke. Someone yelled. I bent close to the floor and took a deep breath, then picked Eddie up and ran toward the voice.

I saw the window just before I would have run into it. I thrust Eddie through the two-by-fours and felt a tug. A voice yelled right in front of me. "I got him. Let go."

I did and Eddie's weight disappeared. The voice yelled to stand back. Before I could move, I heard the splintering of wood, scraping sounds, and then two sets of hands picked me up and pulled me through the window.

"Anyone else inside?" someone asked.

My throat was seared, but I croaked out a no. Someone stuck an oxygen mask over my face and two more guys carried me off.

I remember telling them that I was fine, but they took me to the hospital and I was too weak to fight them. Just as well. I'd rubbed dirt and ashes into my flesh where the skin had been scraped off my chest and arms. They said it needed treatment to avoid infection.

I spent more than two hours in the emergency room and called The Witch from a payphone after I checked out. This time she listened patiently while I told her the whole story, and to my amazement she understood. She even offered to bring Darren to the hospital, but I told her I was getting out in a few minutes. Too late for the ball game — and that hurt more than my chest. It was the first one he and I ever missed. I told her I'd take Darren to the movies, but wanted to check on Eddie first.

Mandy Wilford was talking to a doctor in the children's wing, and broke off just as I came in. "Eddie'll be fine," Mandy said. "No permanent damage. Smoke inhalation and bruised ribs. The doctor doesn't know why he couldn't move his legs, but nothing's shown up damaged and he already has most of his motor control back."

The news was more of a relief than I thought, or maybe I was weaker than I thought, because I collapsed onto a couch. Mandy sat beside me. "Good job you did back there," he said. "Those kids owe their lives to you."

"Brandon okay, too?"

"He's fine, but I don't think Reynolds would have released him after he got whatever ransom money he wanted. We think he set fire to the house because Eddie could recognize him."

"That bastard!"

"Yeah. We know he tricked the kids into sneaking out of the Estate and meeting him at the tenement. We don't know yet if he planned on killing Eddie right away as a warning to Conway, or if he was going to do both kids after he got the ransom, but if he brought the gasoline into the building and then set it on fire, it's Murder One. We'll find out. Anything you need now?"

"A ride to my car?"

"Mo brought it. He bet me ten bucks you wouldn't stay in the hospital overnight."

I stood up. "Gotta pick up my own kid."

"Well, go home and put on a whole shirt first, or you'll scare the hell out of him."

It was past eight o'clock before I arrived at The Witch's house. I was afraid that Darren wouldn't want to go anywhere with me ever again, but he seemed okay with missing the game and took the change of plans in stride. Even had a movie he wanted to see. I was in a hurry to take off with him, but his mother wouldn't stop hugging him. I could see that what bothered her was the same thing that worried me. It could have been Darren in that burning house. Our common fear was that no one would be around if Darren ever needed help.

I told her the whole story again, even the part about my being afraid to leave Brandon alone outside while I went into the building. Darren got tired of the "grown-up talk" and ran off the porch and climbed through an open window into my car. I wanted to follow, but his mother put up a hand. "I try not to get involved," she said, "but Darren misses you. He only sees you on weekends, and he looks forward to them. I know —" she held up a hand to forestall my objection. "You're working days and studying nights and I appreciate it. I'll just be so glad when you're finally a policeman and Darren can sleep over at your house sometimes."

Darren yelled at us from the car. I turned to go, but felt a hand on my arm, holding me back.

"I explained to Darren why you couldn't go to the

game," she said. "I told him sometimes things would be different now that his parents are divorced, but whatever happens, we both love him."

She looked down at Darren in my car and smiled. I followed her gaze in time to catch him making hurry-up motions.

"We're oil and water, you and I," she continued. "I can't live with you, but I . . . I'm glad you're Darren's father. You're a good dad."

Then to my total amazement, she gave me a quick kiss on the cheek and pushed me away.

I stumbled down to the car. "About time," Darren said, "The movie starts in ten minutes. *Bye Mom.*" This last he yelled out the window to his mother, who remained on the porch, watching us.

I pulled a U-ey in the street and headed in the direction of the movie theater. At the last minute I stuck my arm out the window and threw a quick wave to The Wit — to The Ex.

Crestfallen's Getaway

Simon Wood

Crestfallen was enjoying himself, chasing a urinal cake around the urinal with his pee, when the men's room door opened.

"I need your help," someone demanded.

Crestfallen glanced over his shoulder at the accountant type standing in the doorway. This wasn't the usual place he did business, but the detective couldn't afford to be fussy. "Come into my office."

The little guy did as he was told, letting the door swing close. "Are we alone?"

"As far as I know."

Crestfallen zipped up and made the pretense of washing his hands. Something he wouldn't normally do, but it was good business practice. No one liked to shake hands with a man who had just been holding his dick.

"I assume you know who I am?" Crestfallen kept his back to his prospective client and spoke into the mirror. The slight, bespectacled man was in no condition to take him on. He could afford to be nonchalant. He turned off the faucet.

The accountant type nodded quickly. "You're Peter

Crestfallen, the private investigator."

Crestfallen tore off a sheet of paper towel from the dispenser. "And where did you get my name?"

"People said you were a good man to be trusted in a clinch. Well, I'm in one, up to my neck."

People? He didn't remember people from his customer satisfaction surveys. He reminded himself to give people a discount the next time they turned up at the office.

Crestfallen tossed the paper towel in the trash and offered a clean hand. "Well, Mr. er. . . ?"

The accountant type rushed as if the offered hand was a sign of acceptance of his case. A sweaty hand took Crestfallen's and shook it limply. "Noah. Daniel Noah."

"Noah? A good man to have close when the rains come."

"Excuse me?"

I must stop doing that, Crestfallen thought. He had a habit of blurting out abstract thoughts. It had a tendency to confuse or piss off people. Once, it had gotten him shot.

"Well, Mr. Noah, if you would like to come to the office in the morning, we could discuss your case then." Crestfallen fished for his wallet in search of a business card. "I'm actually with someone at the moment."

"She's probably gone by now."

It was Crestfallen's turn to say, "Excuse me?"

"As soon as you left the table, she was on her cell phone calling a cab. I was watching you from the bar." Noah looked embarrassed for Crestfallen. "Surely, you realized. Didn't you notice how many times she checked her watch?"

Crestfallen hadn't. He thought his date was going well. Well enough to think the condoms in his wallet were going to get an airing. Never mind, he was tough. He would live to fight another day.

A man entered the men's room, giving Crestfallen and Noah a sideways glance.

Crestfallen knew how it looked and pocketed his wallet. "C'mon, let's take this elsewhere."

From the pay phone lobby outside the restrooms, Crestfallen watched Jenny leave the restaurant for a yellow cab. That was the last time he picked up a girl in a nightclub. But he always said that.

He went to return to his table, but Noah grabbed his arm. "Where do you think you're going?"

"I was going to pay."

"She paid."

It's a modern world with modern girls, Crestfallen thought. Too modern sometimes.

Crestfallen allowed Noah to lead to him to the fire exit and into the alley behind the restaurant. Noah's eyes were everywhere, as if he expected to be ambushed at any moment.

"I need specifics," Crestfallen said, tiring of the situation. "What is this about?"

"People are after me." Noah took refuge in the shadows out of reach of the streetlights. "They're probably watching us right now and they know I've spoken to you."

Fantastic, Crestfallen thought. "Which people? The same people who told you to come to me?"

"No, of course not," Noah spat. "Can you just get me out of here?"

Crestfallen exhaled. Money hadn't even exchanged hands and this case was already a pain in the ass. "Where's your car?"

"Out front."

"Leave it there. We'll use mine."

"But, it's in a red zone."

"So, it'll get towed. Wait here, I'll be back."

Crestfallen jogged to the alley's mouth. Nobody seemed to be keeping surveillance. And if they were, it was unlikely they were watching for him — yet.

He made a beeline for his Crown Victoria. It came from

a friend in the San Francisco Sheriff's department. He knew the Ford was big and lumbering, but there was a lot of steel between him and a bullet. And, the police interceptor engine was heavy on gas but could always be relied upon to put distance between him and the bad guys. It looked like he would need the car's power for this job.

He crossed the road, but his eyes weren't on the traffic. They were on three guys checking out a Dodge parked in the red zone. They didn't look like car boosters — wrong age, wrong dress, wrong moves — just wrong. And they didn't look like car enthusiasts. No one drooled over a minivan, except for accountant types. One of the Dodge Caravan appreciation club spotted Crestfallen and alerted his buddies.

Let the games begin, Crestfallen thought. Getting into his car, he noted the parking meter. It flashed, EXPIRED. He hoped it wasn't an omen.

Crestfallen rode the sidewalk and flung open the passenger door. Noah burst from the shadows and leapt into the Ford.

"Do you drive a silver '98 Caravan?"

"Yes."

"Three guys were checking it out."

"Jesus."

Crestfallen made a half-hearted attempt at stopping before making a free right turn. Like Noah, he was eager to put distance between him and Noah's friends.

"Are you going to tell me what this is about or do I have to go back and ask your buddies?"

"Money."

"It usually is. How much do you owe?"

"I don't owe. I took."

Crestfallen checked his mirrors. No one seemed to be following. He and Noah were just part of the anonymous flow of city traffic.

"Might I ask who's the unlucky recipient of your thievery?"

"Craig Kleinfelder."

Crestfallen slammed on the brakes. He slithered across two lanes and bounced off the curb. "I'm sorry, pal. I can't help you. No one can help you."

"I can pay you anything you care to name."

Crestfallen flung open the door for Noah. "Anything you pay me would only go towards a nicer funeral. Get out."

"You can't, Mr. Crestfallen."

"But I can. As a business owner, I reserve the right to refuse business to anyone I don't see fit to serve. I'm exercising my right."

"He'll kill me."

"You should have thought about that before you ripped off San Francisco's most lethal crime lord."

Noah latched onto Crestfallen's arm. "Please."

A Lincoln slid by. Familiar faces occupied the car — the car buffs.

It was too late. Noah had left his indelible mark on him. Kleinfelder's guys would be checking out his license plate and would know he was a private eye. Bent cops would be supplying information for a little extra in their lockers on Friday. The bull's-eye was in position. He was Noah's guy whether he liked it or not.

"Close that damn door."

"Thank you, Mr. Crestfallen. Thank you so much."

Crestfallen yanked the selector into reverse and roared the wrong way into one-way traffic to a chorus of blaring horns. He halted at the first cross street and spun the car to point uphill. He punched the gas and left rubber as an apology.

The Lincoln boys lost their cool and tried to copy Crestfallen. They were rear-ended for their trouble. They wouldn't be bothering Crestfallen and his client for a while.

"How much have you taken?"

"Do you know anything about computers?"

Crestfallen knew where to find the on/off switch and how to work an ATM, but that was about it. He left the techno stuff to the right people — five year olds. "Yes, of course I do. What do you take me for?"

"Sorry."

"That's okay. Go on."

"I'm Kleinfelder's accountant."

Crestfallen might have been wrong about his date, but not about the man. He wondered if the adage about owners looking like their dogs applied to people and their jobs.

"I've written accounting software that channels his income into various legitimate accounts."

"And while you were doing it, you thought, why not channel a percentage your way."

"Yeah, well . . . you know."

"Yeah, well, how did Kleinfelder find out?"

"A computer virus. Turned our systems to oatmeal. A side effect was that Kleinfelder was sent a statement listing all the accounts his money was sent to."

"Including your account details."

Noah nodded soulfully.

Crestfallen joined 101 south. "What are you expecting me to do for you? Kleinfelder isn't going to be interested in you giving the money back and he isn't going to listen to anything I've got to say."

"I know. I just want you to get me somewhere safe."

"Is there such a place from Craig Kleinfelder?"

"I have a place in Washington State, north of Seattle. He won't think to look there. My family is from the Midwest and my sister lives in New York."

"We'll see. Now there's my fee. I insist on a retainer."

Noah cut Crestfallen off before he could finish his terms and conditions. "I transferred five thousand to your bank account earlier tonight. I'll pay you another fifteen when you get me to Washington."

"Transferred?"

"It's not hard to hack into people's bank accounts and credit histories. Twenty grand will clear your overdraft and the note on this car, and give you a head start on next month's rent."

Noah wasn't wrong. Twenty thousand would give him a level playing field to operate from. But he wasn't so sure he wanted his life so accessible to the likes of Noah.

Twenty thousand was far more than he expected to charge for a simple babysitting job. But Kleinfelder's presence added points, lots of points. Twenty thousand didn't sound like a lot if this job turned messy.

"I prefer cash. I like to see things. I don't like the invisible world. You can't trust what you can't see. Ask the emperor about his new clothes."

"Do you want more?"

"Is the money Kleinfelder's or yours?"

"A little of both."

"Twenty grand's fine."

Noah exhaled and melted into his seat. The accountant didn't have anything to worry about anymore. He had put his faith in Crestfallen because Crestfallen knew what he was doing, because he would save the day, because he was the hero after all. The detective felt the weight of Noah's fuck-up clinging to him.

"Where are we going?"

"SFO."

"I'm not sure if flying is a good idea."

"It isn't. And this car isn't any good to me anymore. They've got a make on it and I want them to think we're somewhere else."

Crestfallen dumped his Crown Victoria in long-term parking. He bought luggage for appearances and both of them hopped a ride on the next Bayporter bus back to San Francisco. Once in the city, Crestfallen ditched the luggage and bungled Noah onto the first BART to Richmond.

Noah checked over his shoulder. The nearest BART passenger was at the other end of the carriage. "How is this getting me to —"

Crestfallen put a finger to his lips. "To your final destination?"

"Yes."

"Don't worry about it. Let me do the thinking. What I need you to do is keep your mouth shut, don't draw attention to yourself, do exactly what I tell you to do and not piss me off. Okay?"

Noah sighed.

"I'll take that as a yes."

They got off at El Cerrito and Crestfallen hailed a cab. As they slipped into the cab, Crestfallen relaxed. He was hopeful. Kleinfelder's boys weren't breathing down their necks and they had no way of knowing where he was taking Noah. They would never think to look for him in San Pablo.

And as a bonus — he hadn't needed to use his gun. Not that he had it with him. It was a problem he sought to remedy.

The Sikh cab driver asked for the destination for the second time. Crestfallen gave it.

"Why are we going to a gym?" Noah asked.

"You look like you need building up."

The cab pulled up in front of the gym.

"Wait here for me," Crestfallen instructed the cab driver, then tugged Noah's arm. "C'mon, you."

Crestfallen signed Noah in as a guest under a false name. It was a good place to keep his client hidden for a few hours. The place was open twenty-four hours with full facilities. There was plenty to keep Noah busy. Guiding Noah into the gym, Crestfallen filled him in on the next few hours.

"What am I going to do here until morning?" Noah whined.

"Knock yourself out. Have a sauna, a workout. There's a licensed bar. I don't care." Crestfallen checked his watch then left for reception. "I'll be back in the morning."

"Crestfallen," Noah moaned.

"Can't stop, I've got a cab waiting."

Crestfallen told the cabbie to take him back to the El Cerrito BART and he took BART back into San Francisco.

Leaving the BART station, Crestfallen needed a car. He couldn't go back to SFO. Kleinfelder's men knew what he drove and probably where he lived. He needed a car they knew nothing about.

He wandered along a row of townhouses off Geary until he found an unlocked Nissan sedan. Slipping behind the wheel, he attacked the ignition and hotwired the import.

He didn't need much for Noah's road trip but the one thing he did want was a gun. He owned two. One, he kept at his apartment. The other was at his office.

Crestfallen eased the Nissan onto his street and scanned the apartment block. His apartment lights were out, as were most people's. He continued to make a complete circuit of the block. Everything looked okay. But he was unsatisfied and made a sweep of the surrounding streets.

"Shit," he mumbled.

The Lincoln that Crestfallen had lost earlier was parked two streets over. He squeezed the gas and abandoned hopes of a good night's sleep.

If Kleinfelder's little helpers were at his apartment, it was an even bet that more helpers would be in his office. He needed a gun, but he was a smart cookie, he knew people. He could get a gun anywhere. It would be dumb to go to his office now. Wouldn't it? But it was about time he met the neighbors.

Crestfallen left the Nissan in a red zone in front of his

office block. He crossed the road staring at the only lit office in the building — his.

"Evening, Chuck," Crestfallen said, acknowledging the security guard.

The guard refused to make eye contact and mumbled a reply.

"Looks like I have clients, Chuck."

"I wouldn't know anything about that," he replied, still managing not to exchange glances.

Crestfallen could have forced the issue, but the old guy was scared and made minimum wage. Would Crestfallen do any differently if he were in Chuck's position? He doubted it. He pressed a button and waited for the elevator.

As the doors slid shut, Crestfallen heard, "There's two of them."

"Thanks."

Stepping from the elevator, Crestfallen searched for a makeshift weapon, but gave up on the idea. He wouldn't make much of an adversary with a potted plant in one hand.

Anyway, bad guys didn't shoot unarmed men — punks and politicians, yes, but not bad guys. They had ethics.

Or so he hoped.

Crestfallen stepped over the broken glass that was once his door.

"Hey, Nomar. What did I say? A dog always returns to its vomit. You owe me fifty."

Unimpressed, Nomar delved for his wallet. He looked like the kind of guy who lost a lot of bets. A heavy-set guy, a boxer maybe, who once was muscle, until he had it punched out of him in the ring.

The Philosopher rocked back and forth in Crestfallen's chair with his feet on the desk and a Glock pointed at Crestfallen's crotch. Unlike Nomar, the Philosopher wasn't the muscle but the brains, attractively wrapped in Armani.

He snapped his fingers at his partner. Nomar paid up

and slapped a fifty in the Philosopher's hand.

"Hi there. My office is currently closed, but I will be open at nine. So, if you wouldn't mind leaving."

Nomar snorted.

The Philosopher smiled. "I like your humor, Mr. Crestfallen, but Nomar doesn't. And I don't have time for games. My employer is less than pleased."

Crestfallen dropped into one of his visitor's chairs. "And who would be your employer?"

"Craig Kleinfelder. But you already knew that and you know why we're here. Where's Noah?"

"On his ark."

The Philosopher's Glock spat a spearhead of flame and Crestfallen's chair bled stuffing. There wasn't even time to flinch.

"Wrong answer. Try again."

"I'm a private investigator and you might have seen our bumper sticker. PI's do it confidentially."

The Glock spat again and seat stuffing billowed between Crestfallen's legs. It was lucky he had them apart.

"Mr. Crestfallen, I said I didn't have time for humor. We can laugh and joke when I have, but until then . . ." The Philosopher gestured with an open hand and a pained look. "Nomar, take a finger."

The boxer lunged with a speed Crestfallen wouldn't have thought capable from an old bruiser. Crestfallen sprang to his feet and gave it his best shot. Nomar blocked the punch and launched his own. Nomar connected. A pins and needles sensation tore through Crestfallen's body, anesthetizing the crunching blow. But Crestfallen's mom had brought up a strong boy and he didn't faint. His legs buckled instead. It was lucky Nomar was there to catch him.

Crestfallen was just recovering from the first blow when Nomar slammed him into his desk. Crestfallen's chest struck the thin edge of the tabletop. He felt something crack.

He didn't think it was the desk. It had cost a lot of money. It was no Wal-Mart bargain.

Nomar stretched Crestfallen's left arm across the desk top. The Philosopher grabbed it and held it in place. Nomar pulled out an ornate switchblade and a four-inch blade jerked out.

The Philosopher brought his head down to Crestfallen's level. "Crestfallen, are you really going to let this happen? Are you going to allow yourself to lose a finger, or even worse, your life, to protect a worthless piece of shit like Noah?"

Crestfallen wheezed.

The Philosopher shook his head. "Do it."

Nomar spread Crestfallen's fingers to make sure he wouldn't catch more than one. He positioned the knife over Crestfallen's pinky and applied pressure.

Crestfallen's flesh gave way easily under the keen blade. Blood sprang from the wound and crept up the polished stainless steel. He bit back the pain as the knife cut into bone.

"Stop!" Crestfallen screamed.

The Philosopher raised his gun hand and Nomar let up on the knife immediately.

"I'll tell you where you can find him."

"Good. I thought you'd see sense. I couldn't believe a man like you would lose his life without a good reason. And Noah isn't a good reason."

Sweat trickled into Crestfallen's eyes. He blinked it away. "I'll take you to him."

"Of course you will," the Philosopher agreed. "But it's late and I'm going back to bed. You can take Nomar after you've had some rest."

"Rest?"

"Yes, rest." The Philosopher whipped the Glock across Crestfallen's temple.

Crestfallen rested.

Crestfallen hadn't been moved. He still lay where he had fallen, next to his desk. Luck was on his side.

He didn't know what time it was, but it was morning. Light filtered through the windows. It had to be early as the rest of the office floor was still silent. He raised a leaden arm to look at his watch. Hands pointed to numerals, but he couldn't string the numbers together. There was a five in there somewhere, not bad going for a man in his condition.

"Let's go," Nomar demanded, lounging on Crestfallen's bullet-ridden couch.

"Can't a man rest?" Turning on his side, Crestfallen clutched at his desk.

"No."

His arm disappeared behind the desk's foot well.

"C'mon, stop stalling."

"Go fly a kite, I've had a hard night." Crestfallen's hand searched.

"Fuck you, pal." Nomar leapt to his feet and charged towards Crestfallen like someone had called "Seconds out!"

Sensible people keep firearms in a safe, but not Crestfallen, he kept his taped to the underside of his desk. His hand found the snub-nose .38. It slid easily from the holster.

Nomar snatched fistfuls of Crestfallen's shirt. Crestfallen jammed the .38 into Nomar's guts. Nomar froze. Crestfallen spotted the 9mm tucked into Nomar's pants and removed it.

"Take your fucking hands off me."

Nomar did as he was told.

"Back up. Keep your hands where I can see them."

Nomar edged towards the couch.

Crestfallen got to his feet, using both guns as props. He struggled with Nomar's 9mm in his left hand. His blood-encrusted pinky refused to bend, but he was a tough guy. He forced his hand to work. The scab broke and blood drizzled from the wound. He needed stitches but there wasn't time.

"Get those hands higher."

Nomar edged them higher.

"That'll do."

Crestfallen fired both guns simultaneously. It was a difficult task firing two guns of different size, weight and balance. But he was good.

Crestfallen's bullets ripped through both of Nomar's palms. The stigmatic clutched his hands to him and collapsed onto the couch.

"Hurts don't it?"

"You son-of-a-bitch."

"So, I'm told." Crestfallen smashed his .38 into Nomar's face. "Lights out, pal."

Nomar's nose disintegrated. Blood spilled down his face, filling an unconscious mouth.

A man could drown left like that, Crestfallen thought. He pocketed the guns and rifled though his en suite bathroom for his office first aid kit. He tended his finger and bandaged it. There wasn't a lot he could do for the bruising on his face. Why first aid kits didn't keep a porterhouse in them was one of life's unanswered mysteries.

From his floor safe, he took a thousand dollars cash and half a box of .38 shells. What more did a private eye need?

Crestfallen spun the dial on the safe and raced out of his office. Nomar didn't budge. Most definitely, a man could drown left like that, Crestfallen thought. Someone would find him in time.

The Park 'n' Sell at Hilltop was opening for the day when Crestfallen parked the Nissan. When he had left his office, he found it was only six. He had rejuvenated himself in a Denny's, seeking the restorative powers of coffee and eggs. Sliding from the sedan, he wouldn't have said he felt like a new man, more like an old one.

Harry Taub emerged from the trailer and his salesman's face dropped when he saw it was Crestfallen. Taub was an insurance agent turned jalopy car salesman that Crestfallen had worked with years ago. Rather than go in for a dealership, Taub chose to take a percentage from the sale of high mileage cars left on his lot by private sellers. Good business really, he didn't have an inventory to manage, only the lease on a lot to pay for. Taub closed the trailer door.

"Crestfallen, you've got to stop trying to derail freight trains with your face."

"I'll bear that in mind. Harry, I need a car."

"What about the Nissan?"

"It's not a reliable runner."

"And not yours." Taub headed into the vehicle-packed lot. "It's stolen, isn't it?"

Crestfallen smirked.

"Jesus, Crestfallen."

"So, you're not interested in the Nissan?"

Taub shook his head. "You buying then?"

"Borrowing."

"This isn't a library."

"I need something for two or three days. Good on the freeways. I'll bring it back in one piece. I promise."

"People give me their cars to sell, not lend. People trust me."

"Just the way they did at State Farm, huh?"

"Oh, don't try that one on me again. You did me a favor. I didn't do time, thanks to you. How many times do I have to pay it back?"

"Once more."

"You're a son-of-a-bitch, Crestfallen."

"So, I'm told."

"I'm not surprised." Taub jerked a thumb at the Nissan. "Get that thing out of here. Dump it at the mall across the street and let me see what I can do."

Crestfallen stopped a Jeep Grand Cherokee in front of the gym and found Noah working at a PC. He was dressed in the gym's branded sweats and polo. He did a double take when he saw Crestfallen.

"What the hell happened to you?"

"My job. C'mon, let's go."

Crestfallen relaxed; happy to be on the freeway and even happier when they left I-80 for I-5 and the north. It seemed that if Kleinfelder's people weren't tailing him now, then they never would. After a long night, it all seemed to be a letdown. But in Crestfallen's experience, letdowns like this were few and far between. It was good to enjoy them while they lasted.

As the Oregon state line approached, Crestfallen realized he knew nothing of what Noah had done to get himself into this position. When Crestfallen returned to San Francisco, there would be music to face. He deserved some answers.

"How did you wind up working for Kleinfelder?"

Noah placed his Coke in the cup holder. "I applied."

"What?"

"Sorry to disappoint you, but there was no clandestine meeting. I didn't have gambling debts or a compromising kink to pay for. I wanted a new job. The headhunters got me an interview and I got the position. Simple."

"Did you meet Kleinfelder at the interview?"

"Nah. No one meets Kleinfelder. He's a corporation, a ghost. That's why he's so successful. He's never around to get his hands dirty. I stood more chance of meeting the Pope."

"Who interviewed you?"

"Someone from his human resources department."

Crestfallen raised an eyebrow.

"That's his genius. You know who you're working for, but everything is so above board, you can't believe there's anything criminal going on."

Crestfallen found it hard to believe that Kleinfelder's organization was so civilized. He couldn't imagine all these people taking everything at face value. But then again, people believed in governments in the same way. Nobody panicked at the ticking bomb when someone hung a tag off it saying, "Don't worry, it's not really a bomb." People were strange creatures.

"Did you meet Kleinfelder afterwards?"

"No. He never got involved. I still don't know what he looks like after five years of service. He made his presence felt through his intermediaries. That was enough."

Crestfallen thought of the Philosopher and nodded.

"So, when and why?"

"Skimming you mean?"

Crestfallen nodded.

"Three years ago. It was very simple to do, like I told you. Accounting and software allow you to hide a host of sins and unless you understand it, you would never know. Goddamn viruses." Noah fell silent for a moment. "As to why, I don't know. I didn't need the money. My salary was exceptional. Life was good. I suppose I did it because I could. And what harm was I doing? Kleinfelder was a crook. I was stealing from a thief. It didn't count. I suppose you think I'm an idiot?"

Crestfallen shook his head. "I don't judge. People do whatever drives them. Sometimes it works, sometimes it doesn't. In your case it didn't. I'm a simple repairman. I do what I can to fix things."

Noah smiled at Crestfallen's words and settled into his seat, comforted by being in his hands. Crestfallen didn't have the heart to say he couldn't fix everything given to him.

Crestfallen noted the road sign. Seattle was twenty miles away. They had made reasonable time from San Francisco, twenty hours, and without molestation. The only casualty was his thousand dollars. Hundreds dwindled on gas and food from his expenses pot. He used only cash. He didn't want to be traced, which was the reason why they crashed in the Jeep and not in a motel. He left no trail — his Wild West ancestors would have been proud.

"Stop here," Noah announced. "Let me off here for a minute."

"Is this the drop off?"

"No, but I need to do something."

Crestfallen frowned.

"It'll only take a minute."

Crestfallen eased the Jeep to the roadside. Noah hopped out and ducked into a cyber café. Ten minutes later, he returned with two coffees.

"Finished?" Crestfallen asked.

"Yeah. And, you've been paid."

"More computer trickery?"

Noah smiled smugly.

"I like cash."

"I know. Pull into the next Washington Mutual you see."

Crestfallen spotted a bank on the outskirts of Seattle. He did as instructed. Noah returned with fifteen grand in cash. Three stacks of hundreds bound with paper bands. Noah slipped the money inside the glove compartment.

"Thanks, Crestfallen. You did it. You got me here in one piece."

Crestfallen said nothing. His job wasn't complete. Things could still go wrong.

"This is where I want you to drop me."

Noah rattled off a list of directions that led them through the city. Safeco Park was way behind and the Space

Needle dominated their locale. Crestfallen stopped on a busy street of mixed residential and business use.

"This it?"

"Yep. For now, anyway." Noah offered a hand. "Thanks for all your help. You earned your salary."

They shook.

"You'd better get going."

Noah nodded. He hopped out and trotted across the road, making sure to avoid the cross traffic. He pressed the buzzer to a four-story apartment block wedged between a 7-Eleven and a liquor store. He spoke into a speaker and waited.

Crestfallen thought the picture didn't fit. Middle class accountants didn't hang out on skid row. He wondered whom Noah knew. But it was better he didn't. He didn't need to know who Noah's friends were. As long as they got him to safety, what did it matter?

A graying man in his forties opened the apartment door. He offered a hand to Noah and he took it. He slipped inside and the gray-haired man closed the door while checking for watching strangers.

Crestfallen gunned the engine and selected drive. His job was done.

Not quite.

The passenger door whipped open and the Philosopher slipped into the seat next to Crestfallen. He had brought a familiar friend. The Glock found a home against Crestfallen's kidneys. It was an uncomfortable fit but everyone would get along.

"Tag, you're it," he said.

Crestfallen raised his hands.

"No, keep 'em on the wheel. But let's hang for awhile." The Philosopher switched off the engine.

"You're good," Crestfallen admitted. "I didn't tag any of your boys on the way up."

The Philosopher laughed. "We didn't have to follow. We knew he was coming here. Noah underestimated us. He didn't think we'd look further than his resume. Mr. Kleinfelder makes it his business to know everything about everyone."

"They say information is power."

"And they're right. Mr. Kleinfelder thrives on it."

"How's Nomar?"

"A lot worse since you last saw him. I liked the hands thing. You a religious man, Crestfallen?"

"No. Just makes it hard to dial a phone and shoot a gun."

The Philosopher nodded appreciatively. "Has he paid you?"

"In the glove box."

The Philosopher pocketed the fifteen thousand. "Not bad for a couple days work."

"What's to happen to me?"

"Nothing. For now. We've got our money back. You were only doing a job. Mr. Kleinfelder understands that. But we may call on you again."

"And Noah?"

"Matters are being dealt with."

The Philosopher opened the door and slid out while maintaining his aim.

"Goodbye, Mr. Kleinfelder."

The Philosopher laughed. He holstered the Glock and leaned through the open passenger door. "Is that what you think?"

"A wild pitch then?"

"Enough to walk me. You meet Mr. Kleinfelder when it's too late. Certain business he likes to take care of himself."

Crestfallen glanced at the apartment block. The gray-haired man who had answered the door. He was Kleinfelder. Crestfallen murmured his name.

"You've got it, rookie. Later, friend." The Philosopher

banged on the roof and headed towards the Space Needle.

Crestfallen stared at the apartment entrance. He knew some people he could help and some people he could only help so much. Noah fell into the latter category. And continued to fall. He had done all that he could for the accountant.

Gunning the engine, some would have said the Cherokee backfired. But Crestfallen knew otherwise. The backfire had come from the apartments.

Tight Squeeze

Michael Bracken

Keegleman pushed himself off the double-bed and stared down at the blonde's lifeless body. He hadn't meant to kill her — had, in fact, mistaken her death throes for orgasm and had squeezed his thick fingers even tighter around her slender neck.

His flaccid penis, still sheathed in the lime green condom she'd chosen from the assortment in her nightstand drawer, clung to his right thigh. He walked to the bathroom, peeled off the condom, and wrapped it in pink, two-ply toilet tissue. He threw the soggy wad into the wicker trash basket, then had second thoughts and retrieved it. Carrying the soiled condom in one hand, he searched the bedroom for the foil square in which it had been packed, found it half-under the bed, and then stuffed everything into the pocket of his jeans before stepping into them.

He pulled on the rest of his clothes and let himself out of the blonde's apartment, stopping briefly at the mailbox downstairs to discover the blonde's name had been "S. Richardson." He couldn't remember what S. stood for.

"Miss me?" Keegleman asked when he pushed open his apartment door an hour later.

Samantha brushed against Keegleman's legs and purred loudly. He reached down and scooped up the gray tabby, holding her in one arm as he kicked the door closed and snapped both locks into place. Then he carried her to the kitchen, opened a can of Friskies Salmon Dinner, and left the cat on the kitchen counter eating from the can as he stepped into the bathroom and stripped off his clothes.

He showered, lathering and rinsing himself three times before the hot water turned cold. Then he stepped from the shower and toweled himself dry.

Samantha pushed the bathroom door open and stared up at him.

"She asked me to," Keegleman told the cat. "That's why I did it."

The cat said nothing.

Keegleman emptied the pockets of his jeans, disposing of the condom and its wrapper, and stacking his wallet, car keys, breath mints, and loose change on the vanity next to the sink. He left his dirty clothes and his towel in a heap on the bathroom floor.

Then he went to bed.

He lay in the dark, Samantha curled over his legs, the clock on his nightstand ticking away the seconds of his life, and he tried to sleep. Each time Keegleman closed his eyes, he saw the blonde's face — at Singularity with a Stoli's in one hand and a cigarette in the other, against the brick wall of the bar as he slid his hand under her blouse, in bed beneath him as he entered her and listened to her throaty whisper begging him to choke her.

And when he finally fell into a troubled sleep, Keegleman dreamed of fingerprints and DNA samples and every *Columbo* episode he'd ever watched.

Groggy from lack of sleep, Keegleman retrieved the newspaper from the hallway outside his apartment door and spent much of the morning reading every column inch of news. Finding nothing about the blonde's death, he spent the day in front of the television watching college football. He studied the next morning's paper and spent that day watching professional football.

Monday morning, Keegleman called in sick, telling his supervisor at the printing plant that he'd caught the flu. Then he studied the morning newspaper for the third day in a row, finally throwing it against the wall.

Samantha ran from the room, ducking behind the living room couch and staring at him until he coaxed her out from hiding.

He called in sick for the next three days, finally discovering a page three article on Thursday. He read it carefully, finally learning the dead woman's name: Sheila Richardson. She worked as a real estate agent and her body had been discovered when a worried co-worker finally convinced her building's supervisor to unlock the apartment door. The police had no suspects.

On Friday, Keegleman returned to work.

He didn't return to Singularity for nearly three months. By then, he no longer saw Sheila's face when he closed his eyes, no longer kicked Samantha off the bed as he restlessly tossed and turned in the night, and he had begun to suspect that the police knew nothing of his one night with the dead woman.

He bought a drink for a slender brunette who couldn't construct a sentence without resorting to "like, you know," and then bought one for a buxom blonde closer to his own age. Shelly drank peppermint Schnapps, smoked Virginia Slims, and danced close even during fast songs. He learned her name, listened to her complaints about her overbearing boss, discussed the local team's chances of making the Superbowl, and bought her drink after drink.

After last call, Shelly asked if he wanted a nightcap at her place. Keegleman accepted and half an hour later they stood in her bedroom, peeling off their clothes. Then they were in her bed, their fingers and lips exploring each other's bodies, stopping only long enough for Keegleman to slip on one of the condoms he'd brought with him.

Then he moved onto the blonde, thrust into her, and quickly realized that she had no sense of rhythm. He held her face in his hands and kissed her long, deep, and hard. Subconsciously, his hands moved down to her neck, his fingers wrapping around the back while his thumbs rested on her larynx.

And in that moment he remembered the best sex he'd ever had. And in that moment, he tightened his grasp on Shelly's neck. And in that moment, her blue eyes widened in surprise.

Then she began pounding her fists against his back and thrusting her hips upward, attempting to buck Keegleman off.

He rode her until the end, until he erupted within the condom, until her body finally stopped spasming beneath him, until he finally peeled his fingers from her throat and slipped off the bed and pulled on his clothes.

An hour later, Samantha greeted him at the door. He fed her a Friskies Salmon Dinner, showered, then slipped into bed.

With the cat draped across his legs, Keegleman fell into a deep and satisfying sleep.

Souls

James Stevens-Arce

"How does it happen," dis guy at de other end of de bar say, "that there is so much horror in the world today?"

I just get a 2–3–4–4–5 on my first roll, which give me a shot at a straight both way, high or low. At my end of de bar, we are playing Generala — which for some reason de focking gringos call Jahtzee, which is not even English, for chrissake — and dere is twelve dollar in de pot. I look at de guy. He is staring into his glass. I wonder if it is empty and if dat is part of de horror, ha, ha.

Paco, de bartender, glance up from drawing a Tuborg for my shit for brains old lady, Mayra, who think if she drink a foreign beer it make her a lady.

"What horror, man?" he say.

The guy shake his head, like he cannot believe Paco's ignorance. "Look around you," he say with a Nujorican accent, make him sound like de chick who talk through her nose in dat flick about white guys cannot jump. De attitude he take, joo know he think being a Nu Jork Puerto Rican make him better dan us real boricuas who never move to de Mainland. Like it don't matter dat he forget his Spanish living in Spanish Harlem. "Read the newspapers, listen to the radio, watch CNN, man," de guy say. "It's all there."

He point at his glass, which is one a dem cheap souvenir bamboo porquerías with a red devil on de side for de turistas to take home. He want Paco to hit him with another Zombie. I scoop up one of de fours and rattle de die inside de leather Generala cup and blow into it for good luck. Joo maybe think dat's bullshit, but sometime it work.

"Carjacker in L.A. shoots a guy in the mouth," de Nujorican say. "This is after the guy's already handed over the keys to a brokedown '76 Gremlin was worth maybe a hundred fifty bucks, max. Busts a cap on him 'cause the gas gauge was riding on empty. Here's the topper: the carjacker was a brother, from Watts; guy he shot was also a brother, also from Watts. What is wrong with this picture, peoples?"

I flip de cup over, slap it down on de bartop, trap de die underneath. Li-i-ift u-u-up de cu-u-u-up . . . another four. Coño. I should have blow focking harder. Now I got only one roll left. If I hit de straight, I get twenty-five point, but widdout a one or a six, I got shit-on-a-stick, and de gringo asshole sitting next to me, dis pendejo call Dana — which is a focking girl's name, for chrissake — focking Dana will win de pot, he is not even a regular here at El Diablo Rojo, a focking turista from focking Connecticut, man.

"This guy in Milwaukee," de Nujorican say, "quiet, clean-cut, good neighbor, everybody thought the world of him? Turned out he had a thing for the girly-boys, liked to pick them up at malls, bus stations, parks, take them home for a little hanky-panky in this torture chamber he'd built in the basement. When he got bored, he'd snuff 'em, slice 'n' dice 'em, grill him up a little barbecue, store the leftovers in the freezer. Can you imagine? Make love to somebody, butcher and eat them after, go out, do it again? What's the thought process behind that? Cops eventually nailed the sucker, found parts of sixteen, seventeen different bodies —

arms, legs, ribs, buttcheeks — all wrapped up in tinfoil, tucked away in a deepfreeze. In case he ran out of fresh meat, he said."

Paco slide Mayra her Tuborg, bring de guy a fresh drink in a new bamboo glass. I roll a one, get my twenty-five point. Jess, I got de power! Dana, with his discount Madras shirt and khaki shorts from de Lauren outlet on Cristo Street here in Old San Juan, focking juppie geek Dana don't even look worried, like dere is no pressure, like I don't just put de cabrón screws to him, man. Focking gringos think dey own de world.

"Retired couple in Arizona," de Nujorican say, "kept their fourteen-year-old Down's Syndrome granddaughter chained inside a closet, gave her nothing but table scraps to eat until she starved to death. Took her like eighteen months to die, a year and a half living hunched over inside this closet, two feet deep, three feet wide, with nothing but a bucket to pee and shit in. Nobody to talk to, no one to hold her, never seeing the light of day, but all that time hearing the people outside going about their business, dishes and silverware clinking on the dinner table, little Kraut wiener dog yapping, old fashioned hi-fi playing Nat 'King' Cole and McGuire Sisters albums, teevee news talking about Hutus killing Tutsis, Serbs butchering Croats, Russians massacring Chechens. Kid looked like a skeleton just before the end, except for this bloated balloon belly, like the starving babies from Biafra you see on the news."

I am grinning, 'cause de twelve dollar in de pot, dey are mine, man. Only way Dana can beat me now is he roll five-of-a-kind — a focking Generala. And rolling a Generala on his final turn, well, I mean, what are de odds when he got shit-on-a-stick his first roll, a totally worthless 1–2–3–5–6, not even a pair to build on? The dumb cabrón keep de six, sweep up de other four dice, so focking cocky, like de four sixes he is missing are in de focking bag. Right. As if. What make de gringos so arrogant, man? Dey think dere dick is made of gold? Is no wonder nobody don't like dem.

"Assembly line worker in Buffalo, white guy, takes a routine drug test at his plant, turns up HIV positive," de Nujorican say, staring at his second Zombie, he has not jet drink a swallow. "Figures he must've got it from a hooker clipped him fifty bucks for a quickie in the back seat of a rental on a trip to catch a Rangers game with some buddies. Happens the hooker was black. Next thing you know, the guy starts stalking African-American women who live alone. He breaks into their homes at night wearing a red-white-and-blue ski mask looks like the U.S. flag, ties them up, gags them, rapes them in their own beds. 'Captain America,' the tabloids call him, this son-of-a-bitch serial rapist, on account of the mask. When the cops finally catch him and ask why did he do it, you know what the guy says? 'To get even.' That's when the twenty-two women he's raped find out the bastard's given them the AIDS virus, too. What kind of a human being does that?"

Cocksucking Dana roll three sixes and a deuce. Can joo believe dat shit? But! He got just de one roll left, and it got to be de fifth six or he is dead meat. I still like my chances better dan his, joo dig?

De Nujorican start another dumb story. Dis cocksucker don't know when to plug his hole. "Sunday afternoon, the N.F.L. Western Division Championship, Cowboys hosting the Forty-Niners. High school senior in this whitebread Chicago suburb, class valedictorian, president of the Student Council, goes next door during the halftime ceremonies, stabs an 83-year-old woman he's known all his life, old lady he used to run errands for, mowed her lawn, shoveled snow from her driveway, stabs her thirty-eight times with her own kitchen knife." De Nujorican shake his head. "Says afterwards he was wondering what it would feel like, metal hacking through flesh, blood shooting everywhere, like that guy in the movies with the machete and the hockey mask. An experiment inspired by scientific curiosity? You make the call."

Dana is rattling de die inside de cup like he is playing de maracas, chink-chika-chika-chika chink-chika-chika, and I am thinking, Roll de focking die already, moderfocker. Now Dana is blowing in de focking cup so hard I smell de onion from his five-ninety-nine bisté encebollado dinner special, whispering lame shit like, "Baby needs new shoes."

De cocksucker finally flip it over, slam it on de bartop upside down. But he don't show no focking die. Instead, he start to tap de bottom of de cup with de tip of his finger, tap-tap-tap-tap, tap-tap-tap, and say, "Six-six-six-six, six-six-six," making a focking production. I know he is doing it to piss me off and, man, dat piss me off. De Nujorican finally sip his Zombie, make a face like it got too much rum, when joo can't never have too much rum, man, especially in a Zombie, which is suppose to be like five different rum mix together, a couple of dem like two hundred proof, but I got more important shit on my mind just now.

"A mother and stepfather in Queens stuff their five-year-old daughter into the kitchen oven and broil her to death, little girl called Waleska," de Nujorican mutter. "Can you imagine what must've been going through that child's head, man? The agony she must have suffered, and not just physical? And all the while these two bastards, her parents, one of them her natural mother, these two adults who were supposed to care for her, are doing this . . . *thing* to her, committing this . . . this *atrocity?* Can you imagine how long it must have taken, five, maybe ten minutes, the little girl in the oven, pounding on the sides, the top, the door, screaming, skin blistering, flesh charring, not knowing why she's even in there, why these sons of bitches are doing this to her, and all the while these . . . these *Nazis,* with the oven light on, watching through the view glass, unmoved, the stench of burning meat filling the apartment, stepfather bracing the oven door shut with his foot, seeing it through to the end? Then they try to cover it up, and when they can't get their stories straight and the mother breaks down and confesses, they tell the cops the girl wouldn't stop wetting her bed, they were trying to fulfill their parental duty by instilling some discipline. Can you believe that shit?"

Dana lift de edge of de cup, pretend to peek under it, drop it back down when I try to look.

Lemme see what joo got, man," I say, calm, quiet, very cool. Serene. Jess, dat is de word: focking serene. I look de pendejo square in de eye, give him my killer smile. "Joo a winner?" I ask, very serene. "Or a *loser?*"

"I don't know," Dana say. He take his hand off de cup, gesture for me to lift it. "Why don't *you* tell *me?*"

Focking gringo hotdog cabrón. Don't mess with me, moderfocker. I take a gulp of my beer, Medalla, local brew, good shit. Wipe my lip with de back of my hand, tip de Generala cup onto its side, use de middle finger, joo dig, so cute focking Dana know what I think of him.

Cute focking Dana is all smile, on account of cute focking Dana has hatch a focking six under dat cup. Cute focking Dana has swipe my twelve dollar — which I have won square and fair — with some last ditch flim-flam I have not jet figure out how he work it. He got some cojones, he think he is gonna get away with dis shit.

I jawn and stretch, focking serene as hell, and flash dear old Dana my killer smile again. "Look like joo win," I say, pushing de pot over to him. "Can't nobody beat blind luck." I shrug, letting him know it don't mean shit to me. "But, hey, no hard feeling, joo know. Let me buy joo a beer, man." Cool, like, I snap my finger so Paco de bartender look over. I clap dear old Dana on de back. "Fock dat Clydesdale piss joo drinking, man. Paco, give my amigo here a Medalla, let him taste a beer with Latino soul."

"The way I figure it," de Nujorican say, "it's because of a lack of souls."

"What joo mean?" Mayra ask.

What shit is dis? She don't never show no interest in what *I* got to say. Wait, I know. Dis espiritista woman — Hungarian bitch who call herself la Viuda Gitana, de Gypsy Widow, and run a psychic scam up on Luna Street — last week she say Mayra is "an old soul" has live fock know how many past life. De way I see it, dat Gypsy cabrona take her for twenty-five Jorge Washington, but Mayra eat dat shit up.

Dana chug his Medalla, smack his lip, say to me, "Very tasty, buddy. Moo-chaz grassy-ass." I bet he must know also "bway-nose dee-ass" and "eighty-owes." Adios to joo, too, Mister I-Am-Too-Cool-for-School, like now joo speak my language? I don't think so, moderfo —

¡Carajo! De cabrón has focking pat me on de shoulder, which I focking hate, I don't never let no man touch me. Den he say, "Excuse me, I got to see a little boy about a hat," and head for de pisser past de potted bromelias at de other end of de indoor patio, whistling some old R&B song, I think it is call *Soul Man.* Focking asshole has even got to be cute about taking a leak. I hate dat, too.

De Nujorican glance at Mayra. "I mean that while maybe souls are immortal, what if the supply's not unlimited?" Mayra give him dat sleepy-eye look mean her cunt is doing her thinking. He look her up and down before he go on. "If that's true, then when there's more people getting born than there's souls to go around — even allowing for the possibility of reincarnation — some are going to be born without."

De dickhead sip his Zombie and make a face. Focking pussy. Whassamatta, joo? Joo no can handle a macho drink? Joo wanna focking candy bar, order a daiquiri, maricón.

"It's just a theory," de Nujorican say, "but what if the sum total of all human souls in the universe is . . .oh . . . let's say four billion. Hypothetically. So long as the number of people on the planet stayed below that number, there would've been enough souls for everybody. But the day we shot past the sum total mark, demand would've outstripped supply."

Mayra's eyes pop open, like somebody just shove his dick up her ass. "And dat is why everything been shooting to hell on a bicycle!" she exclaim, slapping her hand on de bar top. "¡Sí, sí, seguro! All dem soulless people being borned, more and more every day, more serial killers and child rapers and wife beaters, more carjackers and drive-by shooters and mass murderers, more terrorist bombsetters and dictators who kill dere own people —" she is almost shouting now, jumping up and down like she need to pee so bad she cannot hold it another second "— look at Idi Amin and Milosevic, Saddam Hussein and Ghaddafi — more outlaw governments and big fish drug sellers and bloodthirsty fanatics, all dese peoples who don't give a shit about human life, how could dey, dey got no soul, all dose peoples dragging de world down to de devil, and, and, Jesus, jess, I get it, I get it, dat 'splain so damn much."

"Yeah," de Nujorican say, looking all focking depressed. "Don't it, though?"

I have not see Mayra dis excited since de night she catch me doing Isabel with de pierce nipple and I have to punch her in de face to calm her. I figure focking Dana is gone about enough time to de can already, so I get up and head dat way, real serene. I got something I want to show him, just de two of us in dere. Moderfocker is loco, he think he is going to keep my twelve dollar.

At de door mark Caballeros, I check to see is somebody scoping my act. De Nujorican guy is doing me a favor, though he don't know it. He got everybody looking at him. I start to turn de knob, see Mayra slide off de seat next to mine, swing and sway around to de Nujorican's side of de bar, plunk her fat ass down on de barstool next to his.

"Is dis taken?" she say. Puta.

"It is now," de Nujorican say. Cabrón.

Is all clicking into place. Getting Mayra to spread her leg, dat is what dis pila de mierda has been after with all dat how-do-it-happen-dat-dere-is-so-much-horror-in-de-worl d-today crap.

Focking Dana swing open de john door, bump into me, start to excuse himself. Before he can finish, I knock his focking ass back inside and charge in after. I lock de door behind, pull de boxcutter I carry for special occasion out of my pocket. Focking cocksucker steal my money. I got to set dat shit straight right now. I take care of Mayra and de Nujorican later. Catch up with dem after dey leave de bar and duck into some dark alley to cop a feel. De bitch like dat shit, don't I know it.

Dana pick himself up from de puddle on de black-and-white tile floor. Scumwater drip from his forearm, soak into his up-to-sixty-percent-off Madras shirt and khaki shorts.

"What the hell do you think you're doing, you asshole?" he say, trying to sound tough, but squeezing a hand against his head where he bang himself on de wash basin. He catch his reflection in de cracked wall mirror, see de blood streaming from de cut on his temple. Look worse dan it is, of course, head wound bleed like a moderfocker. Still de cut *is* pretty deep.

"Jesus, you bastard," he say, really piss now, "I'm going to need stitches."

I shake my head and flash my killer smile. Den I show him de boxcutter and start to explain why he will not.

Contributors

Dan Sontup sold his first mystery story back in the 1950s. His stories have since appeared in *Alfred Hitchcock's Mystery Magazine, Blue Murder, Ellery Queen's Mystery Magazine, Hardboiled, Mike Shayne's Mystery Magazine, Murderous Intent, Thrilling Detective,* and many old pulps and digests. His most recent book publications are "The Santa Switch," a novella in the Eppie Award-winning anthology *Blood, Threat & Fears,* and "A Lousy Piece of Toast," in the anthology, *Hardbroiled.*

A former homicide detective, **O'Neil De Noux**'s novels (*Grim Reaper, The Big Kiss, Blue Orleans, Crescent City Kills* and *The Big Show)* have been lauded for their hyper-realistic portrayal of police work. His most recent published work is a short story collection, *LaStanza: New Orleans Police Stories.* De Noux adapted a short story from this collection, which was televised and broadcast in New Orleans. De Noux's short stories have appeared in magazines and anthologies in Canada, Denmark, England, Germany, Italy, Scotland, and the U.S. He teaches mystery writing at the University of New Orleans.

Anthony Neil Smith is originally from the Mississippi Gulf

Coast. He is a fiction editor with *Mississippi Review Web,* and co-editor/founder of *Plots with Guns.* His work has appeared in *Barcelona Review, Blue Murder, Exquisite Corpse, Futures, Handheld Crime, Judas, Nefarious,* and others. He is currently a Visiting Professor at Grand Valley State University in Michigan.

Ann Aptaker was born and raised in New York City. She spent the major part of her adult life in the field of art and design, working in museums, theaters, and art galleries in various cities in the U.S. and abroad. Ann presently resides in the San Francisco Bay area, where she left the art world in order to consumate her lifelong passion to write urban crime and mystery fiction. She recently completed her first novel, *The Woman.*

Percy Spurlark Parker has been a member of the Mystery Writers of America for more than thirty years, and a member of the Private Eye Writers of America since its inception. His short stories have appeared in numerous anthologies and mystery magazines, including *Ellery Queen's Mystery Magazine,* which was the home of his first published work. He recently traded in the ice and snow of Chicago, for the sun and sand of Las Vegas. This is his second appearance in the *Fedora* series.

Gary Bush's first short fiction appeared in *Flesh and Blood: Guilty as Sin* (Mysterious Press). He's completed his first novel, is currently finishing a novel about murder in a ballet company, and is researching a novel about murder in the recording industry. His career has been varied, from teaching history to prisoners at a Federal penitentiary, to working as a human resources director in a large corporation. Once an avid sailor, he was sidelined by an accident and now writes full time. Bush lives in Minneapolis with his wife, Stacey, and their Kerry Blue Terrier, Max.

Dan A. Sproul's first published short story appeared in 1982 in *Alfred Hitchcock's Mystery Magazine.* In all, more than twenty stories have appeared in that publication alone. Additionally, Sproul stories have been published in various anthologies, including the original *Fedora: Private Eyes And Tough Guys.* He has been twice nominated for a Shamus Award by the Private Eye Writers of America. Many of Sproul's stories center around the private investigator (and degenerate horse player) Joe Standard. The Standard stories are set in and around Miami, Florida and, as with many Sproul stories, deal with some aspect of the thoroughbred racing industry. Sproul was born in Defiance, Ohio. After a stint in the U.S. Navy, he entered Defiance College under the GI bill in 1958, He graduated in 1962 with a Bachelor of Arts degree and a major in English. Sproul and his family currently live in Royal Palm Beach, Florida.

Justin Gustainis is a college professor living in upstate New York. His short fiction has appeared in *Bullet Points, Darkness Rising 9, Futures, Over My Dead Body Mystery Magazine,* and *Underworlds.* His work has won awards in contests as diverse as the Raymond Carver Story Competition and the Bulwer-Lytton Fiction Contest.

Brian Evankovich is 27 years old and has been writing since his teens. His previously published fiction includes stories in *Thrilling Detective.* His work as a journalist in the San Francisco Bay Area, in both print and broadcast, along with literary influences like Mickey Spillane and Max Allan Collins, provides inspiration for his stories.

Robert D. Hughes' short fiction and feature articles have appeared in *Blue Murder, Montana, Murderous Intent, Mystery Time, PI, The Cozy Detective, Western Digest, Wild West,* and the first *Fedora.* Five of his published stories feature dauntless Chicago PI Dennis Malone. Hughes recently completed his first novel, a thriller about a murder-prone dinosaur dig. A native of Michigan, he lived on the North side of Chicago for several years before moving to Livingston, Montana, where he and his wife currently reside.

Tom Sweeney has published about three dozen short stories which have appeared in such diverse magazines as *Analog, Blue Murder,* and *Woman's World.* His stories have been nominated for the Pushcart Prize and the Shamus Award. He and his wife live in Portsmouth, New Hampshire, where he is working on his first novel. This is Sweeney's second appearance in the *Fedora* series.

Simon Wood has garnered over seventy short story credits in less than three years. His work has appeared in American, Australian, British, and German magazines and anthologies. In July, 2002, Barclay Books released his first novel, the suspense-thriller, *Accidents Waiting To Happen.* Barclay Books has contracted his second novel, *We All Fall Down,* and Medium Rare Books has contracted his short story collection, *Dragged into Darkness.* Both are scheduled for release in 2003. He is at work on his third novel. A native of England, Simon currently resides in Richmond, California.

Fedora series editor **Michael Bracken** is the author of *All White Girls, Bad Girls, Canvas Bleeding, Deadly Campaign, Even Roses Bleed, In the Town of Dreams Unborn and Memories Dying, Just in Time for Love, Psi Cops, Tequila Sunrise,* and nearly 800 shorter works. He previously edited *Fedora: Private Eyes and Tough Guys* and *Hardbroiled.* Bracken has received numerous awards for advertising copywriting and his short story, "Cuts Like a Knife," published in the first *Fedora,* was nominated for a Derringer Award. Born in Canton, Ohio, Bracken has traveled extensively throughout the U.S., and currently resides with his family in Waco, Texas.

Since his first sale at age 22, **James Stevens-Arce** has published eighteen stories in a variety of magazines and original anthologies, some of which have also appeared in Germany, Italy, Spain, and the U.K. His first novel, *Soulsaver* (Harcourt, 2000), won Europe's most prestigious award for science fiction novels, was named Best First Novel 2000 by the Denver *Rocky Mountain News*, and was included in the San Francisco *Chronicle*'s Top Books of 2000 list. His historical action-drama screenplay *Blind Man, Preacher Man* was a semi-finalist in the 2001 New York Latino International Film Festival's Screenwriting Competition and his contemporary noir detective screenplay *Sins of the Heart* was selected by the Academy of Motion Picture Arts and Sciences as one of the top 300 out of 6,044 screenplays submitted to their international competition, The 2002 Don and Gee Nicholl Fellowships in Screenwriting. Born in Miami, Florida, Stevens-Arce works as an independent writer-producer-director in the advertising industry in San Juan, Puerto Rico.

www.ingramcontent.com/pod-product-compliance
Lightning Source LLC
Chambersburg PA
CBHW020613310726
48979CB00008B/1457/J

* 9 7 8 1 5 9 2 2 4 8 1 8 6 *